DEADLY AIRBOATS

BY M.W. GORDON

THE WESTERN MOUNTAINS TRILOGY

DEADLY DRIFTS

CROSSES TO BEAR

"YOU'RE NEXT!"

THE FLORIDA TRILOGY

GILL NET GAMES

BARRACUDA PENS

DEADLY AIRBOATS

THE WESTERN MOUNTAINS TRILOGY II

(FORTHCOMING)

BARB WIRED

WHITE WATER

DEADLY AIRBOATS

A MACDUFF BROOKS FLY FISHING MYSTERY

by

award winning author

M. W. GORDON

Deadly Airboats

Published in the United States by Swift Creeks Press,
Sarasota, Florida
swiftcreekspress@gmail.com
www.swiftcreekspress.com

SWIFT CREEKS PRESS EDITION, JULY 30, 2015

Most of the geographical locations are real places but are used fictionally in this novel. This is a work of fiction, and the characters are either the product of the author's imagination or are used fictionally. Any resemblance to actual persons, living or dead, or to actual events or locales is unintentional and coincidental.

Library of Congress Cataloging-in-Publication Data
Gordon, M.W.
Deadly Airboats/M.W. Gordon

ISBN-13 978-0-9848723-6-7
Printed in the United States of America

DEDICATION

Josh Dickinson
Jason Fleury
Garrett Gordon
Huntly Gordon
Johnnie Irby
Paul Tarantino

Fishin' friends

ACKNOWLEDGMENTS

Special thanks to Iris Rose Hart, my editor, friend, and patient instructor in English grammar, for persevering in continuing my training in this challenging language that was thrust upon me at birth.

Particular thanks go to Elsbeth Waskom, Josh Dickinson, Marilyn Henderson, Roy Hunt, and Johnnie Irby. And to Paul Tarantino for valued time fishing together on the flats somewhere in the neighborhood of Florida's West Coast. I could be more specific about the location if he wouldn't blindfold me.

To several people who have provided quiet places for me to write, especially Julie and Jason Fleury of Bozeman, Montana.

To my two casting gurus, both Federation of Fly Fishers Master Casting Instructors, Dave Johnson and Dave Lambert.

To Christine Holmes for developing and maintaining my website and for designing advertisements.

To the graphic design staff of Renaissance Printing of Gainesville, Florida, and especially Jim O'Sullivan, for assistance with the cover, bookmarks, and posters.

To the State Archives of Florida for the cover photo and to the photographer Doug House of Everglades City, Florida.

And always thanks to my wife Buff who reads egregiously incomprehensible first drafts and at times of my self-doubt urges me on.

THOUGHTS ON WRITING

"You can write them again."

"No," David told her. "When it's right you can't remember. Every time you read it again it comes as a great and unbelievable surprise. You can't believe you did it. When it's once right you never can do it again. You only do it once for each thing. And you're only allowed so many in your life."

"So many what?"

"So many good ones."

"But you can remember them. You must."

"Not me and not you and not anybody. They're gone. Once I get them right they're gone."

Ernest Hemingway, *The Garden of Eden*

PROLOGUE

Elsbeth's Diary

These pages are the result of my taking notes years ago about what our family was involved with over several decades. Dad and I talk about what has happened, but he tires easily. His short term memory has diminished, although he remembers with extraordinary detail the troubles Lucinda, he, and I faced together.

Lucinda and Dad were devastated by their incorrect conclusion that the murder of U.S. Representative Juan Mendoza and the shooting of Celia Bustamante were done by or under the direction of Representative Elena Mendoza, Juan's sister. Incorrect assumptions included a lack of person-to-person contact, such as not being present at any of the meetings when the three plotting parties—Jorge García García, Alfredo Luna, and Christina Sandoval—met in Miami; insufficient meetings with Elena; and distractions due to other matters in their personal lives—Lucinda was photographing for magazines and Dad was guiding—which all contributed to their wrongful conclusion. Who murdered someone is not a conclusion one may reach and be wrong.

After the earlier gill net deaths in Florida, Dad and Lucinda were in need of and looking forward to some private time together devoid of bodies discovered in the most bizarre places.

I have always thought they should have rejected Elena Mendoza's first request to visit Cuba and remained on either the salt marsh flats of Florida or the creeks and rivers of Montana and Wyoming. But that was not their nature. Nor has it been mine.

My own traveling to Cuba with my best friend Sue, who has spent the last two weeks with me visiting here at the cottage on Captiva, was not intended to interfere with Dad's clandestine trips to Havana and Playa

Larga. Regretfully, I know that I caused them grief both when I was in Cuba and on many other occasions too numerous to count. They always worried that they brought me into a life where Dad's continuing dueling with Juan Pablo Herzog might result in my death. Of course, I would not be writing this if that had happened.

1

A MARCH DAY AMONG THE ISLANDS SCATTERED RANDOMLY ON PINE ISLAND SOUND OFF THE SOUTHWEST COAST OF FLORIDA

"WHERE ARE WE, MACDUFF? ARE YOU LOST?" Lucinda asked, her shoulder length auburn hair blowing erratically as she turned around from her favorite perch sitting on a casting platform at the bow of our eighteen-year-old restored Hell's Bay flats boat.

The boat, a sixteen footer, replaced my first flats boat that was incinerated at our dock by then unknown persons, leaving a charred lump of fiberglass and a blackened corpse that proved a challenge to identify.

Hell's Bay is number one on my list of favored flats boats. It's what a Gulf Stream is to jets or a Ferrari to cars. When someone like a Florida Keys legendary guide is behind a fishing product, you know it works as advertised. But then being a "legendary" anything can promote complacency and reluctance to engage in new challenges. I know—I remained a law professor through a decade of despondency over my wife's death until an unpleasant Guatemalan named Juan Pablo Herzog decided to kill me, nearly beat me to death, and has since tried to find me to finish what he started. He's searched for eleven years. I'm still alive, and he's still searching. Maybe I should thank him for scaring me so much that I left the law and became a fly fishing guide. My circumstances have been wearisome—one doesn't guide for a living unless weariness is irrelevant.

Our current Hell's Bay boat was a windfall acquired from a congenial seventyish man in Sarasota, Florida. More accurately, I bought it from his wife because *he* had suffered a disabling stroke soon after he restored the hull to pristine condition. He hadn't quite finished. He didn't last long enough to install what he planned: a trolling motor and power pole.

The boat owner's wife—soon to be a widow—was reluctant to sell. Every day since he returned home from the hospital after his stroke, she watched him spend hours sitting at the center steering console on the boat parked in their driveway forty miles from the nearest water, thinking he was running across the flats around Sarasota Bay.

She finally moved boat and trailer to the garage to prevent the neighbors seeing him sit hour after hour and at times break down convulsed with tears. She didn't know whether his tears were because he had become an obvious burden to her or he no longer knew what he was doing.

Three weeks ago, as March arrived, the last surge of winter left a thin, white coat on both our St. Augustine cottage and the ground beneath the trees. But two hours after the sun rose, the frost had vanished. While March had come in like a lion, it was struggling not to go out like a lamb.

All thoughts of Northern Florida frosts were gone as Lucinda and I skimmed along Pine Island Sound 250 miles south of our St. Augustine cottage. Good fishing waters are inhospitable to a flats boat that doesn't respond kindly to bone-slapping waves. There is a tradeoff when buying a flats boat. It doesn't provide the comfortable ride of a deep "V" hull, but it allows a penetration into the shallows of the marsh flats where sensible boat drafts range from five to six inches.

A light southwest breeze was sweeping in from the Gulf of Mexico, crossing Cayo Costa, and irritating the usually calm waters of Pine Island Sound. We could feel the wind in a sky clear of clouds that would normally confirm a breeze. Palms on the barrier islands formed long ago leaned persistently leeward.

The temperature and humidity separately hugged eighty and made us realize time was closing in on our facing the Great Plains' inducement to boredom on our cross-country trek to Montana to spend the next six months.

We had launched at Pineland Marina destined for three nights at the Cabbage Key Inn. By Lucinda's standards we carried little baggage. For storage, flats boats are closer to VW Beetles than SUVs. Our fishing gear absorbed almost all the locker space. Three small bags were set in front of the center console. I had one, Lucinda two. But when we were packing, she asked if I had a little extra room for some of her things and proceeded to half fill my bag.

I sat at the small console, sparsely fitted out with steering wheel and throttle, compass, switches for lights, trim tabs adjustment, VHF radio, and one gauge that showed RPM. No speedometer— I run by rpm's. No stereo—I listen to birds and live human voices.

Lucinda often sat alongside me, frequently steering, but when she wanted some solitude, she moved to sit or stand on the foredeck.

"Are you listening to me?" she asked, turning toward me, her brow wrinkling. "Where are we?"

"Sorry, my mind drifted. We're in Wilson Cut. It runs west from Pineland through shallow water, past a couple of islands, across the north-south Intracoastal Waterway, leaving only another couple of hundred yards to our destination at Cabbage Key."

"But you slowed and turned south off the channel. I can see grass. It's shallow. Are you lost?"

"Never! Or maybe rarely. I want to tuck into the water on the west side of Black Key. It'll be shallow, but we're due to view a full moon tonight and right now we're closing in on a very high tide. The two combine to give us moonlighted visibility of a good depth . . . . I want you to show me your skills casting to redfish—look for their tails rising above the surface."

"I can't if we're aground."

"Trust me."

We moved slowly over the grass-carpeted bottom toward uninhabited Black Key, rimmed with high red mangroves that draped over the water from their tenacious connection with the shore. As we neared the mangroves, my helmsmanship wavered.

"What are you doing?" Lucinda asked.

"I'm picking a sand flea off my ankle."

"Aren't they what we call no-see-ums?"

"They are."

"They bite! And they hurt," she grumbled.

"They're like midget vampire bats," I added. "They suck blood. Then they remove the protein needed to lay eggs. Their bite can be a problem. Even start an infection or transfer one of several diseases."

"Why did you bring us here?"

"To fish."

"I won't be hungry enough to eat fish if I have an infection and I'm diseased."

"You won't get sick. I sprayed you with a ninety percent solution of DEET."

"Oh, no! DEET causes cancer. You *are* trying to dump me."

"Not proven. DEET's confused with DDT, which admittedly has carcinogens. DEET may cause kidney or liver damage, but so does your favorite Montana Roughstock Whiskey. DEET also can cause birth defects, which at your age you don't have to worry about, or development effects, but you're already very well developed."

"I don't think I want to talk about that any further. . . . I hear something, Macduff. Do masses of sand fleas sound like millions of mosquitos?"

"No, what you hear is the propeller on a slowly moving airboat. It's around the bend ahead, where we're going."

"That airboat noise sounds strange, like it's muffled. The boat can't be running at full speed," she added.

"If it were at full speed, the noise would be impossible even for my lousy hearing. . . . It should come into view in another minute."

"Aren't we in *very* shallow water?" she asked. "The grass bottom looks like it's at most a foot deep."

"The chart shows one to two feet—'mean lower low water.'"

"What's 'mean lower low?' Sounds redundant."

"However it sounds, 'mean lower low water' is the average height of the lower low waters at a given place over a nineteen-year-period."

"Meaning?"

"Meaning we're almost aground. But don't worry. We can run in less than a foot of water. At least we could if you hadn't brought so many suitcases."

"They're not suitcases; they're canvas bags. And there are only three of them. I have to look presentable at dinner."

"Most anything's presentable at Cabbage Key."

We rounded the northern tip of Black Key and entered a one- to two-foot depth where I'd caught a couple of reds a decade ago. A small flats boat coming out of the area by Black Key moved past us at a surprisingly fast speed. A single person at the helm wore a face-covering balaclava, a good way of hiding from the sun—or from something else. When it passed the northern tip of the key, it turned east out of sight, probably headed toward Pineland where we launched.

"There's the airboat, Mac," she exclaimed, pointing eastward. "Over to our left. It looks like the driver lost control and drove into mangroves on the edge of Black Key! . . . Why would the engine be running if it's lodged in the brush? The boat is being pushed against the mangroves."

"I don't know what happened. Maybe the driver was drinking. Maybe he fell asleep at the helm. Maybe he had a heart attack."

"None of the above," she said, looking through a pair of binoculars. "There's no driver in the raised seat in front of the propeller cage."

"Then why. . . . Hey, the engine's stopped. At least the noise pollution is over for now."

Closing on the airboat, Lucinda abruptly turned around from her perch on the bow and faced me, showing both doubt and fright.

"Mac, do you see what I can't believe I see?"

As we maneuvered closer, we neared a scene we never could have imagined. When the airboat's propeller had stopped, Lucinda exclaimed, "There's a body tied to the propeller!"

"Or what *was* a body," I countered.

We edged closer and idled. The body was tied to the propeller around the waist, at the ankles, and under the arms. The airboat propeller looked to be a standard six footer, and the body matched that length, stretching from the prop tip-to-tip.

What we were staring at *arguably* was a man, not defined by facial recognition but from estimates of height and build and by clothing remnants. Whoever it was had worn jeans and a man's shirt.

The person's shoes were missing because the feet were gone nearly back to the ankle. Thrust outward and slightly to the rear from centrifugal force and the airboat's speed, the feet had been mutilated by the prop's metal cage. Also, the weight of the body strained against the rope tied to its waist and caused the knees to buckle, ripped the jeans open, and crushed the knees.

But not only had the feet and knees been shredded by the cage: the spinning upper body and head had slouched rearward, collided with the cage, and, like the feet and knees, become unrecognizable.

Lastly, the person's arms had not been tied, and the spinning caused them to fly out and hit the propeller cage. There would be no taking of fingerprints because there were no fingers. Or hands. Or forearms.

Strangely, there was little sign of blood from the grisly remains. Blood that had impacted the cage had presumably spun away as a red mist and disappeared into the water, leaving a crimson wake. But enough had landed in and on the boat to suggest a DNA sample would provide the start to an identification process of the body. But not the killer.

"Who would do this, Mac? It's barbaric!" Lucinda uttered, looking away from the airboat.

"No one we want to know. We have to call for help. Use Channel 16 on the VHF. That should get the Coast Guard or some vessel that's monitoring the channel. Don't say who you are and don't use your cell phone. The call to Channel 16 may be recorded, but they won't know who made it."

Lucinda called and in a disguised voice said nothing more than describing the scene and giving the location. When she was asked for her name, she hung up.

In the silence with the propeller stopped and my motor shut down, we watched a few remaining drops of blood falling onto the airboat's afterdeck.

"I've heard of the term 'to bleed out,'" Lucinda observed, "but I never imagined it might happen this way. . . . Mac, what should we do?"

"You've called. Be patient. And check your Glock," I replied, searching for my gun somewhere among the mess in the after storage compartment. Lucinda was sitting holding her loaded Glock long before I found mine.

"Don't say another word," I pleaded. "I found mine. I'm ready. Oh damn! It's not loaded. Got any extra cartridges? Mine may be in here somewhere."

"You're *useless*, Macduff! You could have been shot dead by now. . . . Motor closer and see if we can do anything?"

"Do what? . . . If we touch anything, boat or body, we might disturb evidence and leave our prints and DNA. Let's sit and wait. Hide your Glock," I suggested, putting mine in my fly box."

We waited twenty minutes, watching the sun slant downward over nearby Useppa Island. The noise of a distant motor grew louder and within minutes another airboat, bearing large "FWC" letters on its side—Fish and Wildlife Commission—arrived with two persons aboard. It wasn't dark yet, but the boat was ablaze with flashing lights and strobes so overwhelming it looked like the inside of a punk rock club.

The FWC boat approached the airboat but backed off when the occupants saw what had happened and, slowing their speed, moved toward us. Twenty feet away, the officer at the helm, a fiftyish, bald, muscular male, unsnapped his pistol holster clinging to his belt of many gadgets, leaving his hand on top of the gun.

"Keep your hands where we can see them," he called. He reminded me of a waterborne version of the Southern redneck police chief in *Cool Hand Luke*. "You got weapons?" he asked.

"Who are you?" I asked, ignoring his question. "You're not wearing uniforms. Show us some identification."

He ignored my demand. "We're not wearing our FWC uniforms because we were off duty and taking this airboat to be serviced. We answered the call because we were close."

"Who *are* you?" Lucinda demanded.

"You fish around here you *better* know who I am—Tommy Lee Cartwright. My daddy's a state representative, and my uncle was a wildlife officer who got electrocuted working on one of these goddamn airboats. . . . The guy with me is Brucie Cassell, and he works for *me*. I got a mind to shoot both of you. You killed that poor bastard! But you weren't smart enough to leave. Jeez! . . . Who do we let have a boat these days?"

"Just a minute, Cartwright," I called. "We were heading toward Black Key to fish for reds. We heard noise that sounded strange, came over here and saw exactly what you're seeing now, and called Channel 16. . . . Keep that gun in its holster."

"Tommy," the younger man said, interrupting Cartwright. "*We don't need our guns.* They wouldn't have called on 16 if they were the killers."

"I'll handle this, Brucie boy," demanded Cartwright, without even a glance at his long-haired, skinny, twenty-something-year-old partner.

"Why didn't you try to save the poor guy? Just sat on your asses doing nothing!" Cartwright added.

"We didn't want to touch anything that might be evidence. We arrived only twenty minutes before you did and haven't been any closer to the airboat than we are now."

"You might have *saved* him," he replied.

"Saved what? A hand or a foot? Maybe some teeth? Be realistic, Cartwright."

"Have you determined it was a *him* and not a *her*?" Lucinda challenged Cartwright.

"I'm not stupid," Cartwright answered. "He's wearing *pants*."

"So am I," Lucinda offered.

"Don't sass me, lady. You're both *here*. No one else is in sight. And we got a mutilated, dead body. You're suspects. I'm takin' you in." Cartwright pulled a set of handcuffs from his belt.

"Tommy, they aren't necessary," said the one called Brucie. "At least not yet. Why don't we ask them a few questions? I don't believe they're the killers."

"You work for *me*, Brucie boy. I'm in charge, and I give the orders." Turning to face Lucinda, Cartwright demanded, "Whose airboat is that?"

"We don't know," she responded.

"You towed your flats boat behind the airboat," Cartwright speculated. "And after you drove the airboat into the mangroves, you got into your boat and backed away. That's when we found you. Another crew will be here to take over and check for evidence. I got you red-handed."

"Tommy, I meant what I said," repeated Cassell. "We have no grounds to take them in, with or without cuffs. You haven't even asked for identification. Or why they're here. You assume too much. Aren't you in enough trouble from your bad ass conduct last year? You're on probation for falsely arresting that county commissioner for keeping snook. Snook were in season, and you were dead wrong. You put cuffs on *him* and paid a price. Do it now, and you may be all through. *And lose your pension.* . . . We need to stay here and wait for the evidence experts and someone to take the body down after examining it the way it is now. Let these two get on their way."

Cartwright sat for a moment gloating. I thought he was thinking, but he was fooling with what appeared to be a cellphone. Then he looked up at his partner.

"This is the last case you work on with me, Brucie. . . . But OK. No cuffs. No arrest. Yet."

Turning to Lucinda and me he added, "Get the hell out of here."

I smiled at Lucinda and backed the boat off slowly keeping an eye on the two, especially Cartwright. I turned the bow and pushed the throttle forward to get onto a plane and put some distance between us before Cartwright decided he *was* going to arrest us. When I looked over my shoulder, Cartwright was yelling something at Cassell and waving his arms. I couldn't imagine the FWC hiring or keeping someone like him. The *influence* of his father must be the answer.

"I'm exhausted from that encounter, Mac," Lucinda said as we skirted Useppa Island, centuries ago part of the mainland, now a controlled, limited access, private refuge of wealth.

"Remember Playa Larga?" I asked Lucinda, wanting to take her mind off the unpleasant episode at Black Key.

"Whatever made you mention Playa Larga? Why Cuba?"

"Useppa is where the U.S. trained some of the Cuban exiles for the Bay of Pigs debacle. Maybe they enjoyed Useppa too much. The invasion failed, but to be fair it was mostly due to the lack of promised U.S. air support after the exiles began their invasion."

We turned south on the Intracoastal and passed Useppa as Cabbage Key came into sight.

"That's where we're staying, Lucinda," I commented, pointing ahead while we carefully approached our destination.

"I miss Wuff," she said offhandedly as the few buildings that make up the Cabbage Key complex came into view. Wuff is our rescued sheltie who vies with me for Lucinda's affection. Wuff usually wins. We dropped her off in Ocala at her favorite sheltie farm. She's with about thirty shelties and probably has forgotten about us. But I won't speculate on that to Lucinda, who would be devastated without Wuff around.

"It's good we left her in Ocala," Lucinda offered. "She's not an attack dog. I doubt Cartwright would have been scared of her."

"That's not a nice thing to say. Her feelings would be hurt. She thinks of herself as a ferocious protector of her flock of two."

We were scheduled to stay at the Dollhouse Cottage, which often serves as Cabbage Key's honeymoon lodging, but I didn't tell Lucinda that. I brought our boat to the main dock where we tied up, walked ashore with that wobble that follows being on a boat, and checked in. I think I was a little curt in response to the warm greeting we received; the day was beginning to overwhelm me. A few steps took us to the cottage with its private dock and a couple of spine-teasing Adirondack chairs.

Lucinda and I were tired and thought of leaving our boat at the main dock but soon realized numerous other boats would be jockeying to tie up and unload scores of people for dinner, so we shifted our boat the few yards to the small pier in front of the cottage.

Once our bags were in the cottage and the boat secured for the night, I asked, "Ready for dinner?"

"It's an hour after sunset. I know it's our first night here, but can we go to bed early?" Lucinda asked. "I've lost my appetite."

"I've never lost my appetite for going to bed early with you," I answered, grabbing and holding her as the day caught up to us.

Lucinda began to shiver in the cool evening air.

2

THE FOLLOWING EVENING AT CABBAGE KEY

LUCINDA AND I SAT IN THE RESTAURANT AT Cabbage Key the next evening after leaving our boat at the dock for the day and exploring the island, interrupted by a few cat-naps. Our rented cottage was as encumbered by moss-draped Cuban laurel trees as the restaurant was by dollar bills. Years ago a guest autographed and pinned a dollar bill to the wall and tens of thousands of patrons have followed suit, including Jimmy Buffett, who may or may not have written "Cheeseburger in Paradise" there. There are thought to be some $70,000 worth of separately signed bills. After the walls were covered, the next tidal flow of dollars was hung from posts and overhead beams. Larger denomination bills are gobbled up by the cash register at prices reflecting Cabbage Key's status as a "resort."

Prolific mystery writer Mary Roberts Rinehart built the house in 1929 for her son. Her own winter-season house sat a mile away high on Useppa, which in society's pecking order was notches higher than Cabbage Key. The Cabbage Key home morphed into an inn fifteen years later and for three-and-a-half-decades has been in the capable hands of a family that also owns and operates the Tarpon Inn on Pine Island.

After dinner Lucinda and I carried what remained of our drinks to a quiet table in the front, overlooking the sound. She was sipping a Planter's Punch. My request for Gentleman Jack was declined, and I settled for Jack Daniels with a dollop of bitters.

"I don't know whether to be fighting-angry about our treatment yesterday at Black Key or commiserate with you over the sad demeanor of one of our FWA officers," commented Lucinda. "Cartwright was something else! . . . Are you listening? Why are you opening your iPad? Looking up tomorrow's weather? Remember that we're on vacation."

"I can guess that tomorrow's weather here will be great," I said, "like yesterday's and the day's before, and tomorrow's. . . . I'm looking up Cartwright and Cassell on the FWC list of officers. They're listed by name, but no information is given about them."

"Macduff, look up FWC and recent incidents or crimes."

"OK. . . . Good thought! The first thing that comes up is a release issued today: 'Unidentified Body Remains Found on Airboat.'"

"Read it to me, quietly."

I did:

> *The unidentified remains of a body were found tied to a propeller on an airboat at Black Key in Pine Island Sound off the southwest coast of Florida. Secured at the ankles, waist, and under the arms, the person had been spun to death by the rotating propeller.*
>
> *Centrifugal force from the spinning propeller had caused the feet, knees, hands, and face to come into contact with the stout metal propeller cage as the airboat sped across Pine Island Sound. A positive DNA test conducted during the autopsy may determine the identity of the body—if a match is established.*

The airboat apparently was stolen from its registered owner, Rod Swenson, a resident of Gibsonton, south of Tampa, known as the location where circus and carnival side-show performers have long resided. Swenson and a partner operate an airboat business in Gibsonton, and both they and their boats frequently have been in conflict with the noise ordinances in various counties.

The airboat and body were discovered yesterday by a couple fishing who reported the matter on Channel 16.

Lee County prosecutors are investigating.

"What about Cartwright and Cassell?" Lucinda questioned. "Why aren't they mentioned?"

"Maybe they never reported what they found, in which case we have to worry that they may have been up to no good and will come after us."

"I can't believe they *forgot* to report seeing a body. . . . Macduff, we *can't* get involved. Not again. I haven't recovered from Cuba, much less the gill nets."

"We're already involved. Cartwright apparently passed information on to local Lee County officials or the state attorney's office in Ft. Myers. They may not have given their names because they might have been involved. Drugs? I don't know. The question is: What do we do?"

"Call the police?" she suggested.

"Which police?"

"The FWC? The county sheriff's office? The state attorney's office for this region? Whoever handles crimes?"

"And tell them what?"

"What happened to us," she replied.

"We weren't involved in the killing. We didn't get out of our boat. . . . We didn't touch a thing. That means *nothing* happened to us."

"But we know about the two FWC officers who arrived on the second airboat. A boat with FWC markings. We could at least report that," she suggested.

"We do know a little about them. They know *nothing* about us. They didn't ask for identification, and we didn't show them anything," I responded. "Our boat has state licensing numbers. It was their responsibility to write down the numbers if they wanted them. I suspect they didn't. They told us to leave. We aren't at fault for their shortcomings."

"Could we be in trouble for failing to call the Lee County police and tell them what we know, in addition to our Channel 16 call?" she asked.

"No. We don't know as much as the two FWC officers must have learned. Or at least should have. They must be required to make a report, but from what you've read, they apparently didn't. Why? Something about the FWC is suspicious. Most of all, we don't want our names discussed in the press."

"What do we do?" she asked.

"Pay attention to whatever appears in the papers and keep our lips sealed. If anyone asks why we're interested, we say the incident happened on our way here and naturally we we're curious about such a bizarre event."

"OK. . . . But I can't help thinking that just maybe we could help."

"And just maybe it would mean some publicity-seeking reporter from the press would badger us about who we are and publish it or report it on TV in their desperation to be the first with 'breaking news.' Regardless of any consequent harm to us."

"What do we do?" she asked again.

"Have dinner and test the bed once more."

"The bed works fine. . . . We *are* better off not being mentioned. I think you're right, Macduff."

"Be glad you're not missing feet, hands, knee caps, and part of your face. Someone plays rough."

"That's not going to happen to us."

"No. But think of what might happen if publicity caused us to lose our identity and Juan Pablo Herzog in Guatemala learned about it. He still wants to locate and kill us. We have a good life. I won't jeopardize it."

"You're right. . . . No more talk about airboats tonight."

"Turning to a more pleasant subject, what would my gorgeous bride like for dinner?"

"Gorgeous bride!" she exclaimed. "I like the gorgeous part, but I wonder about the reference to my being a bride. Are you finally admitting we got married? There was a ceremony? With rings? And a cake? . . . And I got to sleep over?"

"You have a one-track mind," I answered.

"You're right when it comes to sleeping over. . . . Because more than a year has passed since we swapped yeses at that church in Oyster Bay, I guess there's no use debating any further. To use your lawyer-speak, an admission of marriage is not rescindable after the first year. . . . Or after a first drink. And we've had two. . . . Do you love me, Mac?"

"Well, I love Wuff and *Osprey* and Elsbeth." Elsbeth is my daughter who is at the University of Florida. *Osprey* is our wooden drift boat, secure for the winter in its shed at Mill Creek. Wuff is my rescued sheltie. "Is it possible to love more than three?" I asked.

"If it isn't, you're in big trouble. . . . Do you still love El?"

El was my first wife who was killed during a boating accident in Wyoming some two decades ago. I was Professor

Maxwell Hunt at the law college at the University of Florida and spent the decade after El's death muddling through my coursework and engaging in unwise tasks abroad for our State Department.

Some trouble arose in Guatemala that nearly resulted in my death at the hands of a local drug lord, Juan Pablo Herzog. Threats to finish what he started led to the State Department deciding to place me in a protection program with a new name, location, and job. A year later, I met Lucinda.

"I'll always love El," I admitted. For years I assumed she died giving birth to our daughter—to be named Elsbeth. A couple of years ago I learned she miraculously had survived. "Elsbeth looks to you for motherly advice. She adores you, Lucinda. . . . So do I," I whispered.

"But I haven't even made *your* top three that include a boat and a dog!"

"You're different. Special. One of a kind. Rare."

"Like a black orchid?" she asked.

"Better."

"The Hope diamond?"

"Much better."

"A Lafite wine owned by Thomas Jefferson?"

"Now you're getting close."

"A wine! You're awful."

"You don't fit *any* classification."

"Meaning I'm unfit?"

"Meaning you're unique."

"How?"

"Looks, personality, intelligence, compassion. I could go on, but I'm not the one with a Ph.D."

"Go on anyway."

"Delectable and scrumptious. I've loved you since you opened your ranch door that Thanksgiving."

"You don't always show it."

"But I always *feel* it. There's a difference."

"Will it last?"

"No."

"No! Am I about to be cast out onto the icy streets of Montana?"

"No. It will last only until the earth disappears into a black hole. It can't be measured in time."

"You're embarrassing me, Mac. . . . I'm all ears."

"Before I change my mind, let's eat."

"What do you want?"

"A burger and fries."

"Not a chance. All those nice words were intended to get me to agree to your eating junk food. *I'll* order for you. Remember that I'm the family nutritionist."

She did order for me, and we shared a smoked salmon appetizer and a Mahi-Mahi entreé. I got to add the caramel turtle fudge ice cream pie for desert, but she ate most of it; she has the fastest desert spoon in the country.

An hour later she asked, "Want to walk the shoreline?"

"Only as far as the king-size bed in our cottage."

"I thought I exhausted you last night," she said.

"I've miraculously recovered. But try to exhaust me again."

"I'll try harder," she said, prodding me along. "If you can make it to the cottage."

"Piece of cake."

3

TWO DAYS LATER AT CABBAGE KEY

DAWN SHOULD HAVE BROUGHT NEW ENERGY and both dislodged from our memories bad experiences and opened our minds to new challenges. But this dawn—our last breakfast at Cabbage Key—struggled to achieve either. We both had our own visions of airboats, and they had kept us from sleeping the past two nights.

The kitchen had barely enough room to make coffee. We stumbled in to start breakfast after our unsettled night. Five minutes later, on the porch with hand-warming coffee cups and facing a chilly sunrise wrapped in bathrobes, we watched Cuban laurel branches bend in the welcoming cool breeze from the northwest. Settling into two wooden Adirondack chairs, we sipped the coffee, staring over the cups' rims at the early departure of two Cabbage Key guests in their Grand Banks trawler.

"Macduff, stop dreaming about a Grand Banks; we have *two* boats. . . . Instead, go online again and see if there are any new developments about the body in the airboat."

I did, looking for and finding the local Ft. Myers *Times*. Ignoring pleas to subscribe to the online edition, I took advantage of free limited access and on page three found a single-column article titled "Airboat Death Remains a Mystery."

"Anything new we don't know?" she asked.

"Yes. The person who was killed was Raymond Prescott. Born in Nashville, Tennessee, he was fifty-one at his death. He lived on Pine Island and commuted to Ft. Myers where he worked as a CPA. Nothing else about him is mentioned."

"Anything about his death on the boat?"

"The authorities don't know much yet, but drugs appear to have been involved. Investigators found traces of cocaine in every compartment on the airboat. If it was transporting drugs, maybe Prescott found out about them, and they cost him his life."

"Or *he* may have been involved in drug trafficking," she suggested.

"Possibly. The *Times* article says the airboat was reported by its owner, Martin Swenson, as having been stolen. Its manufacturer, ABI Company, was furious at being mentioned in some news reports. If Prescott was the one who stole the airboat, plans went terribly wrong, and he lost his life in a most gruesome way."

"If Prescott didn't steal the airboat, how do you suppose he ended up tied to its propeller?" she asked.

"Abducted and, conscious or not, taken to the boat, tied to the propeller, and learned what it felt like to be spun at 500 rpm or more."

"I don't want to think about what he looked like when we saw what was left of him, even from thirty-feet away. I hope I never see a sight like that again," she said, having taken the article when I sat down to drink my coffee.

"Mac, there's more at the end of the article. A boat cushion was discovered hanging from a branch in the mangroves close to the airboat. We had two cushions. The one found was stenciled *Fishhawk*. That's *our* boat!"

"Fortunately, I haven't put the name on our boat's transom," I added. "I brought the letters with me and planned to apply them some morning while we're here."

"That ends that plan. Could the letters be traced, maybe to a store like West Marine?"

"Not if I remember what I said," I answered. "I asked for one *A*, one *F*, two *H*'s, one *I*, one *K*, one *S*, and one *W*. I never referred to the name being *Fishhawk*."

"But the boat *is* for fishing," she said, "Four of the letters we bought spell *fish*. That leaves only four letters. Look in a dictionary for a word beginning with *fish*. Like *fishhook*. Or *fishhawk*, which uses all the letters you bought."

"Don't scare me, Sherlock."

"Let's destroy the other cushion with the name, choose a new name, and put it on the boat immediately," she proposed, adding, "Anything more in the article? *Anything* suggesting who might have killed Prescott?"

"Nothing. . . . Who do you think could have done the killing? After all, you're the family sleuth."

"Too many choices, Mac."

"At least it must have been someone who viewed using an airboat as a convenient method to kill or as a way to send some kind of message to someone else. I don't view it as *convenient*."

"A lot of possibilities exist," she began. "One is the airboat owner, Swenson, assuming he had issues with Prescott. Another could be a neighbor of the airboat owner who was mad at the callous noise made by the airboat at late hours. But why kill Prescott rather than the airboat's owner? Unless one was related to the other. We need to learn more about Prescott and any link between him and the airboat owner or the owner of the ABI Company.

"A third possible killer was someone who stole the airboat to use as an instrument to kill Prescott. Or someone who stole the boat believing cocaine was aboard. Or who wanted the boat, and the cocaine traffickers caught him stealing their drugs and killed him. Or perhaps even boaters who hated his noisy intrusion when they were fishing the quiet flats."

"You have such a fertile mind when it comes to murders."

"That comes from living with you," Lucinda said.

"If my Guatemalan assailant, Juan Pablo Herzog, knew I was protected by you, never again would he try to kill me."

"As John Lennon said," Lucinda proffered, "'As usual, there is a great woman behind every idiot.'"

"This idiot prefers Oscar Wilde—'Women are made to be loved, not understood.'"

"I agree," she said, giving me a well-deserved hug.

"To get back to the murder, all our suggestions could be wrong," I said. "Remember how bad our guess was in the Cuban deaths? We were certain the murders using the barracuda pens were the work of U.S. Representative Elena Mendoza, not—as admitted to much later—the actions by the Cuban Interior Minister Cristina Sandoval. "

"Our conclusions may have been wrong. But we *were* involved in Cuba, or we became involved. We're not involved here."

"Anything more about the airboat in the article?" I asked.

"There is," she answered. "Prescott's pockets apparently were emptied before he was killed. But he was wearing one of those shirts with breast pockets that open by a small zipper along one *side* rather than at the top. Whoever stripped his pockets forgot the shirt pocket; it carried one item—a wrinkled business card."

"What did it say?" I asked.

"It was a card from a fishing guide at Captiva, Mark Sloan. . . . I hate to ask, but do you know him?"

"I hate to answer, but I hired him as a guide to fish for snook off the Sanibel beaches when I was teaching law as Professor Maxwell Hunt. About fifteen years ago."

"That's exactly why we don't want to get involved," she mused. "Anything that brings into the discussion you as Professor Hunt. Sloan could recognize you. Nothing yet has been mentioned about him in the reports, but I assume he'll be investigated."

Lucinda's cell phone rang. It was my daughter Elsbeth, calling from Gainesville, where she attends the University of Florida. She calls me for money. She calls Lucinda for everything else. I didn't mind; I've wanted the two to be close. Elsbeth never knew her mother, and Lucinda couldn't have children because of what her former British husband, Robert Ellsworth-Kent, did to her. Elsbeth and Lucinda have become best friends.

"Elsbeth, what are you up to?" Lucinda began.

"Exams start in a couple of weeks. Can you believe I'll be a junior in the fall?"

"Sue also?" Lucinda asked, referring to Elsbeth's house mate and trusted friend.

"Of course. We're like twins. . . . When are you guys heading to Montana?"

"We 'guys' are heading there soon. Where are you two 'gals' spending the summer?"

"Pestering you and Dad on Mill Creek. We've got jobs again at the Chico Hot Springs resort. And we've been promoted. Sue's job will be to check people into the restaurant; mine will be at the front desk of the resort."

"Congratulations," I interjected. "What will you study in the fall? Don't you have to decide on a major?"

"We've both been accepted to do our junior year abroad."

"Outer Mongolia?"

"*London!* Where Lucinda once worked and allegedly you once taught."

"I'm glad you're not going back to Cuba," Lucinda called out. . . . "Do you realize you've talked four minutes without asking your dad for money?"

"I'll get to that. I want to come over next weekend and see you two before you start west."

"Come ahead. Right now we're on Cabbage Key, but we'll drive back to the cottage at St. Augustine in a day or two."

"Anyone shot or blown up on your flats boat in the past few days?" Elsbeth asked.

I shuddered to think about that.

"No, I answered, but someone was killed on an airboat near here two days ago. *We* had nothing to do with it!"

"You expect me to believe that? See you, Dad," she said. "Oh! Have your checkbook with you next weekend."

Lucinda put down the cell phone, looked at me quizzically, and asked, "Should we have told her more about the body on the airboat?"

"Probably, but it wouldn't phase her one bit after Cuba."

"You were right not to say more, Macduff. Let her concentrate on exams."

4

PARADISE VALLEY, MONTANA—MID-APRIL

WE CHOSE NOT TO RUSH ACROSS COUNTRY with the haste that propelled us during the years of our trips to Cuba because of the barracuda pens murders and to various places in Florida because of the gill net murders. Accommodating weather forecasts for the week urged us to head north and link up to Interstate 90, where we drove and drove across Wisconsin, Minnesota, South Dakota, a corner of Colorado, and partway through Montana toward Livingston. From there we had only a half-hour drive south through the welcoming spring colors and smells in Paradise Valley to our cabin on Mill Creek. But as we passed Billings, I turned to Lucinda.

"We usually race across the country and miss some beautiful scenery and worthwhile places to fish along the streams and rivers that drop down from the mountains. We have a couple of choices between here and Livingston. Interested in a diversion?"

"Why not? Where to?" Lucinda asked.

"In another few miles there's a turn at a town named Columbus to a road that points us south and up into the Absaroka-Beartooth Wilderness. The road more or less follows the Stillwater River."

"What do you know about the Stillwater? A river that looks as placid as a lake, if that's what 'still' water means?"

"I read about the Stillwater in one of the fly fishing magazines," I answered. "It's not 'still' water, at least proportionally to other Montana rivers. To the contrary, it's anything but *still* water.

"It's exceptionally clear water, which is unusual for rivers flowing *east* from the Continental Divide. That includes the Stillwater and our own Yellowstone River. It has to do with the presence or absence of dissolved solids in the water and when present their composition."

"Why are rivers that flow west clearer?" she asked.

"Consider the Missouri that passes Kansas City and twenty-five miles north of St. Louis flows into the Mississippi River, which itself has passed by Minneapolis, and finally dumps its dissolved urban solids into the Gulf of Mexico, after passing New Orleans, where it adds some Cajun crud.

"The path of the Snake River is cleaner, beginning on the west side of the Continental Divide, passing mostly rural land on its way to join the Columbia River, and finally meeting the Pacific Ocean. No Kansas City. No Minneapolis. No St. Louis. No New Orleans."

"Nice geography lesson, but what's so attractive about the Stillwater River? It means we add another day before we reach our Mill Creek cabin."

"The Stillwater flows down from the Absaroka-Beartooth Wilderness and is joined by the West Fork of the Stillwater below the town of Nye. Everything I've heard about Nye is that the landscape is spectacular."

"I'm online searching for Nye, Montana, Macduff," she said balancing her tablet on her lap. "Got it! It has two to three hundred people, including at the last count one Black, a dozen

Hispanics, and a couple of Indians. I guess the rest are palefaces like us. Crow Indians once dominated the area, then trappers and miners and later homesteaders. Today the miners again dominate."

"Why back to mining?" she asked.

"Nye is home to the Stillwater Mining Co., the major U.S. producer of platinum and palladium used for electronics and fuel cells. Meaning the labor force at the mine fluctuates according to forces from places like Russia."

"There's a place in Nye named Carter's Camp. Maybe an hour from here if you turn off at that Columbus sign right ahead of us," she suggested, squinting at the map wearing neither her reading nor sun glasses.

We turned off and stopped for gas for the SUV and bottled water for us, thinking we should avoid drinking water possibly tainted with platinum or palladium. Back on the road, we headed south further into the mountains, following the Stillwater River and wondering what we would find.

"I have the Carter's Camp website on my iPad, and I'm reading about their restaurant," she noted. "Prime rib and karaoke every Friday. The restaurant is ranked number one in town, possibly because it's the only one in town. You'll like the prime rib, and I'll like the karaoke, as long as you promise not to sing along."

"I'll play my oboe."

"Karaoke is sing-along, not squeak-along. Thank God today's not Friday."

We passed through Absarokee—the Stillwater River's 1,200 population metropolis, no longer counting the murdered body found in an alley the week before we arrived—and concluded quickly that there were no compelling reasons to stay and drove on. The natural beauty of the landscape returned as we distanced ourselves from Absarokee and soon entered Nye. And immediately—in the blink of an eye—departed Nye. The welcoming sign said "Entering and Leaving Nye, Montana – Elev. 4825 ft."

Using an online booking agency, Lucinda secured two nights' lodging at a cabin called the Stillwater River Retreat near Nye. The owner accepted Wuff with our assurances that she only barked when her meals were late. I paid for the room and promised to feed her on time.

Settling into our room, Lucinda asked, "What are we going to fish for?"

"For our psychological contentment."

"I'm already contented. I meant what kind of *fish?*"

"The Stillwater comes out of the mountains you see around us. Its headwaters are to the south in the northeast corner of Yellowstone Park. . . . We're close to where the Absaroka-Beartooth Wilderness begins. We won't go that far this trip, maybe another time. The river drops fast heading north out of the Wilderness and then becomes floatable. We're too early to float; enough water to do that comes after the runoff sometime in late May or early June and ends in August as the water level drops. For drift boats that means only a two-month window, extended or diminished by the vagaries of weather."

"Fish! I asked what kind of *fish*? Not for a lecture. . . . What size rods? What kind of flies? Enough *geography*. . . . But it is beautiful."

"There are good size brook trout and rainbows in the higher wilderness area. In this area browns have mostly replaced the brookies; both browns and brookies co-exist with the rainbows.

"Let's use our bamboo rods and 9' 5X leaders," I recommended. "We could go to 12' leaders, but I think the 9's are OK, and they're easier to cast. Remember that we're casting the line, not the leader. The weight is in the line tip. . . . Let's head upriver a little, *above* the mine."

"Because the mine dumps residue into the river?"

"No. Fortunately, the Stillwater Mine mostly is an underground operation. The platinum and palladium are trucked to a smelter at Columbus down near I-90 where the Stillwater joins the Yellowstone."

The landscape-disfiguring mine complex soon came into view, and the monotone of dirt and dust overwhelmed nature's magnificent colors.

Ten minutes later, parked where the owners of our cabin had recommended, Lucinda began to put together the 7' bamboo rod I'd given her the first Christmas after we met. For a year it hung over her Manhattan apartment fireplace mantle and became a conversation piece about the gift she'd received from *that* fishing bum Montana guide. That bothered her; she treasured the rod and had not hung it to induce ridicule.

Lucinda has used the rod frequently since we became a pair. It was the second bamboo rod I'd made, with a few modifications from the first, which I was fishing with.

"Macduff, this is beautiful land; the mountains are much closer than when we fish the Yellowstone. But the bigger distinction is that along the Yellowstone you see huge homes, often misplaced where infrequent but inevitable high spring runoffs will cause flooding. Here along the Stillwater, the view is of farm after farm and smaller homes and cabins. It's too beautiful to last."

"The river looks peaceful but that's deceptive," I noted. "We're getting some beginning snowmelt runoff because of recent warming. Use your wading stick for balance. Remember when you didn't think you needed one on Henry's Fork and you pirouetted into the river in Box Canyon?"

"But I saved my fish. And it was bigger than yours."

"I don't know why I take you fishing."

"Because I show you how fishing should be done. Who catches more fish?"

"That's only because I give up a lot of fishing time to train you and pull you out when you fall in. . . . Why don't you stop bragging and fish?"

"I don't have a fly on my tippet. Put one on, please."

"I'll do more than that. I'll put two on?"

"Hopper and dropper?"

"No, hopper season is a few months away. I hoped we'd arrive here for the Mother's Day caddis hatch, but we have a couple of weeks to go to be certain of seeing it. We might see a mayfly hatch. Save your Brown Caddis #14 and #16 flies for the caddis hatch and similar size Baetis or March Browns for the mayfly hatch."

"There's no sign of a hatch. What do we use while we wait?"

"A double nymph."

"But they will *both* sink, and I won't see a strike."

"You will because I'll add a strike indicator of bright orange yarn just where the fly line and leader join. Then squeeze on a very small BB size split-shot about a foot-and-a-half from the tip of the leader. The larger nymph—my favorite Pheasant Tail—ties on the end tip of the leader, and I'll add a small Hare's Ear as a dropper at the end of another foot-and-a-half of 4X tippet. Both the nymphs have bead heads to get them down, assisted by the split-shot."

"Isn't this too much to cast?"

"It's not as easy as a single tiny dry fly. It's easy to tangle the two, or four if you count the indicator and split-shot."

"You'll untangle me, won't you? . . . What are *you* going to use?"

"A dry fly."

"That's not fair. I have to work harder and can't see what I'm doing while you have an easy fly to cast and the joy of watching a rising trout take it."

"But there may be no rising trout. Granted, I'll be ready, using a #16 Brown Caddis fly if the caddis hatch starts. It's much more likely that as long as the hatch doesn't start, trout near the bottom will take one of your nymphs rather than spend more energy rising to the surface for my caddis fly."

"And what if the caddis hatch starts while I've got all this junk tied on, and you're a few yards away, catching one after another during the hatch? . . . You're deliberately trying to see me skunked."

"I had planned to exchange rods with you if the hatch started," I responded with a quivering voice of rejection. "And then, while watching you catch trout after trout, I would remove all *your* 'junk' and—hopefully before the hatch was over—throw a small caddis like you were doing. I was *planning* to do that because of my undying love."

"I don't know whether to whack you with my wading stick or burst out crying," she said.

I didn't find out which because her indicator submerged in an instant and instinctively she lifted her rod."

"I've got one, Mac!"

"No!" I shouted.

"I do! Look at my line."

"You have *two* on the line, one on each nymph. A solo double! Don't lose them."

"How do I fish them?" she pleaded.

"Carefully."

"That's no help. What do I do?"

"I have no idea; it's never happened to me."

"Take my rod. *Please,*" she pleaded.

"If I broke your bamboo rod, you would never forgive me."

"I promise to forgive you. Take it!"

"OK, hand me yours, and I'll hand you mine."

At that moment a 15" to 18" brown trout exploded on the surface, engulfed my caddis fly, and headed toward Lucinda.

"*Mac*, look what you've done to us!"

"Pure guiding skill."

And at *that* moment my solo trout crossed the line of her duo, her tippet got caught in mine, hers broke, and I was left with three fish on the line.

"Now, self-described skillful guide, what are you going to do with three fish?" she asked.

With that, my brown decided to head the opposite direction her two rainbows chose. The underwater tug of war ended with Lucinda's two breaking off first, and, with an apparently weakened tippet, my brown soon following.

As the water smoothed by the now unperturbed current and no sound came from the pastoral surroundings, Lucinda's Cheshire cat grin overwhelmed me. I took a step toward her, began to lose balance, grabbed for my wading stick, missed and fell, twisting around and landing butt first on a boulder that was decidedly firmer than my rear. I sat in the frigid spring snowmelt water, looking up at her.

"When we first met, I was sitting on my rear, in front of your ranch door on ice you hadn't cleared. Here I am again, the victim of your affection."

She took a few steps to me.

"Take the rod," she said. "I see something in the water by your wading boots."

She reached down into the cold water, grabbed whatever it was, and pulled.

"Look what I have," she said laughing. "It's our tippets and the three flies. The fish didn't break the tippets; they slipped the hooks. It spoke well of barbless hooks."

"I'm freezing," I added, now upright and dripping. . . . "You're more interested in retrieving the flies than retrieving me!"

"I always save the flies I catch fish on," she said. Now, let's get you out of this river and out of your clothes."

"I like the second part."

We had fished for at most twenty minutes; it was barely noon. I disrobed in the car and wrapped up in a blanket we kept in the back for Wuff to lie on. I was sure to have fleas. By noon I'd recovered—benefitting from a quick drive back to the lodge, a hot shower, and coffee plus adjusting to Lucinda's waves of convulsive laughter.

Walking Wuff an hour later, I felt fully recovered but fully embarrassed. Lucinda grabbed my arm and asked, "What other exciting fishing adventures do you have for us, Macduff? Shall we try the river again?"

"I may never fish in a river or stream again and stand in the water within sight of you," I declared. "You're a danger to the good name of fly fishing. A Drusilla in waders!"

"I can't wait to tell people. We're meeting with a dozen Livingston and Bozeman friends in four days for Erin Giffin's birthday. They will love hearing about your most recent guiding experience."

"I may not have recovered by then. . . . Let's have a late lunch in Fishtail. It's not far from here, and we can drive slowly and see more of this area. We'll do a loop to Fishtail, have lunch at the Cowboy Bar, go on and rejoin the river road at Absarokee, and come back here."

"Shall we keep our fishing gear rigged?" she asked.

"Of course, plus some dry blankets in case you push me in again."

That evening we returned to Carter's Camp, tucked between rising Beartooth Mountains' peaks. Carter's served us dinner—whiskey *au natural* followed by whiskey sirloin. Fortunately, karaoke was another night away.

At our cabin we hated to go in but it was too cold to sit on the porch. We stayed in our heated car facing the mountain gap where the Stillwater road disappeared. There was enough moonlight to outline the mountains' fragmented edges rising on each side of the river. A few lights from scattered homes on the lower mountainsides flickered and went out one-by-one.

Lucinda was smiling, not at me, not at the mountains, but at herself for some thought she hadn't shared. Then she turned and said quietly so as not to disturb the landscape, "When we had lunch, Macduff, I noticed a special on the menu I'm going to cook for you at Mill Creek."

"Should I ask? Tofu masquerading as something edible?"

"Nope. Oysters."

"Where are you getting oysters in Montana? Flown in from Apalachicola in Florida or the Chesapeake Bay?"

"Nope."

"They can't be local?"

"They are! They're called Rocky Mountain oysters or prairie oysters."

"I'm beginning to be worried."

"No need to show concern. Montana has spring and fall festivals where they're served. We haven't been in Montana when such events are held. You may know them as Montana tendergroins or cowboy caviar or swinging beef."

"I know what you're suggesting. I'm not eating bulls' testicles!"

"I wouldn't serve you those. You get *calf* testicles which are far more tender. . . . Like eating oysters. You cut the muscle and remove the skin. Then slice them, put them in a frying pan, cover them with beer, and let them cook for about two hours."

"Tell me when you start cooking them. In two hours I can drive a hundred miles, fleeing our dinner table."

"Spoil sport. I give up. Instead, I'll cook you hush puppies."

"Wonderful."

"Made from rattlesnake meat."

"You've been trying to convert me to vegetarian. I think you're succeeding."

5

NEXT DAY - ARRIVAL IN MONTANA

WE WALKED INTO OUR MILL CREEK PARADISE Valley cabin exhausted from driving across our vast country.

"Wow!" Lucinda exclaimed. "Our housekeeper Mavis must have been here today. It's spotless. She left coffee, milk, English muffins, and a dozen eggs. We don't have to go to the general store in Emigrant until tomorrow."

I made a quick check in the music room below the main floor, where I store most of my guns. From behind my music stand in a locked cabinet that—when opened—appears to hold only sheet music and the black cases for my oboe and English horn, I extracted, brought upstairs, and loaded the .44 magnum Ruger revolver that stays in my bedside table drawer, the short 12-gauge double-barrel Coach shotgun that stands in the corner of the bedroom, and the .44 Henry lever-action rifle that hangs within reach over the front door. It's comforting each spring to retrieve and place the guns where they're quickly available.

Lucinda has her own S&W pistol she keeps between the spoons and forks in a kitchen drawer. Our final defensive measures are cans of bear spray by each door, mainly for what they are labeled to stop or at least momentarily distract: curious visiting grizzlies. The cans also should work on uninvited and unwelcome Guatemalans, meaning Juan Pablo Herzog.

My final check was our shed, where our two drift boats rested safe from the menace of a Montana winter. *Osprey*, the wooden drift boat I built my first winter, is irreplaceable. The second and backup drift boat is a Clack-a-Craft, my preference among all the available plastic boats. It doesn't have a name; we refer to it as the "other" boat. It's the boat we use the most.

Osprey is saved for friends and clients who I know will not leave cigarette burns on its gleaming ash, oak, and mahogany. Whenever I check the two boats on arrival each spring and find no winter damage—like rodent nests—I unconsciously produce a sigh of relief "whew" that Lucinda claims she can hear from the cabin.

Our drift boats have paid a price for being in my service. Retired ambassador Anders Eckstrum was shot and instantly killed fishing from the bow of *Osprey*. His assailant was ashore near Deadman's Bar on the Snake River in Grant Teton National Park. *Osprey* suffered no damage, but a few months later there was a shootout on the boat, also on the Snake, that led to several holes in the hull, but, more significantly, left Wuff with a permanent slight limp, sent Lucinda into a coma that she came out of with amnesia we fought for months, and wounded me in several non-vital areas. The shooter died in a way I prefer to forget: I steered *Osprey* so that he was impaled by a pointed tree branch in a strainer in the middle of the river.

The next year *Osprey* wasn't directly involved, but its trailer was used for several brutal murders. Not long after, my Clack-a-Craft was nearly blown up, first on the Madison River, and exactly a year later—on the summer solstice—on the Yellowstone, when Lucinda and I were aboard bound and gagged and covered with a wicker man basket. Our heads were adorned with mistletoe.

I seem to have similar trouble keeping our Florida flats boat in one piece. My first one was the victim of a bombing during the gill net murders. There was nothing left but blackened fiberglass and a charred human body.

Our current flats boat, the restored Hell's Bay, thankfully has not been the innocent subject of attacks by my transgressors and hopefully rests unmarred in its summer storage back in St. Augustine.

My reputation as a guide in Montana and Wyoming has been blemished by our experiences. I say "our" because Lucinda stepped into more than an engagement and later marriage when she convinced me I actually had succumbed to her charms. I knew she was far more attractive and intelligent than I will ever be; I was unaware that she also was a formidable nutritionist who would vastly modify my intake of what I consider proper food but she labels "junk" or that she would become a talented, highly sought-after photographer.

While Lucinda's reputation rises, I struggle to convince people it's safe to fish with me. Increasingly, my clients are interested more in talking about our sordid adventures than in discussing ways to attract cutthroats, browns, and rainbows. Some clients refer to me as "that celebrity guide." I didn't ask for that to happen.

While I finished checking on our weapons and boats, Lucinda poured a Gentleman Jack for me and a Montana Roughstock Whiskey for her. Visualizing six months of "Western" living devoid of gill nets, barracudas, and airboats, we enclosed ourselves in heavy twill pants, long-sleeve flannel shirts, sweaters, and scarves, all topped with blankets, and took our drinks to the porch to watch the sun vanish behind the Gallatin Mountains, sharply silhouetted in the uncluttered air.

"A week ago we sat on our St. Augustine dock and watched a similar sunset," Lucinda commented, happily sipping her Montana Roughstock. "There was an evening mist on the Florida salt-marshes we never see here."

"Montana's drier. We're fortunate to have two exquisite places to divide our time."

Sunset finally drew the shade on a good day. The sky had blackened, and the temperature dropped abruptly. Stars began to arrive high above and soon there were even more, until the sky was massed with stars never seen in Atlanta or L.A.

"Macduff! What's happening? I hadn't remembered the sky could be so beautiful."

"We're not immersed in light pollution like east of the Mississippi or along the West Coast. Little more than a third of the U.S. population ever sees what we're seeing: the Milky Way. Urbanites never get to see this."

"Are urbanites scared of the dark?"

"At least those in Atlanta and L.A., but usually for other reasons."

Mesmerized by the natural night sky—a view that seemed to extend its depth—we never went to refill our drinks and finally realized midnight was near and we were shivering. Not welcoming hypothermia on our first night at the cabin, we went in and prepared for bed.

"I know it's late and you're chilled and tired," she said. "But you should know I went online while you were driving today and looked for anything new about the airboat murder."

"Let's talk in the morning," I suggested. "I love sitting and talking with you, but right now I need to lie in a warm bed and hug you."

"Your wish is my command. Some of the time."

"Any luck in *your* search yesterday?" I asked the next morning at breakfast, refreshed from much needed sleep.

"Yes, but maybe not good luck for us. I didn't want to tell you while we were driving and then the Milky Way was much more exciting and then we needed sleep. . . . To be blunt, someone reported seeing a flats boat carrying a couple in the area where the airboat and body of Prescott were found. It's likely we were the couple."

"Was the boat identified?" I asked.

"It doesn't say yes or no," she replied. "Should we call and say we read about the body found on an airboat and tell them that we were the people on the flats boat? But not give our names."

"We have cell phones but dare not use them. We'd need a public phone to call from, but phone booths mostly are a part of history."

"Anyway, would that help us?" she asked. "It could lead to some intensive interrogation. Would we be believed? Police questions could be accusatory. We've both agreed we don't want to be involved any time we are or might be mentioned in the press. There is a chance any notoriety will help Juan Pablo Herzog find us. Why can't we just walk away from this?"

"We're good citizens. How would we help by letting the FWC know what we saw? Maybe our descriptions of Cassell and Cartwright on the FWC boat would lead to their arrest."

"And *our* deaths."

"So our conscious choice of what to do is nothing?" she wondered aloud.

"Nothing. But we keep checking the news from Ft. Myers until we go back in the fall, and then we'll think about trying to help."

"By talking with the state attorney?"

"Not at first, but by learning enough about the killing to *mail* what we've learned to the state attorney—anonymously."

"If we start investigating and asking questions, won't Cassell and Cartwright try to find us, and maybe attempt something so we can't disclose any more about it or testify against them? They may have been the ones using the airboat to transport drugs."

"We control the situation by taking the first step," I stated.

"And then we become implicated even if only as witnesses," she interjected. "Remember, Mac, that trials are public, and this one would draw a lot of media attention."

"Far too much attention. Another bad idea. We want to keep current about the killing *only* to stay aware of what is likely known by the police."

"And avoid like the plague letting the police know about who we are and even more so who you *were*."

6

EARLY MAY

I WOKE AT FIVE IN THE MORNING, THOUGHT about fishing Mill Creek, and tried but couldn't go back to sleep. At 5:45 a.m. I slipped out of bed and fed Wuff fifteen minutes before her breakfast was due. I hoped her internal clock wouldn't automatically reset her proper breakfast time to 5:45 rather than the long accepted 6:00 a.m.

As quietly as I could, I brewed coffee, filled a large mug, and carefully carried it down the steep stairs to the music room. In addition to my guns, other than those I brought upstairs the previous day, the room also houses—and hides— communications equipment for direct contact with Dan Wilson—my protection program contact in D.C. Lastly, the room is where, when time allows, I practice on my oboe and English horn. But only when Lucinda is away!

Lucinda has proposed that I don't need the guns—she and Wuff will protect me—and that Dan usually uses his cell phone rather than our secret communications. Also, she said I could play the oboe on the cabin porch and scare away any would-be attacker, including Juan Pablo Herzog or grizzlies.

I know the proper fingering patterns on my instruments, and I read music. But what comes out of my woodwinds has not drawn an invitation to join any major symphony or even our local Livingston chamber orchestra. I remain determined to master the works of venerable composers including Albinoni, Bach, Cimarosa, Marcello, Mozart, and Vivaldi. All have been dead for centuries, but if they hear music in heaven, they would unanimously favor exchanging my treasured grenadilla wood oboe and English horn for a harmonica and musical saw.

Comfortably settled downstairs, coffee in hand and Lucinda asleep upstairs, I turned on my computers and went online, searching for recent information about the Prescott airboat murder. As the screen began to look promising, I felt a warm body wrapping around my neck from behind.

"It's too big to be Wuff," I said, ducking an expected blow.

"Macduff, if you didn't need me to get you out of trouble, I'd be working on my tan on a sun-drenched Bahamas beach, maybe lying next to a young George Hamilton look-alike."

"But *I'd* have Wuff."

"Not a chance! She'd never choose to stay with you. She'd be a big hit alongside me in Abaco. Ask her!"

Wuff is my rescued sheltie who has a limp from being shot on *Osprey* during a float with me. She has favored Lucinda ever since and was sitting leaning against Lucinda's leg, her head cocked while we debated her loyalty preference.

Thankfully, some info that looked important popped onto the screen and distracted Lucinda and Wuff from harassing me. It was from the Ft. Myers morning paper.

"You have a fishing client to meet in Emigrant in less than two hours, Macduff. You're driving to the Madison to fish. You haven't hooked up your drift boat. Can't airboats wait?"

"Lucinda," I answered, not looking up from the paper, "look at this from the Ft. Myers *Times*. . . . The FWC had an a call yesterday from an unidentified male who alleged he and his fishing companion saw a white flats boat idling not more than thirty feet from the airboat that held Prescott's remains. He thinks it was a Hell's Bay flats boat. There's a photo, but it's not clear."

"Does it say anything about the VHF Channel 16 call we made to the FWC? she asked.

"No. At least not in this piece."

"The first info we had when we were staying at Cabbage Key stated that the body was found at night by a solo fisherman. That suggested Cassell and Cartwright never reported their contact with us or even their having seen the airboat with Prescott's body. Does that mean *we* have information the FWC doesn't know about?" she asked.

"If so, maybe it should go to the state attorney's office," I suggested.

"Before we make any decision, tell me why Cassell and Cartwright might not have made a report?"

"If they killed Prescott," I suggested, "and left the scene and later returned for some reason. Having seen us, they aren't about to admit being there when we were."

"But why would they have returned in an FWC boat?"

"Maybe they were panicked and not thinking. They could have remembered they left something on the airboat. Drugs? We never went aboard and don't know what that something might have been. They could have overheard our Channel 16 call and decided they had better come back. . . . What does the newspaper article say about the two on the flats boat?" I asked.

"The good part is that the two people the anonymous caller saw on the flats boat both wore sunglasses and long peaked hats. We *know* what they saw. It had to have been Cassell or Cartwright who took the photo, most likely using a cell phone we didn't notice while we were deciding what to do. The photo's here on the screen, and it may have been in some other newspapers."

"Macduff! *That's us!* I had on my favorite sweater that Elsbeth gave me last Christmas."

"Where was it bought? A popular sweater produced in quantity or a one-off by some home knitter and sold at an arts and crafts fair?"

"I don't know. I wouldn't ask Elsbeth where she got a present for me."

I reached into my drawer and found a magnifying glass. We used it to look carefully at the photo.

"I don't see anything that could identify us except for the sweater."

"Your jacket, Mac! The brand must have been sewn on the front . . . but all I can see is an 'S.'"

"That's my Simms guide jacket. I wear it a lot. People who fish with me know that. That worries me. . . . But maybe people looking at the photo will think it's just a couple of guys fishing."

"Guys? One has breasts and long hair!"

"I didn't notice the long hair."

"What do we do?" she asked.

"Lay low. If we're asked about the incident, our answer is we've read about the death and know nothing other than what has been in the newspapers."

"What about our encounter with Cassell and Cartwright?"

"Encounter? Where? When? With who?"

7

THE MONTANA FISHING SEASON COMES TO AN END

LUCINDA AND I SPENT THE SUMMER SEASON looking over our shoulders despite the fact we were twenty-five hundred miles from Pine Island Sound. Nothing of significance appeared in any Florida newspapers we checked for new info about Prescott's death. With that, it was easier for us to focus on fishing and photography.

Lucinda considered several photo requests. She's been in demand from the time her photos of Hemingway's favorite places in Havana and Cojímar appeared in the Canadian travel magazine. But she had to joust with a tenacious Florida state legislator named Fulgencio Ramos who was pushing the federal Justice Department to fine her for violating U.S. law prohibiting trade with Cuba.

"Macduff," she asked one evening, "What have I done to violate U.S. law? I wasn't trading!"

"You annoyed one of the remaining few out-of-touch Cuban-American early exiles who spend their days trying to track down and harass people they don't agree with who are engaged with any activity involving Cuba. Like drinking Havana Club rum when you're in Mexico or smoking a Cohiba cigar in London. They don't limit their activities to matters they believe are unlawful, but raise challenges that will place them in the spotlight when the next election comes around. . . . Specifically, Ramos has complained that you earned money from photographing in Cuba."

"I did. So what? I went to Cuba as a journalist carrying a federal license. CNN sends journalists to Cuba. They appear on TV, and they're paid for their work."

"I think it's partly frustration because you're working with a Canadian magazine company. Countless U.S. citizens travel to Cuba by way of Canada and that irritates the excitable remaining Miami exiles. Our relationships have changed, and a few irrational Cuban-Americans no longer extract political concessions they once extorted. Ignore them. Ramos isn't worth even thinking about. Remember this saying: 'Don't get in a squirting match with a skunk.'"

"Why don't they pick on *you*?" she wondered. "You went fly fishing at Playa Larga."

"And I drank Havana Club rum. Plus, I brought some back. I carried two bottles with me in the Cessna on the flight from Cuba to Key West. And fifty Cohiba cigars. I gave Dan Wilson and U.S. House member Elena Mendoza a half-dozen each. Feds trump Cuban-Americans. . . . Would you like to go back to Cuba?"

"Any time. It's beyond description. You fish, and I photograph. Why don't you invite Ramos to go with us, and you'll teach him to fly fish?"

"Ramos would be lined up against a wall and shot by locals. We don't need to be associated with more shootings or with people like Ramos. Anyway, I don't want him with me fishing, unless I could leave him at Playa Larga to clean out the barracuda pens."

By September Lucinda and I were baffled that nothing more about Prescott had appeared in the Florida papers.

"Is the Prescott murder a dead issue for us?" Lucinda asked.

"No murder is ever officially dead. But this one appears to be in a coma. It's a cold case."

"What do you think the state attorney's office in Lee County or the FWC know that's new?"

"Not much more than what we've read about. And what we saw: an airboat with a maimed body. Raymond Prescott was murdered on an airboat owned by Martin Swenson of Gibsonton. Allegedly it was stolen from Swenson. Cocaine traces were in every locker on the airboat. Someone—probably fishing—apparently came upon the scene and called Channel 16. When the FWC arrived, there was a white flats boat with two people—probably a couple—near the airboat. An unidentified FWC officer photographed the airboat, and in one photo the two yet unidentified people—meaning us—appeared. That's about it. We haven't read what the forensics people in Lee County have learned."

"So we sit and wait?" she asked.

"More or less."

"It's hard for me to forget it," she said. "One can't be forced to forget something like that. Grotesque images endure."

"But don't forget what might happen if we became involved. Maybe forgetting *can* be accomplished by fear—if not by force."

"I've got the fear, Macduff, but I've still got vivid images of Prescott on the airboat. I'm glad I have some photo assignments to do. Keeping busy helps put aside those bad images."

Lucinda had begun her photo essay on the origins of the Snake and Yellowstone rivers. Finding where each river begins wasn't easy and has been debated for years. Her work did tend to focus her mind. Why do two great rivers begin their journeys more or less adjacent to each other, the water from one flowing to the Pacific, but the water from the other flowing to the Gulf of Mexico and the Atlantic?

"Why don't we know *exactly* where each of these two rivers begins?" she asked one morning. I was tying some bead head Prince nymphs. It wasn't going well. My fingers seemed incompatible with size sixteen or smaller flies. Lucinda's question was a welcome interruption.

"Look on your Yellowstone *trail* map," I suggested. "The Continental Divide runs about southeast, passing fairly close to the southern-most corner of Yellowstone Lake. The Two Ocean—meaning Atlantic and Pacific—Plateau Trail, on the west side of the divide, lies south of the lake, meanders about ten miles, and connects with the east-west South Boundary Trail, which more or less follows the Yellowstone's east-west boundary. All of this is in the northeast corner of Wyoming.

"To roughly establish where the two rivers are born, start by heading upriver from known locations of each river. When we drive north from Wyoming's Jackson Hole to start through the park and come home to our cabin here at Mill Creek, we generally follow the Snake River upstream. Starting on the Snake not far north of where it has flowed *into* Jackson Lake from the northeast, it has come *out* of Yellowstone Park not far from the south park entrance road.

"Following the river upstream north into the park, its course turns abruptly east about where the Lewis River joins it from the north. From then on it is no longer near any road. And it looks like its name—Snake—as it winds upstream north to perhaps four miles south of Heart Lake and makes an irregular loop around to the east and heads back south-east. It leaves the park, crossing the South Boundary Trail, wiggles further east and then turns north again back into the park, again crossing the same hiking trail. It ends about a mile north into the park.

"Your trail map shows the Snake's origin to be a pond at about 9,250 feet on the Two Ocean Plateau, which straddles the Continental Divide. The river has come close to but not crossed that divide; thus, the water of this very small Snake River must one day empty into the Pacific, but only after it has headed south to get around the Grand Teton Mountains in Wyoming and then turned west into Idaho, which it crosses to ultimately join the Colombia River. Confused?" I asked her.

"Not with my trail map in front of me. Are there campsites?"

"A surprisingly good number. In the stretch I've described are about ten campsites, each limited to six to twelve campers. The last of the campsites upstream is a little over a mile off the trail at Mariposa Lake. Want to go?"

"Yes, with you, a guide, and a half-dozen cans of bear spray."

"The last is probably the most important, but I wouldn't try the hike without a guide."

"How far a hike to the source?"

"Looking at the trail map, I'd estimate twenty-five miles in to the source, mostly uphill, and, of course, twenty-five miles back out, thankfully downhill."

"So now I know about the Snake River. What about the Yellowstone?"

"When you're at the Snake's origin, near Mariposa Lake, if you walk five miles east, you'll cross the Continental Divide and you'll run into the Yellowstone. Remember that you're walking *across* the mountain that is the divide. That means walking up the west side and then walking down the east or Atlantic side.

"To make it easier, let's start from the southern shore of Yellowstone Lake. The place where the Yellowstone River flows into the Yellowstone Lake is about sixteen miles directly across the lake from where we've often sat on a bench in front of the Yellowstone Lake Hotel. Boats can be hired to take you across the lake."

"Are there hiking trails along the Yellowstone?"

"More or less. The Thoroughfare Trail follows but is usually out-of-sight of the river. But not more than two miles away."

"Campsites along that trail?"

"About eleven in the park. When you exit the park following the Yellowstone upriver against its flow, you enter Bridger-Teton National Forest in the Absaroka Range, and you have a long hike remaining to the river's source.

"And, since you are now on the *east* side of the Continental Divide, the water from the Yellowstone must end up in the Gulf of Mexico."

"You mentioned the Absaroka Range! I thought our cabin and ranch were in the Absaroka Range."

"They are. The range runs north and south from the northeast head of our Paradise Valley—close to I-90 and not far from Livingston—south for 160 miles. It becomes the eastern boundary of the park. The range ends not far from the town of Dubois in Wyoming."

"How far south out of the park can one follow the river upstream to its source?"

"About eight to ten miles, staying east of the divide. Its source is around Yount Peak."

"I assume there are a trail and campsites once you're out of the park?"

"Yes, the Thoroughfare Trail, that started where the river flowed into the lake, continues south outside the park. Do remember that you're heading *upriver*. That means you climb as the water tumbles down past you."

"When do we go? When the aspens turn color and dust the landscape with a gold gilt?"

"When do *you* go? I'm booked with floats. I'll watch the aspens and cottonwoods change from my drift boat or from our cabin porch."

"Wimp."

I set my record for total floats during a season and also for consecutive floats on *Osprey* without losing any clients to shootings or explosions. I nearly lost one client from Louisiana. After losing his balance he fell overboard. He had his fly rod in one hand and a beer in the other. *He* brought the beer; I don't provide it until after the float. Watching him splash around, I thought about what to do for a few moments before deciding to pull him back into the boat.

Another client died from a natural cause—a massive heart attack just before he would have landed the brown trout of a lifetime. The fish survived him, unaware that its battle to survive below the surface caused a death above.

Then there were the usual hooks caught in flesh, a good reason for using barbless hooks. Usually it was my flesh, but sometimes it was the person fishing in the bow hooking the one in the stern or vice versa. I've learned to do minor surgery on ears, scalps, back of necks, and shoulders. *Osprey* is a kind of floating emergency care clinic.

My most significant surgery was not removing a hook. One client, at the end of the season on a very cold day, had a call to nature. I ran the boat ashore and off he went to the bushes. He was wearing underpants, a Patagonian Capilene bottom, and heavy khaki cargo pants that had a zipper. Preparing to pee, he caught himself in the zipper, and I heard a scream from the bushes. Thank God for my Leatherman.

He survived, but blamed me for his "discomfort." As he left, he handed me a $10 tip. I don't know why he complained about my guiding. He came to fish and caught a dozen nice rainbows, browns, and cutties. If his voice was higher after my surgery, it was not my fault!

The season was partly successful because no one attempted to bomb our cabin and I saw no signs of a wicker-man-and mistletoe-covered person on my floats or bodies on my trailer at the end of a float. I didn't see a gill net or a barracuda pen the entire season, not unexpected being in Montana and Wyoming.

Elsbeth and Sue visited us at Mill Creek several times when they were off work at Chico Hot Springs. Elsbeth stayed with us the week before she and Sue flew to London for the forthcoming academic year. The day before she left, we decided to tell her about the airboat death, partly because Lucinda wanted to ask her about the sweater.

When we showed her the newspaper photograph of Lucinda and me on our flats boat in Pine Island Sound, Elsbeth studied the photo carefully, looked up, and exclaimed, "That's the sweater I gave you, Lucinda!"

That didn't make us feel confident until Elsbeth said it came from Macy's, which had probably sold hundreds of duplicates in Florida alone.

But the confidence evaporated when she added, "Dad, as usual *you're* wearing your favorite old Simms jacket."

"You're assuming the 'S' stands for Simms?"

"That's true, but I could tell by the right pocket. You recall that you took a flask of red wine when you went fishing on the flats on a cold January day a year ago? You didn't put the cap back on securely after lunch, and the flask tipped over in your pocket when you caught that big sea trout. Remember? The wine stained the pocket."

"I remember," I said, deciding to leave the jacket in Montana when we headed east in the fall.

"Is there anything else in the photo that makes you believe the two are Lucinda and me? No names are mentioned."

"Not really. But if I were asked to guess their heights and weights, and maybe hair color, I would be giving figures that describe you two. With hats and sunglasses it's hard to guess ages."

I continued guiding on the more moderate days into the first week of November, wearing several layers for the first couple of hours, but by noon often dressed in a light flannel shirt. We were having an unusually warm and productive fall. But the high temperatures were dropping a degree or two each day.

"Should we leave soon for Florida?" I asked Lucinda one noon, after putting on a sweater. "It's chilly."

"Not until we have Thanksgiving dinner," she answered.

"Why is that so important?"

"We met on Thanksgiving not more than a mile or two from here. Don't you remember?"

"I remember slipping on the ice at your front door. I had a sore rear for a month."

"But I invited you in despite your clumsiness, gave you a drink before a roaring fire, and fed you. Your showing up meant a lot to me because you were the only guest who arrived."

"I could have been a serial killer intent on ravaging you."

"And I could have been serially promiscuous and targeted you when I saw you walking along the Mill Creek Road. Maybe the truth is that I never invited anyone else to that dinner."

"If I'd only known! . . . But I knew you were really hurt by the way your invited guests treated you."

"I was," she said quietly, the hurt still obvious these years after.

Her hurt was due to an absence of good manners shown by six of her Manhattan investment broker colleagues, who first accepted her invitation to fly to her Montana ranch for the holiday. Two days before Thanksgiving, they sent one-sentence retractions, abruptly deciding instead to fly on a private jet to Peter Island in the Caribbean—apparently to be seen by other jet setters. I turned out to be Lucinda's sole guest. In time it proved to be the most memorable—and costly—meal of my life.

"I haven't eaten in that room since," I noted. "I assumed it was because you had bad memories of that first Thanksgiving dinner."

"Not bad memories. Just reminders that fate drove me into a relationship of mayhem and murder."

"Don't complain. You're alive. We've been on adventures you never would have imagined."

"Like last year when you took me to Cuba? I didn't get to stretch out on a beach at Varadero and soak up some Caribbean sun. My remembrance of Varadero is that it's next to where we escaped the island one night by taking off from a highway in a fifty-year-old Cessna that had no instruments."

"It was flown by a beautiful woman Navy pilot who thought I was Harrison Ford."

"Ha! She was so scared of you that she asked to be transferred from Key West to Honolulu."

"You loved every minute being in Cuba," I reminded her. "You even went back. And you took some superb photographs of Hemingway's favorite places in Havana and Cojímar, received accolades from your photo journalist peers, and was sent a very nice payment for the photos from that Canadian travel magazine."

"But now you have me in the middle of another murder, a man strapped to an airboat prop and spun to death!"

"We're not in the middle of it—only spectators from the bleachers. To our knowledge no one other than Cassell and Cartwright know we saw the airboat."

"We haven't heard anything about the murder for two months. Do you suppose it's been solved?"

"No, but it would be good to arrive back in Florida without that facing us, if the case has been resolved."

"Do you suppose Dan Wilson in D.C. knows about the murder? We haven't talked to him in months, which probably makes him happy."

"He has no reason to know. Just another murder in Florida. Happens most every day somewhere in that state."

My cell phone rang. It was on the table between us, and Lucinda beat me to it, picked it up, and answered, "This is Lucinda Brooks."

"I thought I was calling Macduff," the voice answered.

"You *are* calling Mr. Brooks. I know who you are, and I don't think he'd be interested in talking to you."

"Who on earth is calling?" I asked.

"Someone whose voice is all too familiar and who we have just been talking about—Dan Wilson."

I reached over and grabbed the phone.

"Dan, it's Macduff. I'm having trouble finding a decent secretary. . . . We were just talking about you."

"And you were hoping I didn't know about your issues in Florida. To be more accurate, your experience with airboats used to commit murders."

"I'm not surprised you've heard about the murder, but *we* were not involved. It was a unique way to murder someone."

"Creative killing, like using wicker man baskets and mistletoe. Or drift boat trailers. Need I go on?" he replied.

"Why do you link *us* to the murder? Lucinda and I were certain that no one knew what we saw. That includes *you!*"

"I didn't know anything about it. I checked some Pine Island Sound lodges' guest lists, mainly asking if anyone named Brooks had stayed there at the time. Does Cabbage Key sound familiar?"

"It's not easy to hide from you and your high-tech spy stuff."

"Now that you've affirmed your presence and I know you have a Hell's Bay boat, tell me more."

We both told Dan every detail we could remember. He listened carefully.

"You two should stay out of this. Don't play detectives. You were innocent bystanders. You may have evidence the authorities don't have—you saw the two with the FWC boat. That's info that should be reported to the Lee County State Attorney's office."

"How do you suggest we go about that?"

"Email me a description of what you saw. Don't include your names. I'll pass it on as credible information from a reliable source that puts your lives in danger if your names are disclosed. I won't give your names, but I'll say it's our opinion the two people were not involved in the killing. They can take it or leave it. They can't do anything to this Agency."

"We'll send the info tomorrow, using a coded address. Unsigned. You'll know who it's from."

"Where are you two going to be in the next few weeks?"

"Thanksgiving is in three days. We're staying here until it's over and leave the following Tuesday when the roads are free of holiday traffic. We'll be in St. Augustine sometime the first week of December."

"Have a safe trip east. Forget about airboats. You were only two people who happened upon a completed murder. Let it go regardless of your history of meddling. Enjoy the winter when you go to Florida."

"That's partly in your hands."

We sent him the information—encrypted—as promised.

8

THANKSGIVING AT MILL CREEK

THANKSGIVING CAME AND WENT MARKED BY privacy. No guests. Only the two of us and Wuff. Lucinda and I sat together facing each other on the sofa, our legs entwined. We reminisced with inaccurate versions of our life together and later called Elsbeth in London. She and Sue had dinner with some new U.S. friends. No British were invited—Thanksgiving was not a British day to rejoice. The Pilgrims didn't disembark and claim the land in the name of James I, the English king; the passengers disliked the Jacobean monarch. The 1620 *Mayflower* voyage was not sponsored by Carnival Cruise Line.

Lucinda cooked a turkey for two at our cabin, and we took it to her ranch. She set the table exactly as it was the evening we met a dozen years earlier. The same china. The same silverware. The same crystal. And she also set six places for the guests who didn't show up that year, their plates turned upside down, their glasses tipped over. We dined at the same end of the table as we had that Thanksgiving and talked and laughed for three hours. The words *airboat, propeller, Pine Island Sound, Cassell, Cartwright,* and *Prescott* were never uttered.

The following morning I opened the refrigerator door, confronted a half a turkey, and turned to Lucinda and asked, "What do we do with all these leftovers?"

"Tonight I'm going to make turkey hash with Brussels sprouts and parsnips. Before you complain, you should know it also includes bacon. You love bacon."

"*If* there's enough bacon to disguise the Brussels sprouts."

"I served you Brussels sprouts two years ago and you loved them."

"They must have been disguised as something else and probably were wrapped with bacon. Why hide the Brussels sprouts? Just serve the bacon."

"Who is the designated family nutritionist in this house?"

"We all make mistakes. You, by serving Brussels sprouts. Me, by agreeing to let you be our nutritionist. . . . What else is in this turkey hash you're planning on serving?"

"Not much. A little sage, some scallions, and jalapeño."

"Jalapeño? It rots your mouth. And your throat. And your stomach. It's like swallowing a mix of Listerine and tequila. Jalapeño should have a label: 'Not to be taken internally or rubbed on skin.'"

"You won't see it. The hash is covered with an egg. A *poached* egg."

"A respectable hen would never lay an egg knowing that it was destined to be poached. Can't you fry or scramble it?"

"No, that's what I'm going to do to you if you complain."

I didn't complain. I ate the meal, preceded by two glasses of Gentleman Jack.

Two days later we closed the ranch and cabin, hugged Mavis goodbye, and faced our SUV more or less toward Florida, taking a southern route through Colorado to New Mexico. We hoped to visit friends and fish for a day or two on New Mexico's San Juan River below the Navaho Dam in the Four Corners area, where Colorado, Utah, Arizona, and New Mexico come together.

We soon discovered the San Juan was so crowded it looked like an Alaskan river on opening day. Combat fishing at its worst. More *people* fishing and fewer *fish* being caught because of silting below the dam, along with the inadequate limitation of special trout water to only a quarter-mile, convinced us to confine future New Mexico fishing—if any—to the Jemez Mountains, the Rio Grande north of Taos, or parts of Carson National Forest.

After two days in Albuquerque with friends, we set out to endure as best we could three-and-a-half long days of driving across six southern states: New Mexico, Texas, Louisiana, Mississippi, Alabama, and finally Florida. We enjoyed Christmas lights turned on in every town we passed through as each day ended, but they made us realize how long we had delayed in Montana before leaving.

Our last night on the road was in Apalachicola, where we savored its namesake oysters at a restaurant on the river. While we were eating, an airboat blew past, its noise causing every person in the place to frown, scowl, or grimace. I had an idea where it was going; a gill net was piled high on the seats.

Discouraged seeing the airboat and gill net prompted us to leave our table, pay the bill, and walk back through the quiet streets to the Gibson Inn.

"Merry Christmas!" Lucinda said turning to me.

"It's two weeks away," I noted.

"But living with you I don't know whether I'll make it to Christmas," she responded.

9

DECEMBER AT THE ST. AUGUSTINE COTTAGE

IF WE THOUGHT WE MIGHT QUIETLY SLIP BACK into a Florida winter of daily sunshine, rare freezes plummeting to 20° (above zero), and idyllic days on the salt marshes, we learned otherwise three days after we settled into our St. Augustine cottage. We had not been reading newspapers or going online during the week we spent driving to Florida, including the disappointing stop to fish the San Juan in New Mexico.

Our cottage housekeeper and friend, Jen Jennings, had placed on our kitchen table a manila envelope with no return address and a note on the refrigerator saying "Look inside," where we found a welcoming bottle of *Orvieto Classico* wine. I chose the wine before the envelope; the bottle was cold, and my hand left a print in the moisture. The cork had the feel of cork, not some composition used on the pretext that cork was in short supply. Slowly, I poured two glasses half-full, handed one to Lucinda, lifted mine, and nodded to her.

Envelopes are less exotic to open than wine bottles. Envelopes don't have an enticing aroma when first opened. But this envelope proved to be far more enriching than the *Orvieto Classico.* Inside the envelope were articles copied from various editions of Guatemala's *Prensa Libre* and the English language *The Guatemalan Times.* On top was a brief note: "Thought you might find these of interest. Have a nice holiday, you two." It was signed, "Dan Wilson."

Since she doesn't read Spanish, I gave Lucinda the *Times* and I delved into *Prensa Libre*. Both featured one event—the recent Guatemalan presidential election. In mid-January the newly elected candidate would be sworn in for a four-year term. The new president was to be Juan Pablo Herzog!

Herzog was once a student of mine—when I was Professor Maxwell Hunt living in Gainesville. With his UF degree in hand, he returned to Guatemala and quickly became the drug lord and most ruthless and feared man in his country. As he gained power, he began to believe I was working with the CIA to prevent him from becoming president. When I went to Guatemala as a visiting law professor at Francisco Marroquin and gave lectures sponsored by the U.S. State Department, Herzog and his friend, Abdul Khaliq Isfahani, were waiting for me. They had been classmates at UF, and Isfahani had become a terrorist in his home country, the Sudan.

Thinking I had acted contrary to his visions of Guatemala, Herzog beat me nearly to death and stopped only when U.S. embassy security personnel arrived. I was rushed back to the U.S. on a state department jet.

Knowing Herzog's intentions to kill me, the U.S. placed me in a protection program, and I became Macduff Brooks, a fly fishing guide in Montana. Events since that time have convinced me that Herzog has not forgotten about me over those past dozen years.

"Macduff," Lucinda asked, "how can such a man be elected president of his country? We've known for years that he's been a crime boss and head of drug trafficking, as well as a murderer from the time he was a mid-teen and killed a convent novice he'd impregnated."

"Herzog would like me to be next on his list of murders. Or, rather, he would like Professor Maxwell Hunt to be next. And by association you and Elsbeth. And you, too," I said, looking down at Wuff, who sat listening with her head cocked. You've never met Herzog, Lucinda. Maybe we should go to his inauguration. I could introduce you."

"Let's not! . . . Do we have to worry during his presidency? He must have more important matters to attend to than seeking revenge for acts long past."

"For the next few years I hope that's his thinking," I commented.

When Lucinda left for the post office and grocery store, I called Dan in D.C.

"I have a couple of questions for you," I said. "How do you interpret the newspaper articles you sent us regarding Herzog's danger to Lucinda, Elsbeth, and me?"

"He won't forget you as long as he lives," Dan replied. "But while he's president, he won't want to be directly implicated in an attempt on your life. He would risk losing U.S. support. Of course, he doesn't know about Lucinda or Elsbeth. We've had plans to take him out several times over the past decade, and we should have. But our presidents have been opposed. Not for reasons of national security, but because the word might get out and reduce their re-election chances."

"Herzog's always been power hungry," I observed. "As a teen in Guatemala, he had to be the leader and also the most dreaded student. When he returned after university training in the U.S., he soon became the godfather in Guatemala; you must remember how he used a chain saw on a tennis court and left the reigning Guatemalan crime boss in several parts, adding blood to the already red clay court."

"Now that he's gained the presidency, he's the most powerful person in the country," Dan replied. "With his background, plus the assassination in the Sudan of his closest friend Abdul Khaliq Isfahani, he doesn't give up when he feels challenged. Without any proof, he blames you for killing Isfahani. And also for killing both his niece María-Martina Herzog at the UF law school in Gainesville and his nephew Martín Paz near the tennis courts on the same campus. Remember, Macduff, he has no proof, but he's right about your pulling the trigger in Isfahani's and María's deaths.

"If you weren't in our protection program, you would have been dead years ago. If I had to guess what may happen soon, it's that he will keep searching for you, regardless of the presidency. Now he has good reason to believe you didn't die of a stroke in D.C.; that pretense survived only for a year or two."

"What's your guess on *how* he might try next to discover what happened to Professor Hunt?" I asked.

"Being president will give him access to resources, including the Guatemalan national security system. They work with us—'us' meaning the CIA. I feel much better having a couple of years ago personally expunged *our* files of any reference to Macduff Brooks. If Herzog gained access to all our *current* records that make reference to Professor Hunt, such as his travel missions for us, he would find *no* mention of a Macduff Brooks."

"I assume the records of Professor Hunt's travel for you will remain as they are?" I posed as a question to Dan. "It's the time *after* Hunt 'died' of a stroke that troubles me."

"Any of our records Herzog gains access to will show that Hunt traveled to Guatemala for us, returned here to D.C., and died of a stroke. They will not state that he survived and entered some form of protection program. We want to keep Hunt's travel record free of any reference to Herzog."

"We concede that Herzog *knows* Hunt didn't die of a stroke and consequently is living somewhere other than Gainesville, and using a name that is not Maxwell Hunt," I said. "Herzog must assume that Hunt is not teaching law or engaged in any form of law practice that requires admission to a state bar after a thorough background check."

"Saying he *knows* is a little too strong," countered Dan. "He *believes* because of unproven facts that Hunt actually survived. That will *never* be confirmed by us."

"Dan, I hope you're saying the fact that the Guatemalan military and civilian intelligence communities will co-operate with the CIA doesn't mean they can ask for certain personnel records, such as the circumstances of Hunt's announced death, and receive copies of whatever your agency has. Just what access will the Guatemalans have? Can they find out that a couple of days after my—or rather Hunt's—death, your agency held meetings with me where I decided what name I would use and where I would live?"

"We routinely don't keep such records. They are purged soon after the meetings. I could go through our records today and verify that *nothing* exists dated after Hunt's announced death from the stroke. It's fair to say I took a risk when I destroyed both the original and the copy so that the name Macduff Brooks does not appear in *any* of our records."

"But that leaves one source that could be a problem, Dan."

"What is that?"

"People at your agency who worked on my case. At those meetings sometimes nearly a dozen others were present. Remember the Alan Whitman problem. Before you shot and killed him, he tried to sell Herzog information that Whitman knew about me. If he hadn't been so greedy, the sale of that information would have been made, and he would have told Herzog who I became and where I was living. I wouldn't be alive today. Nor would Lucinda. Elsbeth wasn't with us until a few years later."

"I understand," Dan confirmed. "I did some checking. Of our people who met during those few days, three have died—including Whitman—four have retired and are living in several places, and four remain active with us. Herzog doesn't know their names. . . . And Mac, *we* didn't shoot Whitman."

"Where are the four assigned who are still with you?" I asked.

"Two are here in D.C., one is at our mission in London, and the fourth heads our mission in Mexico City."

"All unquestionably loyal employees?"

"I think so."

"Where are the four retirees living? In D.C.?"

"Two retired here," Wilson said. "Both have lucrative consulting contracts in the private sector. . . . One of the remaining two lives in Florida, and one retired and moved abroad."

"What does the retiree who moved to Florida do?"

"Cause *me* trouble."

"Why?"

"We clashed over an issue when he was serving as head of our mission in Venezuela. . . . We disagreed with his publically sympathizing with the Hugo Chávez government."

"Was he punished?"

"He agreed to early retirement."

"Did he blame you?"

"Yes."

"Is he still angry with you?"

"Unfortunately, yes."

"What if Herzog offered him $10 million for disclosing what he knows about Professor Hunt?"

"I hope he wouldn't take it."

"*Hope's* a fuzzy word, Dan. Would *you* take it if you were him?"

"I resent that, Mac. You know what I've done for you. And for Lucinda and Elsbeth."

"I'm sorry. I'm frustrated. . . . Would your retiree take it?"

"I simply don't know him that well. He has a very good pension. He would lose that, and Herzog might refuse to pay him."

"He might be smart enough to have the money deposited abroad *before* he told Herzog anything."

"Possibly. . . . There's one thing I haven't added."

"Which is?"

"Herzog *is* ruthless. There's a good chance he would have the money transferred to a foreign account, get the information, and have our agent murdered."

"Then Herzog's out the $10 million, which is sitting in a foreign bank."

"It's not Herzog's money; it would be dealt with as a legitimate Guatemalan government expenditure for something of critical importance to the nation's security. It could even come from the foreign aid *we* sent to the country."

"You said the fourth retiree moved abroad. Meaning where?"

"I wish you hadn't asked. He's in Antigua."

"Antigua, the city in Guatemala, not Antigua, the island in the Caribbean?"

"That's right."

"Maybe this former agent. . . . What's his name?"

"Thomas Davis."

"Maybe from living in Guatemala Davis knows enough about Herzog to stay away from any deal with him."

"I hope so."

"Why did Davis retire to Guatemala?" I asked.

"He had served in Guatemala City at our mission a couple of years before you were there and had your run-in with Herzog."

"Do you know Davis?"

"Yes," Wilson replied.

"On good terms with him?"

"No reason not to think so."

"Tell me about Davis," I asked.

"Living in Guatemala and being fluent in Spanish, he knows more about Herzog than he would had he retired here in D.C."

"*Any* reason to question his loyalty?"

"No. He seems happy being there with his wife. They have one son who's away in college."

"Could Herzog get to him the way we just talked about your retiree living in Florida?"

"Possibly."

"Could Davis be bought?"

"Possibly."

"Or threatened and made to talk?"

"Possibly."

"That doesn't make me very comfortable," I exclaimed.

"I understand. Living in Guatemala, Davis is reachable by intelligence people who report to Herzog. He could use them in his attempt to find you. But I repeat: There is no reason to believe that Herzog knows the names of those eight agents. If he doesn't know their names, we're safe."

"But, remember that immediately before Whitman was shot he talked to Herzog for about twenty minutes."

"And?"

"He might have named one or more of the others present at the discussions about my future," I surmised unhappily.

"Herzog's never contacted any one of them—as far as we know. But he could know their names!"

I wondered if he does. The wine bottle empty, I had switched to Gentleman Jack, poured and finished a glass when Dan mentioned Antigua. My second glass was already half empty.

I didn't remember pouring any.

10

THE SAME WEEK IN GUATEMALA

JUAN PABLO HERZOG RELAXED ON THE TILED terrace of his rambling, Antigua, Guatemala, coffee finca—the largest in the valley that is surrounded by three towering volcanoes. Comfortably dressed in an off-white embroidered guayaberra shirt, the bottom worn hanging outside his tropical weight trousers, he held a glass of his favorite *Ron Zacapa Centenario Gran Reserva.* Herzog's sharp gaze was fixed looking west at the conical slopes of the volcano Agua that over the centuries had episodically menaced the town.

Next to Herzog's side, but avoiding touching him, stood a young lady of twenty-three years, wearing jeans and holding a glass of Italian *San Pelligrino* sparkling water. She preferred to drink a Belgian beer from Leuven, where two decades ago her now deceased father had begun his pilgrimage to the priesthood. But she was terrified of uncle Tío Juan and what he might do to her if he thought she were drinking excessively, which she did when she was sure he wouldn't know.

The young woman was Luisa Solares, the illegitimate daughter of Juan Pablo's murdered younger first cousin, Augustino Herzog, who was better known as Padre Bueno. Once ordained, he took his holy orders seriously, vows which were a self-imposed penance for having impregnated his neighbor's young daughter. It was the first and only time he would have sex with a woman. A few days later he resolved to become a priest.

Augustino had struggled with his decision: Should he marry the mother of the child-to-be or enter the priesthood and under the camouflage of black clerical garments hide from any responsibility for the child. By the time the child was born, Augustino had made his choice, fled Guatemala, and entered the seminary in Leuven, Belgium. Soon he was immersed in his studies for the priesthood, and the child was forgotten.

The child's mother raised Luisa as instructed by Juan Pablo, never questioning his insistence that Luisa learn martial arts and marksmanship at what her mother deemed an inappropriate age.

Luisa was as quiet as she was beautiful. Taller than Juan Pablo, she had dark eyes and pale skin that had rarely seen the burning Guatemalan sun. Juan Pablo patiently taught her to be ruthless and give no quarter to her enemies.

To prove her worth to Tío Juan, Luisa had severely beaten a disliked classmate on the day of her *quinceañera*, when most young Guatemalan girls celebrated their coming of age. Luisa acted as calmly as a hit man carrying out a contract, never uttering a word and walking away from the sobbing and bleeding girl collapsed on the cobblestone street in front of her house.

Juan Pablo shared with Luisa the reasons for his belief that Professor Maxwell Hunt of the University of Florida law college had killed both Luisa's cousin, María-Martina Herzog, as she was about to shoot the dean of the UF law college, and a brief time later another cousin, Martín Paz, by a shot fired from the shadows of a building adjacent to the UF tennis courts close by the law college complex. Luisa did not know that Juan

Pablo was correct about Hunt having shot and killed María-Martina, but wrong about who killed Martín.

Juan Pablo was training Luisa for one purpose—to help find and brutally kill Professor Hunt, wherever he had hidden and whoever he had become. Herzog intended to impose the same penalty on any interfering members of Hunt's family.

"Tío Juan," Luisa said, setting her water glass on a side table and with difficulty trying to look directly at Herzog's eyes. He was the only person she feared, but she adored him at the same time because he treated her in a manner that contrasted with how he treated others, never uttering an angry word to her or threatening her or striking her. But he had never kissed or embraced her or even touched her.

"Will serving as our country's President for the next four years prevent you from pursuing Professor Hunt?" Luisa asked.

"I expect to be president longer than my four-year term. In two years I will seek an amendment to the Guatemalan constitution that will allow me to remain in office an unlimited number of successive terms. Only if the people elect me, of course. But I know they will. That is democracy!

"If denied, I will simply take over the country because I will have the loyalty of our military. I have already increased the compensation of all military personnel. So many leaders in Latin America have done the same over the years. Being a democracy and claiming to be one are indistinguishable.

"As to your question, while I am president, I will not participate directly in killing Professor Hunt, although I have dreamed of personally confronting him and watching him die an agonizingly slow death at my hands. *You,* Luisa, may help do the killing. It *must* be a horribly painful end for Hunt."

"Do you believe I'm ready?" she asked.

"Yes."

"How will you find out whether Professor Hunt still lives, and if he does, under what name? And where?"

"I am certain he was alive as recently as two years ago, when he brutally murdered my dear friend Abdul Khaliq Isfahani in the Sudan."

"But, Tío Juan, I've never heard that Hunt did that killing."

"Hunt is an expert marksman; there are few who could have shot Isfahani from such a long distance. I am convinced Hunt was the shooter. But I view Hunt's impending death not as revenge for Isfahani—it's for your cousins' murders that you will help obtain closure for our family."

Maybe closure for *him*, she thought. "How will you find out where Hunt lives?" she asked.

"I will be president in a matter of weeks. I'm weighing two separate ideas for locating Hunt. As president I will be head of our intelligence service and have access to our country's discussions with members of the U.S. CIA mission in Guatemala City. The U.S. mission works closely with us on drug traffic issues; it wants us to curtail drug trade, but I seek to work with the Mexican Zeta cartel and preserve such a lucrative source of income.

"These days our family's wealth comes more from controlling drug traffic passing through Guatemala than what first made us the richest family in the country, owning most of the coffee and other agricultural production. You and I will use my presidency both to prevent the U.S. from reducing the flow of drugs through Guatemala, and—as part of that process—to gain the information I seek about Professor Hunt."

"You said you have *two* methods of dealing with Hunt. What is the other?"

"There is a man named Thomas Davis living here in Antigua not more than three blocks from this house. He is an American who retired here, lives quietly, obeys the law, writes articles and books on Antigua, and often travels to the U.S."

"How can he help us?" Luisa asked.

"Davis doesn't know anything about my interest in him—yet. A year ago he retired from working for the U.S. CIA and moved here.

"Several years ago I traveled to Washington to meet with a CIA agent who had been involuntarily retired. His name was Alan Whitman. He was angry he had not been promoted and for a price offered me information about Professor Hunt. But his price was too high, and I insisted on negotiating a lesser amount. While we were sitting across from each other in the back room of a D.C. bar, discussing the amount I was willing to pay, Whitman was killed by a shot fired from an adjacent building. Maybe the bullet was meant for me. Nothing ever was reported in the media about the killing, which I believe was because it was done either directly by a CIA agent or by engaging Professor Hunt's marksmanship skills."

"Why would Hunt have agreed to do the shooting?" she asked. "He was living somewhere in the U.S. under a new name and doing some kind of work that I doubt was for the CIA. Maybe law teaching, but not killing people. I don't think he would have wanted to be involved."

"You do not know that, my dear Luisa," Herzog responded. "Professor Hunt remains obligated to help the CIA when he is asked. If he refused, he knows his protection might be reduced or eliminated."

"Is that the way the U.S. works?"

"I am sure it does, much as we would do in a similar case."

"Why is Davis important? He is only one of thousands who worked for the CIA and retired without further incident."

"Davis was mentioned to me by Whitman before he was shot. He told me that a colleague of his, Thomas Davis, was present at Professor Hunt's meetings to discuss his new life: what he would assume as a new name, what he would do to earn a living, and where he would live."

"That's perfect. What do we have to do to get that information from Davis?"

"I've been thinking about that for years. Unlike Whitman, Davis served his full CIA career, was awarded the agency's Distinguished Career Intelligence Medal, and lives comfortably here in Antigua. He has both his generous U.S. government pension and considerable money his wife inherited. But she is not in good health and is confined to a wheelchair. He dotes on her, remaining very much devoted to her—and her money. I believe he would not risk her life for *anything* we might promise. All we can promise is money."

"Or you might encourage him by threatening to kill him," Luisa suggested, "leaving his wife without his assistance and affection. . . . Or you might threaten to kill *her*."

"You have been trained well, Luisa. I have thought of those alternatives and watched Davis and his wife since they retired here, hoping she would succumb from her ailments. That may come soon. I've talked to her Guatemalan doctor about what to prescribe for her. When she dies, we will pressure Davis to tell us what he knows."

"Tío Juan, how can I help? I know how busy you will be as President. I want to be of use."

"I will consider that during the next few days, Luisa, and tell you once the inauguration is over."

11

MID-JANUARY AT THE FLORIDA COTTAGE

OUR CELL PHONE CONVERSATION WITH DAN Wilson did nothing to lessen our anxiety about ultimately having to confront Guatemalan president-elect Juan Pablo Herzog. Although I'm convinced he doesn't know I am now known as Macduff Brooks, he is searching for the name and address of whoever replaced me when I was Professor Maxwell Hunt. He came close to learning about me when CIA agent Alan Whitman in Washington was about to tell him my name but was shot and killed. When someone is so determined to kill you, it seems natural that it would focus your concentration.

Unlike our present knowledge about the airboat murder, there has been little if anything Lucinda and I could do about Herzog without Dan's involvement. The two matters are very different, but Herzog is far more threatening.

For nearly a dozen years, dating from when Herzog failed to finish me off by the nearly fatal beating he gave me in Guatemala City, he has not been successful in killing me, much less even finding me.

The airboat murderers are less concerned with Lucinda and me than with avoiding identification and arrest. At least we are proceeding on that belief, but with some conjecture about how we are viewed by Cassell and Cartwright. If they were the killers and had returned, only to find us next to the airboat, we need to worry about them. And they need to worry about us; Lucinda and I easily could identify them in a police lineup or a courtroom.

Lucinda has been more troubled than I am about the duo's threat to us due to our inadvertently having come upon the airboat. She is certain that the two were involved in the death of Prescott and that consequently they are interested in and looking for *us*. They may be looking for us while at the same time we have not decided whether to inform the police about our seeing *them* at the airboat incident. For quite different reasons than is the case with Herzog, neither Cassell nor Cartwright knows *who* we are.

We did not see Cassell or Cartwright take the cellphone photo or write anything down, such as the Florida registration numbers on my boat. But the registration numbers are not large, and our boat was mostly facing them and thus not floating at an angle that would allow easy reading of the numbers.

Were persons other than Cassell and Cartwright involved? The answer has to be yes. They may have hired someone to drive the stolen airboat. Or perhaps they paid someone to drive a chase boat—which we didn't see—to pick up the airboat driver once Prescott was dead. What we did see was a flats boat race past us as we entered the area where we encountered the airboat with Prescott's remains.

"Lucinda," I asked as we drove to Emigrant for groceries, "why Prescott? He was a certified public accountant in Ft. Myers, a highly regarded professional liked by clients, colleagues, and friends. He had no record, not even one recorded traffic ticket! He didn't fish mainly because he didn't enjoy boats or being on the water. He spent most of his personal time reading or playing golf. How could he have ended his life by being whirled to death on an airboat?"

"Someone had it in for him," she surmised. "He must have done something disagreeable to someone. Maybe a business dispute or conflict with a neighbor. He might have used drugs and owed money he borrowed to support his habit. Or the murder was the act of a jealous woman he was having an affair with because he refused to divorce his wife and remarry. He might even have lost at golf and didn't pay up. Prescott could have been killed for any number of reasons. But by being spun to death on an airboat?"

"You're grasping for reasons," I replied. "A golf debt? Please! Besides, everything we've read about him to date is positive. He had no business conflicts with colleagues or clients. His neighbors liked him. He had no record of drug use. Seemingly he was content with his wife. . . . You have to come up with better reasons. But I agree with your doubt that, if he had enemies, he would have met his end in the propeller cage of an airboat."

"Should we concentrate on learning more about Cassell and Cartwright?" she asked. "We don't know very much detail about either of them. But we know one thing the authorities apparently don't know. Whoever Cassell and Cartwright were, FWC officers or not, they *were* there at the scene."

"But they weren't there when *we* arrived," I replied. "And they didn't arrive until after we called the FWC. Does that implicate them? Or were they just two FWC officers who lacked tact and good sense?"

"What if they had nothing to do with the murder, but were trying to find or steal drugs, and they thought the drugs were on the airboat?" she asked.

"Do the authorities believe any drugs that were on the boat were not removed until sometime *after* the murder—even after we left?" I replied with another question.

"We're guessing at too much," she answered, uncertain. "The drugs could have been removed from the boat *before* Prescott was tied to the propeller and by persons unrelated to those who murdered him. Cocaine leaves lasting traces. The drugs and Prescott may not be connected, but I agree it seems logical to believe that they were related."

"We've made this so complex," I said. "Are we overreacting?"

"No," she responded, with hesitation. "We were involuntarily drawn into this by the accident of time—by our being there and seeing the body. . . . We need more facts before we reach any conclusions," she suggested.

"I'll go online and try to find out more about Cassell and Cartwright," she proposed. "You take on Prescott; you may find out something he did that could have been a motive for murder. And you might check on the boat's owner, Swenson."

"I have doubts about your premises, but I'll try," I agreed.

"One more possibility," she noted. "Could Prescott have been the wrong person murdered by a paid killer who didn't know what his victim looked like?"

"That sounds like science fiction," I said.

12

TWO DAYS LATER

TWO EVENINGS LATER AFTER I FINISHED MY search about Prescott and Swenson, I placed my notes on the small table in our cottage kitchen. From my rattan chair I looked out the large window at the salt flats with sea grasses waving in a slight southeast breeze born in the Atlantic and lifted over the dunes, spreading pungent salt smells throughout the marshes.

Lucinda had brought her notes about Cassell and Cartwright. I uncorked a bottle of an Argentine *Familia Rutini Chardonnay Mendoza* and set it on the table along with two Scottish crystal wine goblets cut with a subtle thistle design. Using them brought from my memory the wild Orkney Islands. The wine soon squelched bad memories of the Scottish Druids' practice of atonement that included the use of wicker man encasements festooned with mistletoe.

"Crystal glasses! Is this special wine?" she asked.

"Apparently. The *Wine Spectator* says it's 'fresh and crunchy.'"

"I'd prefer aged and not crunchy. Do I sniff it and then chew it?" she wondered aloud.

"You know sommeliers who are always searching for new adjectives so their wines will be distinct, calling some wines 'chewy' and others 'crunchy.' Would you prefer chewy?" I asked.

"No, I think I'll stay with crunchy," she said, sipping the wine very carefully but not hearing any crunchy sounds and happy she could swallow after sipping and not having to chew.

"Find anything useful about Prescott?" she asked, setting her glass on the table and looking at me expecting some answers.

"Not one bit of information suggesting that *anyone* had a motive to kill or harm in any way Mr. M. Raymond Prescott," I began. "He was born and raised in Nashville, Tennessee, by devout Presbyterians who were affectionate parents and owned the city's most admired independent bookstore.

"Prescott had a business degree from the University of Tennessee and an M.B.A. from George Washington in D.C. He passed exams to become a C.P.A. and worked in Tampa for a decade before moving to Ft. Myers and becoming a partner in a medium size, highly respected accounting firm. He lived on Pine Island in a modest, restored, 1920's plantation-style house that sat on a Calusa mound.

"I decided to pay for a more thorough online search on Prescott and found nothing negative. Not one record of an appearance in either criminal or civil court. He devoted time to several organizations, such as Wounded Warriors and Habitat, and coached a kids' soccer team for five years. He didn't like sports, so he took up golf and was only average. He was not attracted to the water, neither the ocean nor lakes. He was so ordinary I wonder if the killer had made a mistake in identity.

"I also found details about the boat's owner, Rod Swenson. He claimed his boat was stolen while he was at lunch and about to demonstrate the airboat to a prospective buyer. He has an airboat business in Gibsonton south of Tampa, with one partner. Both the partners have often been in trouble—noise ordinance violations, drug dealing, and bar fights. But Swenson had no immediately apparent reason to kill Prescott. . . . No reason even to ever meet him. Swenson occasionally may be a problem, but he is no paid killer. What did you find about Cassell and Cartwright?"

"Cassell was easier," she began. He's thirty-four. Melbourne High School grad. Worked at a number of jobs. Off and on he was a low paid deckhand on a shrimp boat out of Fernandina, Florida. Went to Alaska and was a deckhand on a boat that fished for halibut out of Homer. He stayed several years, came back, and worked at various jobs. Then he enrolled in a course to become a FWC officer. Surprisingly, he did well, finishing first in his class. He joined the FWC soon after.

"But there's a dark side to him. He has a short temper and was involved in bar fights when he worked in Fernandina and Homer. He drank a lot. With another deckhand in Homer, he allegedly stole the payroll from the boat they worked on. No charges were filed; the matter was settled. Cassell was terminated and agreed to leave Alaska. He came here and seems to have gone straight. Apparently, he met Cartwright only last month when he started with the FWC."

"What about Cartwright?" I asked.

"Tommy Lee Cartwright is sixty-three. His father was a state representative in Tallahassee and then a minor Lee County official with a reputation for influence peddling. He dropped out of high school and never returned. But later he received his high school equivalency certificate and married a gal named Tommie Lou! . . . He has sold drugs in one form or another—mostly trafficking using boats to import drugs from Mexico's Yucatan.

"Cartwright was charged with attempted homicide three years ago and placed on leave. That's where it gets interesting. The attempt was against one of the two owners of an *airboat* company south of Tampa—in Gibsonton—on the east side of the bay. The company sold new ABI (Air Boats Inc.) boats and refurbished airboats, usually on consignment. Rod Swenson was one of the partners in the Gibsonton company.

"The attempted homicide charge against Cartwright was dropped when a man a week away from execution at Starke confessed to the act. Despite some objections from senior FWC officials, Cartwright was reinstated by the FWC."

"Does any of what we discovered help?" I asked.

"Maybe some of the info about Cassell and Cartwright. But why didn't they tell us we were right to call them on Channel 16, and that they would take care of the matter and we could go on our way before it got dark? Why they acted the way they did didn't make sense. Were they nervous, trying to think how we might have been involved? Whatever their reasons, we can't ask the authorities about them unless we disclose what we saw. That opens the door to the state attorney adding us to the list of suspects. What should we do?"

"Keep reading the newspapers for new information," I suggested. "Maybe visit Cabbage Key for a few more days and ask around about the latest rumors on the killing."

"Cabbage Key sounds good. Will we take our boat?"

"Yes, but with a new name on the side, and it won't be *Fishhawk*."

13

RETURN TO CABBAGE KEY IN MARCH

I PHONED THE CABBAGE KEY RESORT, ASKING to reserve the Dollhouse Cottage where we had stayed nearly a year earlier after the airboat incident. We were fortunate. All the cabins had been booked for the end of this busy season that started four months ago in December when the Northern invaders arrived, seeking the sun and warmth that all but disappear for that time from their homes in places called Saginaw and Sheboygan. The Dollhouse favored us by a fortuitous cancellation for five nights. We reserved all five.

"Lucinda, are we crazy to come back here?" I asked a week later as we shifted our bags from the SUV to our flats boat, which had its new name—*Sandpiper*—in small letters on each side. We launched at a private marina at Bokeelia on Pine Island rather than a dozen miles to the southwest at the Pineland Marina we had used the day of the airboat murder. We didn't want anyone at the marina to ask: "Weren't you here last year, the week of that murder on an airboat?"

This time we headed across Pine Island Sound straight to our destination at Cabbage Key. No deviation for seeking tailing redfish, where we might encounter something we didn't need adding to our entanglement with the airboat murder. We had to remind ourselves that Herzog was our greater threat, with the airboat murder a distant second. We couldn't risk acting in a way about the airboat murder that put our faces before the public and a possibility that we would assist Herzog's search.

"How far do we have to go, Macduff?" asked Lucinda. This flats boat wasn't made for anything more than water that's—well—*flat*. We've got waves, and I'm getting a sore butt."

"Complain and I'll trade this in for an airboat, with a propeller blade about your length."

"My butt feels better already. But you didn't answer how far we have to Cabbage Key."

"It's almost a straight southwest run from where we turned out of Bokeelia. What you're looking at ahead is Patricio Island. That about marks the beginning of Pine Island National Wildlife Refuge, which goes south some fifteen miles to the other end of Pine Island and more or less where Sanibel makes its curve east at its southern tip. The west side of the sound that protects us from the Gulf has a bunch of islands north to south that were once isolated sand dunes. . . . To answer your question we have about four miles left to Cabbage Key."

"Why is this called Pine Island *Sound*, but Tampa has something similar called a *bay*?"

"You ask too many questions."

"Meaning you don't know," she asserted.

"Meaning go online and see what Wikipedia says."

Two minutes later, after dropping her cellphone twice from the bouncing of our boat, she turned and shouted through the unkind head wind. "Wikipedia is more confusing than *you.* It says a *sound* is larger than a *bay*, deeper than a *bight*, and wider than a *fjord.*"

"That helps only if you're part English and know about *bights* and part Norwegian and know about *fjords.*"

"It also says that a *sound* is a narrow sea or ocean channel between two bodies of land and is also known as a *strait.*"

"What does it say about a *bay*?" I asked.

"You don't want to hear this, but you asked for it. A *bay* is large, but if it's even larger than ordinary large, it may be a *sound* or a *gulf*—like the Gulf of Mexico to our west—or a *sea* or a *bight.* If it's small, it may be a *cove.* If the land sides are steep, it's a *fjord*, which also may make it a *sound.* Got that?"

"Got the gist of it, which is that Wikipedia needs help. And, if we believe it, this area should be Pine Island *Bay* and Tampa should be Tampa *Sound.*"

"One other thing, Macduff, shouldn't a *sound* have to be deeper than a foot or two? The charts for Pine Island Sound show very shallow water except for a few places, such as where the dredged Intracoastal Waterway runs north and south. . . . If you dredge a *sound* or a *bay*, does it become a *sea*?"

"How can you ask me a three dimensional question—about depth—when you've often called me one dimensional?"

"I withdraw that question," she said.

"Thank God. We're almost there. Any other questions to take up the rest of the time?"

"One final question," she said. "How does a *bay, sound, bight, fjord, cove,* or *sea* differ from a *lagoon*?"

The last mile of the trip was marked by noticeable silence on my part.

Rule: Never marry someone with a Ph.D. Especially when she's smarter than you even without the Ph.D.

14

THAT SAME EVENING AT THE CABBAGE KEY BAR

“IF I REMEMBER FROM OUR LAST VISIT, THERE’S neither Gentleman Jack for me nor Montana Roughstock for you! I’ll bet they don’t even serve Moose Drool beer.”

“What will we drink?” Lucinda asked, reading the drink menu as we sat at a small table in the Cabbage Key bar.

“Something appropriate for our visit,” I suggested. “To make our time here especially romantic.”

“I’ll have their Cabbage Creeper,” she said. “It reminds me of you.”

“And I’ll have a Bay Breeze. Does that mean we’re no longer in the sound but have entered a bay?”

“No, it means we have crossed the western-most perimeter of the sound, passed through the Straits of Useppa, missed grounding on the Spoil Area Bight, and, as we approached, came in sight of the Great Bay of Cabbage at the western end of the key, almost in sight of the *Sea* of Mexico.”

“I’ll need a second drink,” I announced. “This time I’ll have a Fuzzy Navel, which complements your sore butt.”

“And I’ll have a Sea Breeze, which differs from the Bay Breeze you had because there was pineapple in your Bay Breeze, and there’s grapefruit in my Sea Breeze. That must mean that grapefruit thrive around seas, and pineapples thrive around bays."

"I'm through drinking; let's go to bed."

"We haven't eaten, and the Sea Breeze has made me hungry. What would you like?"

"A burger and fries, the dinner of the common man."

"I'd say go ahead if the burger were bison. But I doubt the waiter would know what you meant if you asked."

"What are you having?" I asked.

"Sautéed shrimp on angel hair pasta with dill and mango salsa. And homemade garlic sauce."

"And you'll breathe on me all night and I will gag and won't sleep. I'll have to go and sleep on the porch in a chair."

"Promise? I'm tired and need an uninterrupted sleep. . . . Why don't you have the bronzed Mahi-Mahi?"

"It would break my teeth. I'd rather have it grilled. But OK. I'll have that, with an equal portion of garlic sauce as a defensive measure."

"Macduff! Do you have any idea how hard it is to live with you at mealtimes, especially when we go out?"

"You should be able to figure out how to deal with me. After all, you're the one with a Ph.D. . . . I'm *so* impressed. . . . I chose so wisely."

"Your meal?"

"My wife."

"I think I like that. . . . But if only I was more like Beyoncé."

"*Were*."

"What?"

"If only I *were* more like Beyoncé. Shame, doctor!"

15

THE FOLLOWING MORNING AT BREAKFAST

As I WAS SIPPING THE LAST OF MY COFFEE, THE Cabbage Key manager came to our table, apologized for not talking with us the previous evening, and sat down.

"I'm Ted Sweeney. You asked me when you arrived if we might talk. What's it about?"

"I'm Macduff Brooks, Ted. This is Lucinda. We were here almost a year ago on the day of the murder on the airboat over at Black Key. Can we talk about it?"

"Sure, are you a reporter? Or with the FWC or police? Or a private investigator?"

"None of those. I'm a curious frequent visitor to the area who's concerned about any threats—like airboat murders."

"I understand," he said. "I haven't thought about it for months. Most of what I know is a confused mix of Ft. Myers newspaper reports and rumors. Where do we start?"

"There certainly hasn't been much in the local papers since the week after the death," I noted.

"You're right. It was a bizarre murder, but interest soon dropped off when nothing more was reported."

"What exactly do you know about the murder?" he asked.

"We're aware that it involved an airboat and was discovered near midnight by a guide fishing with a friend. The victim,

I recall his last name was Prescott, had been dead since noon. He was a CPA in Ft. Myers and lived somewhere around here, maybe Port Charlotte. The boat was owned by a guy named something like Swanman—but I know he lived in that zany town near Tampa called Gibton. . . . That's really about all I know. . . . Wait a minute. The Ft. Myers paper later stated someone reported seeing a white flats boat in the water near Black Key. That's really shallow water."

"The owner was named Swenson, and he did live in Gibsonton," Ted clarified.

"The only names we've mentioned are the guy that was dead, Prescott, and the boat owner, Swenson. Have you heard any other names?" I asked.

"I can't think of any."

"Who would do something like this? It takes a twisted mind to strap someone to a prop on an airboat and start the engine."

"I'm surprised that there hasn't been another copycat airboat murder," said Ted. "There are plenty of crazies on the water. . . . Sorry I'm not of much help."

"Thanks. I guess we're OK wandering around Pine Island Sound. Where do you suggest we fish tomorrow?"

"It's a little early for tarpon in Boca Grande Pass. May and June are the months to do that. You hardly need to leave our docks to get reds, trout, and snook. With your flats boat I'd suggest spending the day most anywhere along the inner coast of Cayo Costa. You fly fishing?"

"Yes."

"Try the east side of Mondongo Island if you like trout."

"We'll let you know later how it went."

16

NEXT DAY IN PINE ISLAND SOUND

PINE ISLAND SOUND HAD SETTLED DURING THE night and remained a glossy film when we looked out to see the sun's first rays.

"Where are we going?" Lucinda asked.

"To breakfast," I answered. "I can't wait. Free of your nutritional restraints."

"Don't be too sure about that, but I meant *fishing!* We came to fish, not to eat."

"No breakfast?"

"A quick one, before the hundreds of daytime visitors trudge off the tour boats arriving like miniature tourist-encrusted Carnival Cruise Line ships from Pine Island, Captiva, Punta Gorda, and Boca Grande."

Few high spots—if less than a hundred feet can be considered "high"—are on the lands surrounding the sound, not the Calusa mounds at the north of Pine Island, nor the rises on Useppa Island, nor the modest hill behind our Cabbage Key complex. But it doesn't take much height to see the vastness of the sound between Charlotte Harbor on the north and San Carlos Bay on the south, eighteen miles apart. Pine Island itself is a single island that serves as the eastern boundary of the sound;

the west, about six miles from Pine Island, is made up of four barrier islands running north and south—Cayo Costa, North Captiva, Captiva, and Sanibel. Sanibel curves to the east, enclosing the sound's southern end, where San Carlos Bay begins.

The depth of this largest inland sound on Florida's West Coast is deceptive because much of the water comprises a thin veneer to a bottom that lies in most places only a few feet below the surface. For an angler whose experience with the Intracoastal Waterway has been along the East Coast, where the track lies mostly following a few narrow rivers and artificial channels, the ICW path crossing Pine Island Sound looks like a scattering of channel markers in an otherwise undisturbed expanse of water.

Without dredged channels, like Wilson Cut out of Pineland, connecting the deeper water of the sound with marinas on Pine Island and the islands to the west, access to most of the land surrounding Pine Island Sound would depend on bridges from the mainland to the islands, such as the one leading to Sanibel, also the bridge to Captiva at Sanibel's northern end, another from the mainland to Matlacha, and one from Little Pine Island to the much larger main Pine Island.

We dressed and walked to have breakfast at the Old House, Cabbage Key's open-air, three-meals-a-day, 365-days-a-year restaurant. No more than twenty guests relaxed at the tables, far fewer than would arrive for lunch. Our table was in a corner, beneath the walls plastered with guest-signed dollar bills. I think we inscribed one the night before, but not until we were under the spell of Cabbage Creepers and Fuzzy Navels.

"Coffee, please," Lucinda said, smiling at a taller-than-six-feet waiter. She would have said more, but she was speechless in front of this college age Adonis.

"Anything else?" he asked in a baritone better than *Il Divo.*

"You serve eggs, if I remember from the menu." She had looked at the menu for at least five minutes before Adonis arrived. Eggs were prominently featured in several variations; she already *knew* they served eggs.

"For you, we will cook eggs however you wish."

"Give her two poached eggs. She's from London," I interjected.

"No!" she said, objecting. "I want them scribbled," she responded, dreamy-eyed.

"She meant scrambled," I corrected. Like her brain, I thought.

"How would you like them scrambled—I recommend with a drop of almond milk and a touch of cheese," Adonis suggested.

"Whatever you recommend," she whispered with her best Lauren Bacall accent. Adonis smiled and left.

"Isn't he gorgeous?" she asked, leaning on her elbows and watching him disappear into the kitchen.

"Are you searching for a suitor for Elsbeth?" I inquired.

"For Elsbeth?"

After breakfast—now that Lucinda had returned to earth from her starry-eyed service by Adonis—we took Ted's suggestion and ventured off for a day of sight fishing on the flats near the east side of Cayo Costa, the island directly west of Cabbage Key. Cayo Costa is home to a boat-access-only state park, about six miles long, close to a mile wide at the north end and a dozen yards across at the south.

Word was that Spanish mackerel and bluefish were massing in the passes. Both, plus sea trout, were in the water where the grasses were beginning to show their spring growth. A few tarpon had showed up in Captiva Pass, a number that would soon multiply and be many.

We crept along slowly on an incoming tide west toward Primo Island. When the depth finder read two feet of water, I shut off the engine, climbed onto the poling platform, and took the end of the push pole Lucinda handed to me.

"Macduff, it's not very deep, and it's very clear."

"The benefit of no dirty river-sourced water and the constant flushing tides."

"What do you see from up there?" she asked.

"A couple of fish moving toward where we're headed. We'll be close enough to cast in another hundred feet. You ready?"

"Of course. Do you want to do the cast?"

"Nope. I'll fish soon enough. I want to put you on to whatever is ahead. Got your rod ready?"

"Always."

"Look at about two o'clock."

"I see something making ripples. Seventy-five feet. More than I can cast."

"By the time you do a false cast and get your line out, we'll be forty feet away. Well within your range in salt water, even though you're throwing a fly a lot heavier than a #14 Adams we often use in the West. Cast ahead and beyond the disturbance; then strip the fly in to cross in front of the fish."

She tossed a nice cast, but the fly landed not more than three feet in front of whatever the fish was. I guessed a trout or snook. Whatever it was, it scattered.

"Macduff, I messed up!"

"Capital offense. You'll pay the price tonight."

"In that case I may miss a lot more!"

"There's another off to your left, about nine o'clock."

"What should I change in my cast?"

"Nothing, except get a little more line out on your false casts. I'm letting us drift with the tide. The fish is coming against the tide, waiting for something tempting. Get ready."

"Now?"

"Yes!"

"This time she had good length. She stripped the fly back and said, "Something's pulling!"

"Pull yourself! Set the hook. This is not a ten-inch cutthroat on the Snake in Wyoming."

I was sure she was too late, but her line began to strip off, and her rod bent, showing she was onto something that was clearly no ten-inch fish.

"Macduff! It's pulling hard."

"Hang on! It's slowing. Don't increase the drag, and get ready to crank if it turns back. . . . Now it's turning! Crank hard, keep the rod bent, and don't lower the tip."

She turned to me with a determined look. "I'm boating this one, Macduff. Have that net ready. And your ruler!"

"It may be a while. It's not tired."

"What is it?"

"Spotted sea trout. It's a beauty."

It *was* a beauty. I saw in Lucinda's look and movements an ecstasy. Two gorgeous creatures at opposite ends of the line, both determined to be the victor. The salt water spotted sea trout's color differed from the fresh water Western trout. The body of what is most often called simply a trout is silver on the bottom at the front, but at the tail has changed to a gold that started on the top behind its eyes and dominates its sides and back. Its numerous black spots stand out.

I stayed on the poling platform to maneuver to Lucinda's advantage—tilting the scale in her favor. In a few minutes the trout tired and came unhappily to the boat. I stepped down from the tower and slipped the net under most of the fish.

"Macduff, I've never had a trout this size. Its colors are beyond description, every bit as spectacular as a cutthroat or brook trout in fresh water. How big is it?"

"Twelve inches. I don't need to measure it; my judgment is accurate."

"Twelve inches! You're not getting away with that this time. Remember when you wouldn't give me the ruler when I caught a bigger trout than you did out West?"

She set down her rod, pulled from her bag a plastic ruler, laid it on the deck, grabbed the net from me, slipped the fly, lifted the fish carefully, and set it along the ruler.

"It's twenty-seven inches! Agreed?"

"Oh, well. I'll spoil you this time. It's twenty-seven inches."

"She carefully set the fish in the water, head toward the incoming tidal current. In seconds, it turned abruptly and was gone. I put my hand up to high-five her, but she pushed it aside and hugged me. Her body was trembling with excitement.

"Let's do this again," she said, flashing her best smile.

"This doesn't happen every day when we're fly fishing," I said. "That was a great fish."

"Macduff! I didn't photograph it!"

"I did, with my cell phone."

"You're a love."

"A copy of the photo will cost you."

"Money?"

"I wasn't thinking of money."

"You're incorrigible. Let's fish some more, after a sandwich."

I lowered the Power Pole, leaving our small Danforth anchor in its locker. The bottom was grass, and retrieving a traditional anchor would damage the grass bed.

We sat together and ate lunch, looking at each other and communicating without words. Expressions, a cocking of a head or a touching of a hand, were enough. The sun was high overhead, and a light southwesterly breeze floated off the Gulf. I listened as the incoming tide slapped rhythmically against the hull, an osprey screamed at us for being in its private fishing grounds, and high overhead in the wake of a silent jet, ice crystals formed contrails that soon scattered.

By mid-afternoon I was tired poling. Lucinda had caught three more fish, including another decent trout and a small snook. But it was the third—a Spanish mackerel—that provided the best fight of the day.

If one practices catch and release, as we both do, the preferred fishing may be for the fighters rather than some tasty but docile fish that come to the boat easily. Tarpon, Spanish mackerel, bluefish, jacks, and the toothy barracuda all forcefully resist their capture.

Lucinda's Spanish mackerel was only about eighteen inches, but it fought better than a mammoth grouper, flounder, or redfish. Whether her mackerel should have counted became the subject of some debate.

"How did you catch the mackerel?" I asked as we worked the flats boat along Primo Bay for our last fishing of the day.

"You know how. I had a Clouser Minnow; I think a size 2/0 hook. You tied it on for me."

"Did you get a good cast to it?"

"Of course."

"How long was it between your cast and the strike?"

"A moment or two."

"Would twenty-five minutes be accurate?"

"I think I know where you're headed."

"Which hand did you have the rod in when you caught the mackerel?"

"You know I put the rod down for a second."

"Like for ten minutes. . . You were *trolling*. You weren't fishing."

"I was on a *fishing* boat. I had a *fishing* rod in my . . . near me. It had a *fishing* fly tied on. I was, therefore, *fishing*."

"OK. Our records will show you caught four fish. But there'll be an asterisk next to the mackerel."

"Spoil sport."

"Pick up your rod," I said a half-hour later. "Check your fly, and stand up on the bow. This is the last time I'm going to pole today. Be ready."

"You do your job; I'll do mine. You're supposed to sight the fish for me. I can see something sixty feet off to the right. About two o'clock. . . . Can't you see it?"

"It's probably nothing, but I'll pole us over there."

I saw what she was watching. It *was* a fish, slowly moving past us. I began to pole the boat more to the right, keeping an eye on the fish at the same time. At the moment I turned on the poling platform to face the fish, Lucinda stepped to the other side of the bow, and the boat tipped to the left. I knew what the result would be. I was heading in. I landed feet first in a splash, hit the bottom, and fell over to one side, immersed from head to toe.

Lucinda turned to cast. "What are you *doing,* Macduff? Why did you jump in? I have a fish in view."

"Drop the anchor," I yelled as the tide began to take the boat away from me. I was standing in two feet of water holding onto the pole."

"Swim or wade," she called. "I've got a fish on the line."

"The anchor! *Please.*"

I'll never know whether she tossed the anchor over because she was concerned for my safety or because the fish broke off and she had nothing better to do. I waded the twenty yards through a sand and sea grass bottom. Alongside the boat, I handed her the pole.

"Do you want me to help you aboard," she asked condescendingly. "I would have landed that fish if you hadn't decided to jump into the sound and splash around."

"I didn't jump! I fell when you leaped from one side of the boat to the other. You flipped me in."

"You're a guide. You should know how to deal with that."

At that moment I realized Lucinda was no longer fishing just because I was. She loved the challenge of fly fishing. . . . If something happened to me, she would grieve, not in the pews of a church, but on the salt flats of Florida or the creeks of Montana.

By the time I climbed aboard the boat, without assistance, I was laughing and smiling. I grabbed her, squeezed her, and buried my face in the fragrance of her auburn hair.

"Wow! I should flip you off more often. . . . Let's go home."

17

TO GIBSONTON

WE SAT ON THE DOCK OF THE DOLLHOUSE four evenings later; our time at Cabbage Key had nearly run its course. The wind was not even whispering. The temperature was a welcome seventy-two degrees with no perceptible humidity. Visibility was limited only by the horizon. Another day in Paradise.

"Lucinda, I have an idea."

"Does it merit my thoughts? I'm enjoying the last of this delicate Gulf Coast sunset."

"Maybe my idea is not important. It has to do with who might want to kill us. But it's a thought that can wait. It probably won't happen for a day or two."

"Now you've spoiled my communing with nature," she said. "Not to mention stolen the last sip of my drink. Go ahead. Scare me."

"Let's make a slight deviation tomorrow on the way home."

"Taking me to lunch at the Columbia Restaurant in Tampa sounds wonderful."

"I was thinking more along the lines of an Arby's on the Interstate."

"Is Arby's now serving flan? I'd want some flan for dessert."

"Cross off Arby's. I'll trade with you. We leave here early in the morning, and we'll have dinner at the Columbia."

"So you have something planned between here and Tampa? It's not an all-day drive."

"I have something in mind. I want to stop in Gibsonton. Or Gibton as its residents call it."

"Where and what is Gibsonton? I've never heard of it."

"Gibsonton is ten miles this side of Tampa, very close to I-75. It's where Rod Swenson's airboat store and repair shop is located. From its website it's less a building than the side yard of his trailer close to a river. Remember that three years ago Cartwright allegedly attempted to kill Swenson on an airboat he was demonstrating on Tampa Bay."

"Allegedly?"

"He was detained, charged with attempted homicide, and placed on leave by the FWC, but released and reinstated when a death-row inmate confessed to the act."

"What are you going to do? Tell Swenson we encountered Cartwright at Prescott's death?"

"No. Pretend I'm looking to buy a used airboat for our place on the marsh in St. Augustine. And see if and what he knows about the Prescott death."

"And if he does?"

"Try to get him talking."

"Will I be with you?"

"No. I don't think that's a good idea. If you drop me off in town, you can visit some of the town's historic sites, such as where the carnival sideshow celebrity Lobster Boy lived and where his wife and stepson had him killed."

We arrived at the I-75 turnoff for Gibsonton at noon, welcoming the deviation from one of our gridlocked interstates. A mile or so west took us to where Gibsonton Road crossed U.S. 41. Excited about seeing sideshow carnies, we cruised slowly south a few blocks and turned around and went north a few blocks, finding nothing along U.S. 41 that would identify the town as the notable satellite circus town where the old post office had special low countertops for "little people," then acceptably known as "midgets."

Next we tried driving through the residential area, which seemed to have no streets named for men, favoring instead Shirley, Anna, Gloria, Alma, Vera, and—what apparently was the longest street in town—Lula.

We had seen no less deprived areas on U.S. 81 crossing north Texas. In both places yards filled with junk were surrounded by chain link fences to keep the treasures safe. Gibsonton's eclectic yards were even the storage places for circus animals, endowed with legal status by favorable zoning laws.

Dogs represented mostly unidentifiable breeds, and poorly maintained small houses or trailers were covered less with paint than with mold.

There were no outward signs of Gibsonton being the haven for side-show freaks. It was impossible to describe the town and be politically correct. Nearly a hundred years earlier, the carnies flocked to live here because of its relative proximity to the circus city of Sarasota, home of Barnum & Bailey.

Carnival side-shows gave way in the 1930s to movies and later to TV, but Gibsonton retained a place in entertainment history where one could encounter live characters including Percilla the Monkey Girl, the Anatomical Wonder, and the Lobster Boy.

"Macduff," Lucinda asked, searching wide-eyed for signs of the town's culture. "Why are we here? What does this have to do with us?"

"You know whose airboat was stolen and used in the Prescott murder?"

"Remind me."

"Allegedly, the airboat was stolen from Rod Swenson's place here in Gibsonton!" I added as I pulled off, opposite a trailer along the town's north border, the Alafia River. "See any airboats in the yard?"

"I do," she responded. "Is this Swenson's place?"

"It must be. There's a small sign on the front fence."

"'Swenson & Prescott Airboats,'" she read. "But the name Prescott has been crossed out. . . . What do you expect to learn here? How does this relate to the airboat murder? We know Cartwright allegedly tried to kill Swenson three years ago. Here?"

"Not on the river. Out on Tampa Bay less than two miles west of here. Apparently Swenson was demonstrating a used airboat Cartwright was thinking of buying."

"Why is the name *Prescott* here on the sign? He was the one killed on the airboat. On a stolen airboat allegedly owned by Swenson. Or by Swenson *and* Prescott? Why is Prescott's name crossed out? I thought he was a good guy who didn't even like the water? Looks to me as if Swenson believed Prescott stole his airboat, maybe after some business or personal dispute. That's a motive. Are the police aware of all this?"

"Lucinda, slow down! We may find out some answers. I suspect the police have talked to Swenson about his boat being stolen. But they may not have considered his business relationship with Prescott."

"What do we do? I've taken a photo of the sign with my cell phone. Can we go?"

"Not yet. I want you to take the car and wander around the town, drive up and down streets. Get a feel for the place that may help later. I'm going to try to talk to Swenson, if he's here and willing. I'll call you when I'm ready to leave."

Lucinda drove off, and I walked through the chain link entry, keeping an eye on a pit bull with a face scared from being vanquished in numerous fights. One ear was frayed and partly missing. I thought the dog might have lost an eye. It was straining in my direction on a chain attached to a telephone pole in the yard. Its barking drew the attention of a man who came out the trailer office door.

"What you want? I got no airboats for sale. Come back some other time."

"Get out of here. Now! Before I let the dog loose."

18

DISCUSSION WITH SWENSON

ROD SWENSON WAS A FORTY-YEAR-OLD WHO would never understand the concept of social graces. Merely being unshaven—it was becoming common among young men—was not a problem. But unshaven joining unkempt and disheveled best described Swenson. He was shirtless and sweating, and his right hand held a beer can. He smelled like a landfill and probably couldn't remember the last time he had a bath. A bath might not have helped; sand blasting might have been better.

I motioned to turn around and heed his advice to leave, more because of the dog than the odor of the owner.

"Sorry to have bothered you," I said over my shoulder in an apologetic tone. "I would have liked you to take my name and give me a call if you heard of a used airboat for sale," I added, after a pause and while backing away toward the gate.

"Wait a minute, damn it. I were busy fixin' another boat and dropped a wrench on my foot when Killer started barkin'. Don't fuss. He weren't gonna pull off the chain. Come in my shop."

His "shop" did not merit the name; it was more rusting tools scattered around the floor and on old doors laid across saw horses that served as work benches. Liquids of various colors and compositions had spilled on the concrete floor over the years and left a vision worthy of contemporary art.

"Some guy called me last week and asked if I wanted to buy his twelve-year-old Moccasin airboat. Told him I'd do it on consignment, but he were after cash in a hurry. I got his name and phone number. Interested?"

"Yes," I answered. "I know very little about airboats. Wasn't a Moccasin the kind used for that murder last winter around Captiva? Or was it an ABI?"

"You do know airboats. It weren't a Moccasin. It were an ABI. Helluva killin', weren't it?"

"Not a pleasant way to die. Who owned the boat? Probably not the guy who was killed."

"It were my boat, damn it. Got stolen from *this* yard. Damned dog ain't worth feedin.' He didn't stop the robbery."

"Do the police know who did the killing?"

"They don't know nothin'. They came by and asked me a few questions. I told them I filed a report with the police when the boat were taken. They were surprised and asked for a copy. I gave it to 'em. They left and I ain't heard a damn thing since. Dumb cops."

"Do you think the person who stole your boat did the killing?"

"How the hell should I know? Someone else coulda stolen the boat from the first thief. I got a suspicion a guy that were here the day before the boat were taken mighta done it."

"Do you remember what the guy looked like?" I asked, wondering if he were Cartwright.

"You ask too many questions. But if you must know, I ain't never saw the guy. My partner Prescott talked to him."

"Your partner was named Prescott, the same as the guy murdered? Have you seen your partner—his name is crossed out on your sign out front?"

"It were *my* partner that got hisself kilt. He ain't been back since the killin' so this mornin' I crosst off his name on the sign. Didn't like him much anyway. Ain't gonna miss him."

"Sounds like *you* might be a suspect?"

"That's enough. You don't accuse me nohow. Get your ass out of here before I let the dog loose. I ain't fed him today."

I carefully walked past the dog to the street. Lucinda had returned and parked the car across and down two lots. She was sitting a hundred yards away on a piling on the public dock on the river. Starting the car, I watched Swenson head back to his shop, swinging a foot and yelling at the dog as he passed. When I drove to the dock, Lucinda got into the car and crouched down to hide as we drove back and passed Swenson's shop. He was standing in his door watching.

"Have a nice tour of the town?" I asked as we left Gibsonton behind.

"I did. I stopped for coffee near where the Giant's Camp Restaurant once was operated by the town legends—the Tomaini couple. Eight-foot-plus tall Al and his two-and-a-half-foot wife Jeanie ran the restaurant when they weren't touring as sideshow freaks. One of Al's size 22 boots once graced the front yard."

"You could become a tour guide here."

"If I did, I'd make up a story about a freak fishing guide from Montana who. . . ."

"Enough! It wasn't such a good idea. Let's go to Tampa for dinner. I'll tell you about my conversation with Swenson."

"Macduff, I don't understand something," she said as we rejoined I-75 and headed north toward Tampa.

"This sounds like trouble."

"*Who* was killed on the airboat?"

"You know that. Raymond Prescott."

"Maybe yes, maybe no," Lucinda stated.

"What do you mean?"

"The notes you made when you researched Prescott referred to M. Raymond Prescott."

"Same thing. M. Raymond Prescott or Raymond Prescott. Call him whichever you want."

"Is it? What did the sign on Swenson's airboat place say?"

"Swenson and Prescott."

"Below was more smaller writing. Do you remember what it said?"

"I assume just Raymond Prescott or maybe M. Raymond Prescott."

"Neither one."

"What do you mean?"

"The sign said *Martin* R. Prescott. I checked some records on my cell phone, and he's Martin Raymond Prescott, but goes by Ray rather than Raymond."

"Are you suggesting that. . . ?"

"I am. There are *two* different Prescotts!" she said.

"Swenson never mentioned that."

"Maybe he doesn't know."

"That's not possible," I said. "Swenson would know when his partner named Prescott—Martin R. Prescott—came back to work *after* Swenson learned that another Prescott had been murdered."

"Assume that Swenson's partner, Prescott, had a couple of days off and that the first was the day that the *other* Prescott was murdered by mistake. And assume Swenson's partner Prescott then learned of a Prescott being killed on Swenson's stolen boat. Swenson's partner Prescott likely believed he was the intended target and fled. Then Swenson read about a Prescott being murdered, and his partner Prescott naturally didn't come back to work because he fled. Prescott was crossed off the entry sign by Swenson. He thinks Prescott hadn't returned because he was dead, but his partner actually was hiding somewhere. And still is."

"Why would Swenson's partner Prescott act that way and why didn't he tell the authorities?"

"Because he was scared. He may not have known who wanted him dead," she said.

"Or he may have known and hoped the other Prescott's killers didn't believe the wrong Prescott was killed," I responded.

"Wouldn't the killer have known when he tied Prescott to the propeller on the airboat?" she countered.

"Not necessarily. It could have been a hired killer who hadn't been told much other than the name Raymond Prescott," I offered.

"Let me toss out a couple of wild ideas I haven't thought through," Lucinda offered. "Martin R. Prescott and his partner Swenson didn't get along well. Apparently no one got along with Swenson. Remember his spat with Cartwright? Swenson hires someone to kill Martin R. But Martin R. survives because of the killer's mistake. Worried Swenson will learn that the killer murdered the wrong Prescott, Martin R. goes into hiding, hoping Swenson happily but wrongfully thinks Martin R. is dead. The real killer is not found. Swenson's pleased, thinking Martin R. was killed.

"Swenson has paid off the killer and told him to leave the area. Martin R. obviously is pleased he's not dead and has fled the area for good. But, angry that Swenson intended to kill him, he calls the state attorney's office and says *Swenson* killed Prescott. It might lead to the state attorney figuring out what we know—that there were two Prescotts. . . . Swenson had no motive to kill M. Raymond Prescott, but M. Raymond is dead because of the mistake by the killer. And Martin R. is alive.

"So what happens? Swenson is charged with murder and convicted, believing he got caught arranging the murder of Martin R. The actual killer thinks he did a good job and doesn't know Martin R. Prescott is alive. How extraordinary!"

"You're confusing and losing me, Lucinda. . . . That's why we need to stay aware of developments," I responded. "We are *not* involved, but possibly we know more than the police *and* Swenson. And we know about the Prescott who has disappeared."

"What do you think the police believe?" she asked.

"They don't know what we know," I replied. "Maybe Dan Wilson in D.C. will leak some info to them. But I'd rather he didn't."

"The police must think that Prescott was killed because someone had a motive to kill M. Raymond Prescott," she suggested. "Someone who had nothing to do with Swenson and his partner Martin R. Prescott. But the authorities haven't put two and two together."

"*What* do you suppose the police think about the *missing* Prescott?" I asked.

"They don't know about him! Swenson's not going to tell them anything other than he's sorry his partner was so brutally murdered. *Who* do you think the police believe killed Prescott?" she asked, changing the discussion from Prescott to his killer.

"I don't think they know much. Less than we do. . . . If the police believe the drug residues were involved with the murder, they will be looking for whoever might have been involved in a drug deal. M. Raymond Prescott? Not likely. Why kill him? Has the state attorney shown any knowledge of what a legitimate motive might have been for killing M. Raymond Prescott? I don't think so."

"Maybe Martin R. Prescott was dealing in drugs using an airboat. Maybe Swenson as well, but the state attorney's people apparently haven't talked to Swenson other than briefly the day after the murder. I wonder why."

"Lack of resources. If it's complex and nobody's putting on pressure, they might put the case in the cold file section. I think I read that M. Raymond Prescott was a bachelor and there were no family members who would have been interested in his death."

"This is beyond belief, Macduff. I'm exhausted. Let's talk about it in the morning."

On the rest of our after-dinner drive back to the cottage, Lucinda dozed while I thought about my conversation with Swenson and the confusion over two Prescotts. At dinner we had gone over the Swenson conversation again and again, but didn't discuss whether or not it made any difference if we remained silent about the airboat murder. Until a few hours ago, we hadn't talked about the possibility of there being two different Prescotts.

Could there have been two? I wondered.

19

THAT AFTERNOON AT SWENSON'S

SWENSON SAT IN HIS RICKETY CHAIR, OPENED A can of Milwaukee's worst bought in clusters of forty-eight at his nearby Walmart, and emptied the can in one gulp. He thought about his brief talk with the man who had just left. Swenson realized he didn't get the potential buyer's name, but only the cell phone number he'd been given.

He first called the owner of the used airboat, who told Swenson he was anxious to sell and would take $15,000 cash for the boat that the trading ads suggested was worth $24,000. It was too good a deal for a buyer to pass up.

Immediately after hanging up, Swenson dialed the cell phone number the potential buyer had given him. He was surprised when a recorded message said that number was not in service. He dialed again and got the same answer. Swenson cussed, not knowing what to make of this situation. He sat back in his chair, lighted a cigarette, took a sip from another beer can, and stared at the ceiling, thinking.

Then he dialed a different number.

"This is Swenson," he said, "Got a minute?"

"Yep. Shoot!"

"I just had a conversation with a guy who came by and said he were interested in buyin' a used airboat. I told him about an airboat that were for sale here in town. I called the owner. He told me to sell it even for a helluva lot less than his original wantin' price. So, I called the guy usin' the number he give me. But a recordin' said the number were not in service."

"What's your problem, Swenson?"

"My problem is that the guy asked me questions about the airboat murder. I didn't tell him nuthin'. No names. *Nuthin'*."

"Tell me *exactly* what you two did say."

Swenson related the conversation as best he could.

"Why the hell did you keep talking to the guy? Was he a newspaper reporter? Police? He could have been a private investigator."

"I dunno. He seemed like he were a nice guy."

"Did you see his car? Was he with anybody?"

"Come to think of it, he didn't got a car. When he left he walked north toward the river. He coulda left a car by the burger shack on the river. I never seen a car or whether he were with anybody."

"He hasn't tried to call you?"

"I guess not. . . . Ain't heard from him."

"Did he ask about Cartwright?"

"Nope. Only 'bout me and Prescott."

"Prescott's dead."

"I know that. I took the bastard's name off the sign on my fence. If he ain't dead, he will be when I see him."

20

A FEW DAYS LATER IN GUATEMALA

JUAN PABLO HERZOG STOOD ON THE BALCONY of his 14th floor condominium on Avenida Las Americas in Guatemala City, watching planes land and take off a few miles south at La Aurora International Airport. A glass of his favorite local rum was in one hand, a Cuban cigar in the other. A light breeze from the southwest slid over the slopes of the volcanos, cooled the March evening air, and carried toward Herzog subtle airport sounds of jet engines landing. He loved his country, but sometimes thought it was not a good place for families because of the drugs. But he was accumulating a fortune from that drug trade.

In a few days Herzog would be inaugurated as the president of his country. To local newspaper pundits, it was a toss-up whether he was elected because the voters were terrified what would happen to them if they voted otherwise or because they were persuaded by his rhetoric that promised them what they should have known could never be forthcoming.

Herzog brought to Guatemala an envious intellect and endless energy. Both had helped to make him the wealthiest man in the country, the most ruthless crime boss the Western Hemisphere had ever known, and the loneliest man in Guatemala because no one—male or female—was comfortable in his company.

In his youth Herzog had murdered a schoolmate, in his young adulthood he had used a chainsaw to dismember the then drug lord of Guatemala, and as an adult allegedly he had caused the death by his own hands of dozens of people by whom he felt threatened. Nothing daunted him.

One goal Herzog pursued for nearly a dozen years had been frustrated and led to the death of both a niece and a nephew. And, he believed, to the death of his closest friend, the Sudanese Abdul Khaliq Isfahani. Herzog's goal was to kill former law professor Maxwell Hunt of the University of Florida law college in Gainesville. Herzog had beaten Hunt severely because he believed Hunt was working for the U.S. CIA and challenging interests dear to Herzog's ambitions.

Herzog was one of the very few people who refused to accept the announcements by the UF law college and the Department of State that Hunt, saved from the beating carried out by Herzog, was taken to Washington for medical care and died of a massive stroke induced by the trauma of the beating.

One other who agreed with Herzog's view that a death had not occurred was Hunt himself, who was brought to D.C., cared for until he recovered, and placed in something similar to the Witness Protection Program, but for compromised good agents rather than crime bosses.

Professor Hunt, internationally praised for his teaching and his writing on the law, became Macduff Brooks, a quiet and reclusive fly fishing guide who lived in a small log cabin on Mill Creek in Paradise Valley, Montana, near the hamlet of Emigrant with its roughly five hundred residents. A mere thirteen were other than white, and more than half of the modest population had lived there since birth. Diversity in Montana meant differences in favorite beers and guns.

Disliking the cold Montana winters and missing Florida, Brooks bought a cottage on the salt flats south of St. Augustine near Matanzas Inlet. There he began to spend his winters.

Herzog was certain Professor Hunt had survived the beating, did not succumb to a stroke, and was living somewhere using a new name. Five years ago Herzog had offered the UF law college $4 million to establish a chair to honor Hunt. All Herzog claimed that he wanted was a thorough report on what had actually happened to Hunt.

When the true motive of that offer became apparent to the UF administration, Herzog attempted to murder the law dean and the university president. He had trained a niece, María-Martina Herzog, to shoot the two from a law building roof overlooking the dedication ceremony for a new wing. Someone never identified intervened and shot and killed the niece. Juan Pablo was certain that her killer was the person Hunt had become, whatever his name. That assumption was correct.

The following year Herzog tried again to find Professor Hunt in his new identity. This time Herzog used a nephew, Martín Paz, but that effort also was thwarted, and Paz was killed. Herzog was convinced Hunt was the killer. This time he was incorrect.

Herzog also believed Professor Hunt, in his new identity, tried to kill Herzog's best friend Abdul Khaliq Isfahani of the Sudan. He was the subject of an assassination attempt while visiting Herzog in Guatemala eight years ago. Herzog correctly believed Hunt was responsible for the attempt.

Two years ago another long distance sniper rifle shot ended the life of Isfahani as he stood in front of a mosque in Omdurman in the Sudan, being admired by his terrorist followers. Again Herzog correctly believed Hunt was the shooter.

Herzog continued to defer any further attempt to discover Hunt's new name and residence only because he was working to become Guatemala's president. If elected, he would be busy during his four-year term. But recently his hatred of and determination to kill Hunt's successor caused Herzog to renew his search regardless of the demands of his presidency. Perhaps he could use the powers of the presidency to achieve his goal.

The president-elect realized that it had been more than a decade since he severely beat Hunt. Herzog did not want to read about whoever Hunt had become dying of natural causes, thus denying Herzog the pleasure of being the executioner and watching Hunt die. But Herzog knew he would never risk his presidency by killing Hunt; thus, he would have to postpone the task or have assistance.

That assistance was to come from another niece, Luisa Solares.

21

THE FOLLOWING WEEK IN GUATEMALA

LUISA SOLARES PARKED HER ARMORED, BLACK Suburban in a private, guarded area of the Casa Presidencial in Guatemala City. Walking to the building, she inhaled the fragrances in the extensive gardens of the residence and thought how much she loved her country.

One of the guards called President Herzog to inform him she had arrived and was her way up to his rooms. A guard carrying an automatic weapon escorted her to the second floor private study where her Tío Juan could spend uninterrupted time when he was not at the ornate 350-room presidential palace on the Plaza Mayor in the heart of the city.

The security guards had already come to know Señorita Solares, and she passed quickly to her Tío Juan's rooms. A servant met her at the door and escorted her to the living room where Herzog was browsing the most popular serious Guatamalan newspaper, *Prensa Libre,* specifically looking for the first wave of criticism of his initial week in office.

"Buenas dias, Señor Presidente," Luisa said, smiling but not being offered an embrace. She had learned to expect that separation, caused by a mix of Herzog's reluctance to become too close to anyone and to accept her being an illegitimate child.

"I like the sound of that," Herzog responded.

"But I will always call you Tío Juan," she stated. "Have you appointed me Attorney General yet?"

He laughed. "Don't you think you ought to finish your law studies at Marroquín before you become a member of my cabinet?"

"I guess so, but I'm impatient to work for you."

"And before you serve in my government, I want you to do something after you receive your degree here this summer."

"Of course, Tío Juan. What is that?"

"Something similar to what I did years ago. Spend a year studying at the University of Florida law college. . . . I was not at the law college but in the agricultural school. I took one course at the law college."

"Which is where you met Professor Hunt?"

"Yes, he was my favorite professor. . . . And he is mainly the reason for *your* going to Gainesville."

"What good can I do? Hunt no longer teaches there or even lives in Gainesville. It's been a decade since he allegedly died."

"He did not die!" Herzog stated cryptically, causing Luisa to look away and tighten her hold on the arms of her chair. "He may live in Gainesville. Learning if he does live there is part of what you will do."

"I'm sorry, Tío Juan. . . . What do you wish from me?"

"I want you to be a good student and attend to your studies; that will help you to serve me when you return here. We struggle with our relations with the United States, but we have much to gain from playing their games and periodically reassuring them that we are making progress in recognizing and applying the rule of law."

"Are we making progress?" she asked, aware that it might draw another irritated response.

"Of course we are, dear niece. We have always respected the role law plays in helping to maintain a public impression that we are governing for the people's benefit."

"Tío Juan, I cannot start in Gainesville until mid-August. I have almost six months to prepare. What should I be thinking of that will help me learn about Professor Hunt?"

"I want you to leave for Gainesville in late July, rent an apartment, become settled, and begin your studies. You must live alone because you will have materials about Hunt with you, and occasionally we will talk on the phone. A roommate would only interfere and ask embarrassing questions.

"Before you leave Guatemala, we will talk, and I will give you a list. It will include information such as the address of the house where Professor Hunt lived, which ironically is also the house your cousin Martín rented when he was there several years ago—before he was murdered by Hunt."

"I wonder if the current owner knows much about the house's history," Luisa pondered.

"You may talk to the current owner in your search for information about Professor Hunt. In fact, you should find out as much as you can about his two decades living in that house. It's from that house that Hunt left on his final trip here to Guatemala.

"Also, you must visit where both Martín and María were killed, and the soccer stadium that continued to draw Professor Hunt back to Gainesville after he was given a new identity. Perhaps it still attracts him to games. . . . Plus, we must have information about a person with whom you should be careful—Dean Hobart Perry at the law college. I believe he is the only person at the UF law college who knows exactly where Professor Hunt now lives and what name he has taken."

"Now, Tío Juan, I need to attend to my studies here at Marroquín. And I must apply and be admitted to the LL.M. program."

"Is there any doubt that you will be?"

"None. You know we Herzogs always have performed well in school. I *will* be admitted."

"One last matter, Luisa. You must never talk about your being related to me. If anyone asks you about me—after all, I am the president—you must say you have never met me."

Luisa was escorted from the building, and when she reached her car, she could not stop shaking. She sat for forty minutes before she regained her composure and felt able to drive. Tío Juan would do anything *for* her, but also anything *to* her if she did not obey him. She looked forward to being away from Guatemala City for the next academic year; it was becoming more dangerous each year to live there, the reason being the drug traffic, which her family controlled.

She was very worried that she might not obtain the information that Tío Juan sought. What would he do to her? She recalled the Spartan mother saying goodbye to her son, leaving for battle to protect Sparta: "Come home with your shield or on it."

When she reached her home, she entered quietly, went to her bedroom, and tried in vain to relax before joining a friend for dinner.

22

THE SAME TIME IN ST. AUGUSTINE

LUCINDA RELAXED ON OUR TWO-SEAT SOFA IN late afternoon, enjoying studying some results of photographing the salt marsh flats of Northeast Florida. Several of the photos would soon be in the monthly Jacksonville magazine.

"You look tired. Let's go to dinner," I suggested, sitting down next to her."

"Where?"

"Your choice," I offered.

"Sardi's on 44th Street. I can taste their sirloin steak with horseradish whipped potato."

"Lucinda, we are *not* at our Manhattan apartment. If we were, I'd not only take you to Sardi's, but I'd swap my horseradish potato for your sirloin. Seriously, please choose a place a little closer. Like somewhere in North Florida."

"How about the A1A Alehouse? We can sit outside on the upstairs balcony."

Getting out was good for both of us. I had been replacing boards on our dock; she had been repainting our bedroom when she wasn't in the marshes photographing.

The night was balmy; the view from the balcony at the Alehouse always enthralled us. We looked over the harbor to the east and the plaza to the north. There were few diners on the balcony. The weather report had been worse than the weather, and we chose our favorite corner table.

"Do you remember the last time we sat in this same corner of this balcony?" Lucinda asked, as I pulled out her chair. I leaned against the back of her head and smelled her freshness.

"Give me a chance to think. I don't want to risk an admonishment about when we were last here. I don't want trouble," I said guardedly.

"*When* were we here and *why* were we here?" she demanded, knowing she was succeeding in testing my rambling memory.

"Anniversary? Your birthday? Celebrating the day we met? I think I've got it. It was when we were both teens, and my family had just moved into town. I saw you in a shop and fell madly in love for the first time in my life. Dinner here was our first date."

"You're good. You could write romance novels. But I remember it a little differently. And more accurately."

"Fill me in; I may have missed a fact or two."

"I distinctly recall that you told me that you never set foot in Florida before you finished college, the Navy, law school, and practice in Connecticut. A teen? If so, you were a teen with gray hair. We were *not* teens. It was only *eleven* years ago."

"So I remembered wrong. But I was close."

"*Not close.* We didn't meet in a shop; we met on the doorstep of my Montana ranch. You slipped and fell. You may have been drinking."

"I do remember that. It was Christmas."

"No, it was Thanksgiving."

"It was a beautiful evening, full of stars. We could see forever."

"It was snowing, and you couldn't see three feet in front of you."

"I was dropping off a letter that had been mistakenly delivered to my cabin."

"You were invited to join me and my guests for Thanksgiving dinner!"

"I remember now. You never introduced me to your other guests."

"No other guests showed up. They went to the Caribbean instead."

"Oh, yes! Now I remember that evening. We were alone, and you seduced me."

"That didn't happen until months later, in Manhattan. . . . You have a terrible memory."

"Only when it's to my advantage."

"Why were we on *this* balcony?"

"You visited me from New York for a few days of the Christmas holiday. We came here for dinner."

"Your memory has improved. Do you remember what happened during dinner? It was strange."

"You dropped a coconut shrimp in your drink!"

"Your memory has faded again. Something happened that made me wonder what I was getting myself into being with you. After we sat down, two women came in and sat at a table behind me."

"Yes, I know now. One was a former neighbor of mine in Gainesville—when I was Professor Maxwell Hunt—a time you didn't know much about. I didn't want the woman to recognize me."

"You put on sunglasses, even though it was quite dark."

"We dined incognito."

"You remember very well, Macduff. It's been a few years."

"And a lot of scars," I added.

"Don't remind me. Most are on me or Wuff," she replied, with a look that suggested she considered them battle scars from just wars.

"Do you remember what we ate that evening? I do," I said.

"No," she replied."

"An A1A specialty, grilled seafood paella."

"How did you remember that?"

"The paella dinner was intended to be for two. You took more than your share."

"I don't remember that," she said, reaching with her fork and taking most of my Caribbean rum fried custard.

23

A DAY LATER AT THE COTTAGE

THE SMELL OF BISON BURGERS COOKING ON A charcoal grill below our cottage porch made me think of Montana. We were due to leave Florida in two weeks. Lucinda had arrived a half-hour earlier from visiting a friend in St. Augustine.

I had an extra glass of Italian *Pinot Grigio* in one hand, waiting as she came up the steps to the cottage's main floor. I thought it was the wine that attracted her attention, but it wasn't. She sensed that something had happened.

"You look perplexed," she said. "Anything you want to tell me?"

"Yes, about a phone call a half-hour ago."

"From?"

"Ted Sweeney."

"Sounds familiar. Do I know him?" she asked.

"You should. He's the manager and sometime bartender at Cabbage Key."

"I remember him. Are you insinuating that I spent most of my time at the bar when we were at Cabbage Key?"

"Of course not. I get in enough trouble without insinuating anything. I was just making a provable conclusion."

"You still show occasional moments when you regress and act like a lawyer, despite ten years of my efforts to humanize you."

"Do you want to hear about the phone call, or do you prefer to continue to harass me?"

"The harassment is fun. I can continue that later. Tell me about the call."

"Sweeney called to tell me about a conversation he had with a customer."

"Named?"

"The man didn't give his name. Sweeney described him as white, maybe in his 60's, graying crew cut, and tanned probably from the sun like people who spend lots of hours on the water. He had on sunglasses, and thus Sweeney never saw his eyes. He wore khaki pants, a Columbia fishing shirt, and—most tellingly—a cap with FWC letters above the brim."

"That sounds like Cartwright."

"It does. Sweeney said it was the same hat they often wear, even off duty. But how many people wear a Nike or John Deere hat but don't work for either company? Too many to count. He added that a couple of FWC officers he knows personally stop in occasionally. But he'd never seen this guy. I asked Sweeney if he knew a Tommy Lee Cartwright. He said he didn't."

"What did the man ask Sweeney about?" Lucinda inquired.

"He wanted to know if Sweeney knew anything about a couple who a few hours after Prescott was murdered might have arrived and eaten or stayed the night at Cabbage Key. Sweeney said the guy described the couple as if he were describing the two of us."

"That's not good, Mac. What did you say to Sweeney?" she asked.

"That he was describing a *lot* of couples who might eat or stay at Cabbage Key. Then I asked him what he told the guy."

"Which was?"

"Sweeney said, 'I told him he was describing a lot of couples we see here at Cabbage Key.' And that was it. . . . Sometimes leaving a big tip pays off. As I recall, I remember you said I was being very generous."

"I was wrong," she admitted. "You should have given him more."

"Next time. . . . What was your impression of Sweeney? That he would talk if the tip were right?"

"Can't tell, but I doubt it," she said. "We've been there twice in the last year. We stayed ten nights in the Dollhouse cottage. He must consider us good customers. We were nice to him; the guy he talked to apparently means nothing to Sweeney. But I'm sure he doesn't welcome murderers for dinner or lodging."

"Let's hope the guy doesn't go back," I added.

"Any chance he talked to people other than Sweeney at Cabbage Key? And showed them the picture of us?"

"I don't know. Sweeney did say he saw the guy leave on a boat as soon as they finished talking."

"A FWC boat?" she asked.

"No, it wasn't, and Sweeney wondered about that. He said it was an old Mako, about nineteen feet."

"I was enjoying my drink when you gave it to me as I arrived," she said. "Now I've finished it and don't remember taking even one sip after you started telling me about Sweeney. What a waste of good wine! . . . May I have another glass, please? What should we do, if anything?"

"I'd like to know who the guy was wearing the FWC cap," I said, pouring her more of the *Pinot Grigio* she had not remembered drinking.

"My guess is it was the Cartwright character we were confronted by at the airboat murder site."

"My guess is you're right—as usual."

"You're so sweet."

"I work at it."

24

THE FOLLOWING DAY AT THE COTTAGE

EVERY FEW DAYS OUR CONVERSATIONS STUCK on why there was nothing new in the Ft. Myers *Times* about the grisly airboat murder on Pine Island Sound. Week after week the paper was devoted to local politicians taking bribes, federal congressmen arm-in-arm with lobbyists, NCAA sports violations, DUI's, divorces, and obituaries.

But one day news appeared about another death in Florida on an airboat. It not only made headlines in our local St. Augustine *Chronicle,* but also it was reported in dozens of other newspapers inside and outside Florida. The unidentified murderer often was referred to as the serial airboat killer.

"Macduff!" yelled Lucinda, running up our cottage's steps two at a time and waving the local paper.

"I don't *believe* this!" she added, pushing the crumpled paper across the table to me where I was absorbed in the new issue of *Fly Fishing* and dreaming of early fall days stalking lunker brook trout in Labrador.

"Do you see the headline?" she blurted.

"All there is on the front page—except for the headline that says *MUTILATION ON THE MARSHES*—is an unrecognizable photo that appears at second glance to be an airboat.

Below the photo is a note that one should turn to page eight. I don't think I want to go to page eight and read further," I said, disturbed that the paper had upset Lucinda.

"I started to read it in the parking lot when I was putting my bags in the rear," she blurted, "but I gagged after the first paragraph and dropped a shopping bag. The description was so graphic a woman pushing her cart of groceries stopped by me and asked if she could help. I shook my head, got into my car, and drove off."

Hesitation caused by the vivid memory of the body we found in Pine Island Sound made me sit and stare at the folded newspaper. Despite the recent call from Cabbage Key manager Ted Sweeney, Lucinda and I both believed we were through with that murder. After all, we were never *directly* involved, but we did come upon the crime scene and may know facts the police do not.

But now there was another murder. Sooner or later I would have to read the full article. I unfolded the paper, laid it across the table, and turned to page eight, realizing the front page photo had been retouched to reduce the shock to readers. I put on my glasses and began reading:

> *Late yesterday afternoon, a single fisherman paddled a kayak he had launched at Marineland in Flagler County far into the salt marsh flats north of Pellicer Creek. Only kayaks or airboats can go there except for an hour or two on both sides of a high tide, when a flats boat drawing no more than six inches can avoid the oyster bars and make the trip.*
>
> *Sitting low in the kayak, the fisherman could not see beyond each successive bend in the channel because of high sea grass. As he rounded the last bend before reaching the western shore, he no-*

ticed an airboat that had been run up into mangroves along the far shore. The airboat appeared to be deserted.

The kayak fisherman was aware that a year ago an airboat was found driven partly into the mangroves on an island in Pine Island Sound in Southwest Florida. Inside the propeller cage was a badly disfigured body later identified as a Ft. Myers CPA.

When the kayak fisherman paddled closer, he stared in disbelief. A body was in the propeller cage on the airboat. Not a full body or even one like that found in Pine Island Sound. This body was mutilated and appeared to be only the torso, one leg, two arms, and a partial skull. The body must have come loose having been tied to the propeller, causing most of the person to be shredded by contact with the heavy metal frame. Little blood was on the boat because whatever drained from the body was blown into the water behind the boat. The victim has not been identified.

According to the registration number, the boat was owned by a Franz Gerber, who lives deep in the pine woods off U.S. 1, north of the St. John's county line and the Faver-Dykes Park. Gerber was apparently out-of-state on business and has not been contacted. The boat was found near Gerber's twenty-acre lot.

The airboat was a popular model made by Moccasin Airboats, located in Ocala. Because of its sound, it is often referred to as the Harley of airboats, a reference to the noise of the motorcycle.

The identity of the fisherman who discovered the body has not been disclosed. He was admitted to a local hospital in a state of shock. No further information has been released.

"Macduff, this happened in *our* area, not on Pine Island Sound. The boat and body were found near Gerber's land! Gerber's property touches our north line. Should we contact the St. John's County police or Grace Justice?"

"And tell them what? We know *nothing* about this murder and it ultimately would bring into the discussion what we know about the Prescott murder on Pine Island Sound. We don't have an alibi, Lucinda. We were here alone."

"Except for our meal at A1A in St. Augustine. . . . So, it's keep quiet again, regardless?" she asked.

"Depending on what you mean by 'regardless.' Not if we know who the victim was."

"He?"

"Or she. . . . The police may identify the body using DNA. It doesn't mention whether any fingers or teeth were found."

"Then let's wait. . . . And watch," she suggested.

"Where would you like to do our waiting?" I asked.

"Let's escape. Where Butch Cassidy and the Sundance Kid hid. Out West in the mountains. We have our own 'hole-in-the-wall' on Mill Creek."

"I talked to my old fishing friend Park County Sheriff Ken Rangley in Livingston yesterday; he said the Yellowstone River is blown out and won't be fishable until early June. I have some clients booked then."

"Let's leave next week," she suggested.

25

TWO DAYS LATER

GRACE JUSTICE, ASSISTANT STATE ATTORNEY based in St. Augustine, called me as I left a gas station on U.S. 1 and headed the last few miles south to our cottage. I really didn't want to be disturbed and turned off the phone; I was listening to Placido Domingo sing "E Lucevan Le Stelle" from *Tosca* and lost in the graces of memory seeing him play the role of Mario Cavaradossi at the Met in New York twenty years ago. The opera took my mind off the new airboat murder. Grace could wait, and I turned the phone to off until the aria was over. When I turned the phone back on, it rang within a minute. It was Grace.

I met Grace Justice some three years ago after Lucinda left me to return to work in New York City and live in her apartment. Weeks passed without any conversation between us. She didn't answer my calls. I assumed our relationship was over.

Grace was investigating one of the gill net murders, specifically the fire that destroyed my flats boat and part of my dock, as well as the person wrapped in a gill net and left as human charcoal in the boat.

She was an avid fly fisher and we started to fish together. One such occasion led to our having a few too many drinks at her condo at Camachee Cove in St. Augustine after a day on my flats boat. She talked me into staying over because I wasn't fit to drive, and one thing led to another.

When Lucinda and I got back together, Grace and I dropped further liaisons and, surprisingly, Grace and Lucinda became friends when they both helped solve the gill net murders. We see Grace occasionally; she still lives in the condo north of the city, and our cabin is twenty-some miles south on the lower edge of St. John's County.

I always looked forward to seeing Grace, but, in view of her call coming soon after the airboat murder, I answered the phone expecting it to be to join her for some social event. It was not.

"Did you turn off your phone, Macduff? I tried to call you fifteen minutes ago. . . . Any idea why I'm calling?"

"You need a fly fishing casting lesson?"

"*I'm* the Master Casting Instructor, not you. Try again."

"Something to do with an airboat not far from our cottage?" I asked.

"It is. What can you tell me about an airboat?" Grace asked, her tone shifting from pleasant to inquisitive.

"Well, mainly it makes too much noise. It also tears up sea grasses."

"That's not what I meant. You know I mean the airboat that dismembered someone on the flats not far from your cottage. I assume you've read about it in the newspapers?"

"We have, but we don't know anything more than anyone who reads the *Chronicle*."

"You must have read about the earlier airboat murder in Pine Island Sound."

"Yes."

"Yes? Is that all you have to say?"

"Yes."

"Are you not telling me something about either murder that you two know?"

"Lucinda and I don't know much. We were gone to Montana for much of the time."

"Where were you when the Pine Island Sound murder took place? In Montana?"

"We were here in Florida."

"Do you know Pine Island Sound?"

"A little. It's a big sound. I've fished a couple of times near Sanibel and Captiva."

"Ever heard of Cabbage Key?"

"Yes, it's a small island with a big bar and a lot of dollar bills hanging on the walls."

"Ever been there?"

"Yes."

"When?"

"Where are you heading with this, Grace?"

"I'll tell you where, dammit. The day after the airboat murder in Pine Island Sound, I called your cottage land line. You weren't there. But Jen Jennings was. She was doing some housekeeping for you as she has for as long as you've owned the place. She said you and Lucinda had taken a few days to go fishing."

"And?"

"That you were staying at Cabbage Key and fishing in Pine Island Sound. Anything to comment?"

"No. You've obviously read the Ft. Myers *Times*."

"Are you going to be as frustratingly evasive about the new murder here?"

"Lucinda and I were here at the cottage. I told you what we know about this recent murder is what we've read in the *Chronicle*."

"Damn you, Macduff. I'll find out what I want to know without you. Give Lucinda my love. You go to hell."

"Grace, don't leave us like this. You know what Lucinda and I have to lose. Please don't push."

"I have a job. You're not making it easier," she said, her voice fading as she hung up.

I felt terrible for being evasive. But Lucinda and I had decided to stay out of both murders. We can't gain anything from publicity, but we can lose if we're in the public eye and the wrong people hear about us.

Our only danger remains Juan Pablo Herzog. There is still a wall between Maxwell Hunt and Macduff Brooks—a wall Lucinda and I have to keep in place. . . . Maybe I worry too much, but Herzog is clever and now has all the tools of the Guatemalan presidency to use to find us and then to. . . . I don't want to think about it. If it means losing Grace as a friend, that's the way it has to be.

I realized I had been sitting motionless behind the wheel of my car next to the cottage. My conversation with Grace had so disturbed me that I didn't remember even a hundred yards of the drive home after getting gas. That included stopping to unlock and open our gate and closing and locking it after driving in. Plus, maneuvering past a few dozen pine trees close to the road, any one of which would win a collision with my SUV.

"Macduff," Lucinda called out from up on the front porch. "Are you going to sit there the rest of the day, staring out the car window?"

"Collecting my thoughts. I just had an unpleasant phone conversation. More an inquisition than a conversation."

"Are we behind paying some bill? It sounds like Verizon or our bank."

"Neither one. With Grace Justice."

"You were talking with Grace? . . . Did she invite you to sleep over?" she asked. I could see her sarcastic smile from the car.

"That's mean. She invited me to tell her what we know about both the airboat murders."

"We shouldn't say anymore to Grace than we do to anyone else who asks."

"She knows we stayed at Cabbage Key the day the first murder happened. . . . I told her we were here in the cottage when the second murder occurred. Pour me a Gentleman Jack, and I'll tell you about our talk."

"Come up here, and I'll pour you two. One so you'll tell me; the second so you'll forget you told me."

That's what she did. But even after the second glass, I still was unsteady, and it wasn't from the drinks.

26

THE NEXT DAY AT THE COTTAGE

IN THE MORNING DURING BREAKFAST ON OUR cottage porch, Lucinda, still in her bathrobe, looked at me over the rim of her coffee cup, and declared, "Macduff, we've treated Grace Justice unfairly. She's an excellent state attorney, and she helped us with the gill net murders. She's a friend. We've been as equivocal with her as we have with everyone else. But except for Grace, they're all people we don't really know."

"What have we done to hurt her?" I asked.

"That's a surprising question. We've withheld information we know about and she doesn't. She doesn't know we were the couple who were likely the first to arrive after the Pine Island Sound airboat murder. And she doesn't know about your conversation with Swenson at Gibsonton. Also, we both talked to Ted Sweeney at Cabbage Key. We know a few details. And we've *never* shared any of it with Grace."

"Do we know who killed the two on the airboats. Or why?"

"No, that Grace's job. But she could do it more effectively if she had all the information we have."

"What should we do?"

"What we *shouldn't* do is what we've been doing all along: withhold information and hurt a good friend who won't compromise us."

"Should we call Grace?" I asked.

"It would be the decent way."

"Do you want me to do it?"

"Yes. She was in love with you once, Mac, and she respects you for the honest way you treated her, not knowing whether we would get back together."

"I'll call her and ask if we can meet."

"She'll be relieved. We owe her, Macduff, for what you and I are."

"How much do we tell her? Everything we know or only what she asks about?"

"Everything she asks about. But if she misses something important, we fill it in. OK?"

"Let's try."

27

THE NEXT MORNING AT THE COTTAGE

GRACE AGREED TO COME TO THE COTTAGE. Lucinda had called her—much to my relief—and apologized for my behavior. She didn't remember setting a time, so I assumed Grace would come early and get our discussion over with.

I was tying flies, salt water Clousers and Lefty's Deceivers, and listening to Riccardo Mutti lead the Berliner Philharmoniker in playing Debussy's *La Mer,* with a vision of seeing Hokusai's woodblock *The Great Sea* before me. I wasn't paying attention to my fly tying, and the consequence may be that the fish won't pay attention to the flies.

"Macduff! . . . Macduff!" called out Lucinda. "Can't you tie flies with less symphonic background? Maybe listening to one of your favorite Marcello oboe concertos—the way it should be played, not the way you play it.?"

"You know I like music when I tie."

"Yes, but why one tying session with Debussy, another with Lakota ceremonial songs, then one listening to Jimmy Buffett or a Mozart piano concerto, followed by Placido Domingo singing Puccini, or Allan Jackson doing his favorite country music songs? Maybe Handel's *Water Music* or Charles Aznavour or Mexican mariachi. Or *Carousel* or *Evita.*"

"Don't forget Carla Bruni."

"She can't sing."

"Agreed, but she looks great on the CD jacket."

"Then turn on Julio Iglesias or Il Divo for me. And give me the CD jackets."

"Iglesias must be seventy!"

"Not when they took his photograph for his CD covers. Macduff, is there any music you don't like?"

"Yes, but I don't want to mention them and offend their fans. . . . I'll turn the volume down on *La Mer* and maybe replace it with some military marches since our policewoman friend Grace will be here sometime today."

"A car door just slammed," exclaimed Lucinda. "It may have come off the hinges. It must be her."

"It is," I said, peeking out the window.

"She's going to charge through that door without a kind word," Lucinda warned.

"She would," I agreed, "and not in any mood to listen to our continued persistence in claiming we knew nothing about either airboat murder."

Barely missing driving into a giant pine tree, she parked in front of the cottage stairs so closely that she stepped from the running board of her SUV directly onto the second porch step.

There was no knock. The door flew open, banging loudly against a table and knocking over a ceramic pot filled with orchids—an admired gift from friends.

"I've put up with you two enough!" she said loudly, not closing the door behind her. "Look at this!"

She threw a newspaper at me, put her hands on her hips, and glared.

"What's wrong?" I asked, aware that to her *much* was wrong.

"This is another article from the *Chronicle* that describes both the airboat deaths. Grantedly, with some speculation, especially about the murder here, because the body still hasn't been identified. While my office is trying to do that, I want to learn everything about the Pine Island Sound airboat murder of Prescott, and you're not helping! Look at the photo on page three."

I quickly turned to page three, trying to hide behind the pages. "I see it," I said. Lucinda glanced over my shoulder and prodded me in the back.

"So what's the problem?" Lucinda interjected firmly, her voice edgy. "It's a photo of two people on a boat purportedly in Pine Island Sound. Neither person is identifiable. I don't know why our local *Chronicle* would have a photo from Pine Island Sound."

"Lucinda, look at the sweater the woman is wearing. Recognize it?"

"I don't think so, but I really don't know."

"You damn sure do know. I helped Elsbeth buy that sweater for her Christmas gift to you last year."

Lucinda sat down on the edge of the sofa, bent over with her head in her hands, and whispered, "Sorry, Grace."

"Sorry! You have a lot more to say to me than that. Start now!"

I stepped forward between Grace and Lucinda, looked at Grace, and said, quietly, "We have a lot to tell you."

"I'm all ears," she answered, pulling out a seat at the small dining table and laying a legal pad and pen in front of her.

"Please, Grace. No notes. We'll answer all your questions, but I don't want a written record," I insisted.

"Agreed. . . . For now."

Lucinda and I joined Grace at the table. Lucinda put her hand on Grace's arm and looked at her."

"We should have let you know. We truthfully didn't think you should be brought into the Pine Island Sound murder. We thought of calling you for advice, but decided not to bother you."

"You doubted that I should be brought in? The second murder was on *my* turf. That makes the first one important. How do you think I feel based on what help I've received from two friends?"

"Grace, let's drop the accusations," pleaded Lucinda. "We can discuss those another time if you wish. Macduff and I agree about filling you in. What do you want to know?"

"Don't do that, you two. I'm not going to start asking you questions. *You* start from the time you launched your boat on Pine Island heading for Cabbage Island."

"*Key*. It's called Cabbage Key," Lucinda said, reservedly.

"Start with Pine Island and don't stop until you tell me about the murder *here* a few days ago!" Grace insisted, folding her arms and leaning back, ready to listen.

Over the next forty minutes, Grace sat silently as Lucinda and I shifted back and forth, trying to remember everything we had seen or heard. We held nothing back. Lucinda and I started on the wrong foot after the second murder by not calling Grace immediately. We lost her confidence and our credibility. We owed her more than we'd offered. When we finished, Grace said she wanted to ask some questions.

"Two Prescotts!" Grace exclaimed. "But it makes sense when you think about it. I'm glad I finally got you to talk. Now I want to hear your views about who did each murder. Who killed Prescott and why? Who killed the person left mutilated not far from this cottage and why?"

"I can't help you with who did either murder," I said, Lucinda nodding in agreement. "We don't know."

"Can you tell me who you suspect?"

"We can tell you some names, but not that we suspect any one of them."

"Go ahead."

"The owner of the boat we came across on Pine Island Sound near Cabbage Key was Rod Swenson from Gibsonton. He disliked his partner Prescott, and we assume he didn't know it was *not* his partner who was killed, but a different Prescott.

"Cartwright is another possibility. He's a strange character. How the FWC puts up with him is a mystery. But we know of no link that's been established between Cartwright and the Prescott who was killed. In fact, we have come across no name of anyone who might have wanted to kill the man who died on Pine Island Sound—M. Raymond Prescott. We haven't attempted any investigation about that. We don't know who stole Swenson's boat that was used for the murder, if it were stolen.

"As to the second murder, it's impossible to say who might be a suspect when the victim hasn't been identified and all we know is what was in the first *Chronicle* article."

"That's it?" Grace asked.

"Yes."

"Then you really don't know much."

"That's what we've tried to tell you," I said, adding, "As far as we know, the state attorney in Ft. Myers has made no connection between Cartwright and the airboat incident. For all we know, they might not be aware it was Cartwright in the FWC boat that confronted us at the scene."

"We haven't helped you," Lucinda said apologetically.

"Not much, if anything," Grace commented.

"Where to now?" I asked.

"The state attorney's office in Ft. Myers may go after you for withholding evidence. Now, about the murder here," she said, shifting the focus. "Were either of you involved in *any* way?"

"Nothing other than Macduff sometimes helped Gerber with some project on his pier or dock."

"What kind of projects?" Grace asked.

"Lucinda, I didn't mention that on the way home about a week ago I stopped at Gerber's place. He had called and again asked for help. I don't like him, but I wanted to be a good neighbor."

"Help with what?"

"He was installing a new propeller on his airboat. He needed someone to hold it while he placed and tightened the bolts."

"My God!" Grace exclaimed. You're prints must have been all over the boat, and especially on the prop."

"Maybe."

"Turk Jensen will not believe you weren't involved in the killing."

"Turk Jensen?"

"You know him. He hates you for how you embarrassed him when your last flats boat was burned along with the body wrapped in a gill net."

"How's Jensen involved?" I asked.

"If you'd read our paper more, you'd know Jensen is now the chief county sheriff. How he was elected is beyond me.

He'll claim jurisdiction in the airboat case and try to take over the investigation."

"I guess I should call Bill Muirhead, again. I used him in the gill net murder. He's a good attorney, and Jensen hates dealing with him," I said.

"You guessed right. Call him first thing if Jensen contacts you."

"I'm glad we talked, Grace," I said.

"What now?" Lucinda asked.

"Lunch," Grace suggested. "And then I have something personal to tell you."

28

SAME DAY AT LUNCH

LUCINDA AND I WERE EMBARRASSED WE HAD not helped Grace. Our lunch with her was at a small restaurant squeezed between A1A and the beach in Flagler County, a dozen miles south of our cottage. Teetering on a disappearing dune, the popular restaurant is less likely to fail for lack of diners than to fall into the Atlantic during the next hurricane.

Our table conversation concentrated on fly fishing, decorating small living spaces, and engagement rings. Then it shifted to Turk Jensen, and rapidly deteriorated. So we asked Grace about what she planned to tell us that was personal.

"I'm engaged to a guy named Valtr Krall," she began, a smile breaking out. "He works in St. Augustine at Northrop Grumman—a large St. Augustine unit of the maker of advanced aircraft. Valtr is Czech, emigrated to the U.S. in his teens, received both a B.S. and an M.S. in environmental engineering, and has nearly twenty years of experience at Boeing in Seattle and Lockheed Martin in Virginia. He creates product solutions for unmanned systems. In Florida he designs solutions to prevent cyber threats from becoming cyber attacks."

Grace's hands were on the edge of the table. Lucinda looked at them and asked, "Don't Czechs believe in engagement rings?"

"If I remember you telling me," Grace answered, "Macduff was painfully slow to give *you* a ring and only long after he proposed."

"That's not correct," I interrupted.

"Macduff proposed to me in a very oblique way after we were together for a couple of years," Lucinda explained. "When he realized giving an engagement ring was not an option, he gave me a black velvet covered box with a ring that had no diamond. The ring setting was twisted. It made me wonder."

Lucinda slipped off her ring and handed it to Grace.

"It's still twisted!" Grace exclaimed. "But this one has a beautiful emerald cut diamond. Was Macduff too cheap to give you a new mount?"

"I wouldn't trade this mount and stone for anything, Hope diamond included."

"It must have a special meaning."

"Macduff had this first set with a diamond exactly like this one, in a black velvet covered box, ready to give to me the evening after we finished a float on the Snake River in Wyoming. But it was a horrendous day. A former client named Salisbury was trying to kill Macduff. Salisbury and his wife floated a year earlier with Macduff, and when Salisbury clubbed a cutthroat to death, knowing it was illegal, Mac kicked him out of the boat and made him walk out the last few miles.

"He vowed to seek revenge and, ultimately, wearing a disguise on a later float, pulled a gun and shot Macduff, Wuff, and me. I shot Salisbury. Macduff claims he did, too, but what he did was steer the drift boat into a sharp limb protruding from a pile of tree debris stacked in the middle of the river—called a strainer. Salisbury was left hanging from the limb, dead.

"Macduff and Wuff recovered quickly, but I was in a coma for days and then dealt with amnesia for weeks. I learned about the ring months later. When Macduff was first shot, a bullet hit the ring box and knocked the diamond out of the setting. The diamond disappeared into the river. When he proposed and told me about the ring, I insisted he give me the old setting. I didn't complain when he had a new diamond added."

"That's some story," Grace said. "Mine is less dramatic. Valtr is from an old, wealthy Prague family. They lost their land and businesses during the Communist period. One thing the government didn't get from them was a diamond ring that had been in the family for years. Valtr's mother left it to him on her deathbed, hoping it would be passed down. It's in New York now. An exact copy is being made for every-day wear. The original will reside in a safe except for very special occasions."

"When do we meet Valtr?" I asked.

"He's in London on business. . . . I'd love to talk more about our rings, but I have a couple of final comments about the two murders. OK?"

"Your last chance until next fall. We're going to block all incoming calls when we get to Montana," kidded Lucinda.

"Lucinda doesn't mean we won't use the phone," I added. "But we hope Montana will be free of airboat issues."

"About Prescott's murder," Grace added. "The Ft. Myers state attorney's office has been searching for the boat in the photo that includes you two. They downloaded a list of all Hell's Bay flats boats registered in Florida. They're considered the top-of-the-line and expensive, so it's not like tracing most flats boats.

"They started with an area around Pine Island Sound. They discovered that all that area's Hell's Bay boats were accounted for on the day of the incident. Some were at shops having repairs made or new equipment installed.

"When they struck out, they shifted the search to South Florida, which proved to have the largest number of Hell's Bay boats registered. None were near Pine Island Sound on the day of the murder. Many are used in the Keys by guides, and they don't trailer clients northwest as far as Pine Island Sound.

"The next group was the Florida Panhandle. Only a few were registered there, and the authorities found nothing that matched.

"That left Northeast Florida. They're starting that search next week. How did you register your boat?" Grace asked, looking at me.

"Using our St. Augustine address," I responded.

"The state attorney's office will have you listed for this last portion of the registrations being reviewed. There are probably not many Hell's Bay boats in this area, but it does extend from the Georgia border south to around Cocoa Beach. Titusville, home of Hell's Bay, is in that area. It wouldn't surprise me if a lot of people in the home area have chosen the boat. . . . So what do you do if the state attorney's office calls you?"

"Answer their questions truthfully," Lucinda added. "If we don't like their attitude, we'll call a lawyer to help us. You and I know there is absolutely no reason for them to believe we were involved in Prescott's murder."

"But they're struggling with the case. It's going nowhere. Yours is the last district for the search. If they find the slightest reason to bring you in, they will."

"We'll be in Montana when they get to us. Maybe they'll cool off by the time we're back."

"And maybe they won't wait. They could get a warrant for your arrest and ask Montana to send you here."

"That's not encouraging. . . . I'm exhausted from all this. Are we finished?"

"No. One quick matter, the second murder here on my turf."

"Something new?"

"People in Turk Jensen's office have tried to shift the focus to hassling the boat owner—Franz Gerber—for no reason other than they can't identify the body or find a suspect. I hope I can convince them to be reasonable. But you know Jensen. And who knows what he'll do when he realizes you live next to Gerber and especially if he finds your fingerprints are on the propeller?"

"Is there anything *you* can do to find the victim's identity?" I pleaded.

"I'm personally doing that part of the investigation. A forensic specialist from UF in Gainesville is intrigued by the case and offered to help. We're starting this weekend to go over the boat—it's still in our possession. Then I want to go everywhere the boat may have gone, starting with Gerber's dock."

"Thanks for telling us."

"Go home," Grace ordered. "You both look terrible."

We went home, finished packing and began the twice annual drudgery of moving between our Montana cabin and Florida cottage that sit 2,200 miles apart.

29

THE FIRST WEEKS IN MONTANA

MONTANA WAS IDYLIC FOR TWO FULL WEEKS after we arrived and remained hidden at our cabin among the ponderosa and aspen trees lining Mill Creek. Each day we quietly fished somewhere along the creek.

Crossing the U.S. from Florida has become more tedious each year. Friends have suggested we fly and leave vehicles at each end. Our answer is Wuff. We won't have her suffer flying. If you can imagine the conditions for pets being worse than those that people face in economy class, you are close to describing how animals must fare.

Heading west we have tried a southern route, a northern route, and a middle route. Whichever we chose, it remained four days before we saw the welcoming faint outline of mountains begin to appear incrementally rising above the horizon in the distant west.

Of those four travel days, the first two meant mixing with frantic, commuting urbanites and eighteen wheelers, and the second two meant boredom watching amber waves of grain and trying to stay awake until we passed out of the flatlands. Three times I've offered to fly Lucinda west alone while Wuff and I endured the drive, but each time she refused. A mix of self-inflicted road torture and love.

One morning two days after we arrived at Mill Creek, I sat on the front porch after breakfast and put together my seven-foot bamboo rod. I'd finished rigging Lucinda's and added a tiny #18 Royal Coachman fly to her nine-foot fluorocarbon tapered leader. Fluoro for me won the nylon versus fluorocarbon debate. Price favors nylon by far, but nylon is easier for fish to see, looking up from the bottom. Fluoro is more abrasion resistant. Maybe all this is more a product of my imagination enhanced by too much advertising, but it does help to use the line, leader, and tippet you *think* are best. I've chosen to go with fluoro and replaced all my nylon.

One rule I learned soon after I started to use fluoro is to tie on a fly with an *improved* clinch knot. Fluoro doesn't accept a knot as well as nylon does. And a final word—if fluoro is your choice, it takes a very long time to decompose. Good practice is to carry something like a ziplock bag for old tippets and leaders, whether fluoro or nylon.

Viewed from the side, a Royal Coachman fly has a bright red silk body and subtly sparkling green tufts of peacock herl at each end, a few fibers of Golden Pheasant feather at one end for the tail, and some white duck quill for the wing that rises from wraps of brown hackle. I wondered how my fingers, that repeatedly missed the proper keys on the oboe, nevertheless made the correct moves to finish this fly. Priorities, I guessed.

Lucinda joined me as I tied on her fly and affectionately put her hand on my shoulder.

"It's beautiful, Macduff. I've always liked the Royal Wulff; it's the first fly you tied on for me when you took me fishing up Mill Creek."

"It's not a Royal Wulff, my love; it's a Royal Coachman."

"What's the difference?" she asked.

"No Golden Pheasant for the tail on the Wulff, just some dark moose hairs."

"Do the fish know the difference?"

"Such worldly questions are better left for smarter brains than mine. You have a Ph.D. Didn't you study those questions in graduate school?"

"We studied Issac *Newton*, not Izaak *Walton*," she answered, smartly.

"I chose the Coachman, thinking I was picking out a Royal Wulff, but by the time I tied it to your tippet, I realized it wasn't the Wulff but the Coachman. I was too lazy to change it."

"So what *I* fish with isn't important?" she asked.

"It may be to you, but I have doubts about whether it is to one of our native cutthroats. Let me try something. I'll leave you with the Royal Coachman, and I'll use the same #18 in a Royal Wulff. OK?"

"OK, only if mine catches more fish," she answered.

"So if I catch more fish with the Wulff, you'll complain that it was because I put a poor choice of fly—the Coachman—on your rig?"

"Right!" she said. "And if *I* catch more fish with the Coachman, it's because your initial thought of using a Wulff was inept. You gave me what I should have had in the first place, but you thought it was something else."

"I'd agree if I could figure out what you're saying. Let's fish! You go downstream from the cabin; I'll go up."

"I'll go up, and you go down. I don't trust you," she declared firmly.

"You think I came out and chased all the fish upstream?"

"Exactly. . . . Ready?"

Watching Lucinda disappear around a bend upstream while I remained in front of our cabin, I started with a cast to a pool behind a large boulder on the far side of the creek. The fly bounced on the boulder and within seconds of landing on the water went under. Under? It was a dry fly that was intended to float! I realized I hadn't put floatant—the magic dust that makes a dry fly dry—on either of our flies. Would Lucinda know? Unquestionably, when her fly sank on her first cast. Should I go find her and add floatant? No, she'll accuse me of another subterfuge even though she carries floatant in her vest pocket.

Before I could pull my fly out of the water to correct this deficiency by adding floatant, a tug caused an involuntary reaction of raising the tip of my rod. A native cutthroat had taken the fly. The cutty rose from the bottom and was intrigued by the sinking fly that imitated an insect that should be floating.

The fish broke the surface. I was delighted to know I had caught one and hadn't yet heard any yells from Lucinda. But twisting and turning in mid-air, the fish and fly parted and went their separate ways. My reaction had been too hard, and while the fish dropped down into the depths out of sight, my line floated loosely in an unkempt pile in front of me. I was one for one at hooking a fish and zero for one at landing it.

I tied on another Royal Wulff and moved downstream fifteen yards to where a bush hung out three feet over the water. The shade under the bush looked inviting, but only two feet were between the bottom of the bush and the water's surface.

My friend, Master Casting Instructor Dave Johnson, had worked with me on developing a sidearm cast, and this was a good place to try it out. The forward cast would shoot along two to three feet above the surface and thus under the overhanging bush. I wasn't bothered by trees behind me, so I didn't have to figure out how to combine a sidearm cast with a roll cast.

A single back cast while I stood midstream took my line off to my right and behind me on the downstream side. As the line straightened out and was about to settle on the surface, I cast forward in a sidearm motion that kept my rod tip in a forward sweep only a couple of feet above the water.

The fly moved toward the open space below the bush. Concerned that I might be casting it into the bush, I instinctively pulled the rod up short, and the fly dropped in a pile ten feet in front of the bush. If I hadn't been so timid, I might have had a perfect cast. I pulled in some line to avoid disturbing any fish and recast.

This time the fly sailed right into the slot below the bush, alighted on the surface, and was consumed by a fish that never showed its colors. But, as luck would have it, the fish headed downstream where the bush dipped into the water, and my line broke. I could see a foot of tippet dangling from the bush and glimpsed the red body of the tiny fly before it slipped away and began a float that might take it a couple of miles to where Mill Creek joined the Yellowstone River, and thence on a long journey to New Orleans and the Gulf.

My count was now two for two on catching and zero for two on landing. I waded to the creek bank and sat on a boulder, dejected and wondering if I was headed to being a three-time loser.

I wanted to keep my fly on the surface, but not lose it in the brush. I waded down to where the creek widened and became a nice riffle for about twenty yards. I decided to add a tiny #20 bead head Prince nymph as a dropper fifteen inches below a third Royal Wulff. I flipped the flies across the creek, but well short of the bank, mended the line to give a longer float, and watched the small dry fly bob through the riffles until it reached the end of the float where I let it swing across the creek before recasting.

After each attempt I moved a few steps downstream and repeated the process. Five times I tried without success, but on the sixth, as the fly reached the end of the float and swung across in a manner that many who fly fish think is unattractive to fish—given the unnatural drag on the line—a cutthroat I thought was too big to survive in our creek hit the nymph and started back upstream toward me.

When it passed and I struggled to crank in line and keep on some tension, it turned and crossed into the strongest part of the riffles and disappeared. I thought I had enough tension to hold it but not too much to break the line and lose a fish that had to be fourteen inches. But I was wrong; the line broke and not because it was wrapped around a boulder—there were none in the immediate area. Nor was it caught on brush—the bank was devoid of any.

What could I expect? Zero landed for three hooked trout. I decided I'd had enough for the day. When I reeled in my line, I looked at the tippet to see where it broke. But it hadn't broken. The Royal Wulff was there, and attached to the curve of the hook were the fifteen inches of tippet. At its end where I had tied on the Prince nymph, a half-dozen tiny coils told me the knot had slipped. What I thought was a perfect improved clinch knot was not perfect. Not even barely adequate. At least I could blame it on using fluoro!

I sat on the bank near the cabin and for my penance tied a dozen clinch knots while waiting for Lucinda. I must admit it was harder than reciting a dozen "Hail Mary's."

When Lucinda arrived, she was all smiles.

"Three cutthroats in my net," she exclaimed. "I have cell phone photos of each. I called you to tell you, but you didn't answer. The Coachman fly was great; I never lost it. And I'm glad I went upstream. I caught the first trout by dropping the fly softly in the eddy behind a boulder; the second, tossing a perfect sidearm cast below an overhanging bush; and the last, letting the line float through some riffles. How did you do?"

"Nothing," I muttered. "Skunked. Let's go to town."

30

AT THE MONTANA CABIN

SEVERAL MONTHS HAD PASSED FOLLOWING THE second airboat murder. We heard no news about the body being identified beyond being a male of an age somewhere between thirty and fifty. Even knowing that much was surprising because nothing was left other than the portion of the body that was still tied to the airboat propeller, plus two arms and one leg, which were on the bottom of the propeller cage. The arms had no hands. The one leg had no foot. And the head was no more than half a skull. The teeth were gone, removing any identification by dental work.

Presumably, body parts that ended up in the boat and water were consumed by any one or more varieties of creatures from either land or sea. The medical examiner discovered some DNA on the propeller cage and created a DNA profile, but she found no match in the databases.

One discovery narrowed the field, however. The victim had at least one knee replacement. The only leg found was missing the half below the knee, which included the metal tibial component. Protruding from the remaining upper portion of the leg was the metal femoral part. It proved to be titanium, part of a joint made by a company that produces thousands each year. Orthopedic surgeons do not autograph their artistry; but parts are usually numbered. The number on the remaining femoral part proved unidentifiable.

Because the propeller had cut off the fingers and toes, no fingerprints could be taken. Also, none were found on the airboat propeller cage. The propeller was discovered to have been wiped clean before the body was tied—quite likely by the killer—to remove any prints.

The victim's clothes—now rags—consisted of remnants of mass-produced Patagonian shorts and an Izod knit shirt. We know the size of the pants from a label inside the belt area. It was one of the most popular sizes. The tag that usually was sewn on the inside shirt collar was gone. No trace of anything was found in any pockets. The most the coroner could report was that the victim was a white male about six feet tall with brown hair and knee replacements. The ears were torn off; thus, it couldn't be determined whether the victim wore hearing aids.

The collection of a few body parts was the most unusual the medical examiner had ever seen. She had done the best she could laying the remains on her examining table; they formed a three-dimensional jigsaw puzzle that was missing key pieces.

31

LATE JULY IN GUATEMALA

LUISA SOLARES ENJOYED THE PROSPECT OF A day in Antigua at the invitation of Tío Juan, especially a promised lunch at the Casa Santo Domingo, one of the architecturally transcendent convents in the Americas.

Casa Santo Domingo sits near the middle of La Antigua—the city as a whole designated a priceless UNESCO World Heritage Site. Luisa viewed Antigua as a marvel of Colonial art and architecture and an expression of her country's heritage mixing Mayan and Spanish cultures. She thought it the most beautiful city in the world. Her uncle Tío Juan, however, thought of it only as a place where good food and drink were available and where the great stone walls that surrounded the Casa kept out the poor.

Antigua held complex memories for Luisa: It was where years ago her father, endeared as Padre Bueno, was murdered by Tío Juan, as Padre Bueno led an Easter Week Passion of Christ procession through the city's cobblestone streets, decorated with a colored sand carpet.

Luisa had been born as the illegitimate daughter of Tío Juan's first cousin, Augustino Herzog, who, shamed by impregnating a local girl, would soon thereafter enter the priesthood and ultimately become known as Padre Bueno. To avoid embarrassment to the Herzog name, Luisa would take the surname of her mother—Solares.

Luisa and her Tío Juan sat at a 17th century wooden table in the main dining room, overlooking the volcano, Agua, which last erupted at the moment Tío Juan had murdered Luisa's father.

"Luisa," began Tío Juan, "you leave tomorrow for Gainesville. I'm giving you a file with information about Professor Hunt and the law college where you will spend the coming academic year. Several years ago I offered to fund a $4 million chair in honor of Professor Hunt. I wanted only one thing in return—a report on what happened to Hunt after he was injured and flown back to D.C. on a private jet. The CIA and the University of Florida both insisted that he died of a stroke. I have never believed that, and the past few years have produced evidence that Hunt did not die. I *must* discover where he is.

"I believe he was placed in some form of protection program where he was given a new name and location. I have not been able to find out anything further. That is where you come in. The file you have also has various reports by me and others on the issue of Professor Hunt's death and the murders both at the law college and by the tennis courts of your cousins María-Martina and Martín. A map of Gainesville is included, with notes showing the locations of those murders, plus the house where Professor Hunt, and later Martín, lived. I expect you to report to me regularly what you discover about the present name of Professor Hunt, any members of his family if he remarried, and where he now lives."

"Tío Juan, I have some news for you already. I met a man named Thomas Davis, Jr."

"Is he the son of the Thomas Davis who resides not more than a few blocks from where we now sit? I know that the elder Davis was present when Professor Hunt assumed a new name and location. Davis worked for the CIA and when he retired he moved here to Antigua."

"Tío, he *is* the son. Do you know any more about the senior Davis?"

"Some. And about his invalid wife. She is not expected to live long. When she dies and he is mourning, I will talk to him and make him an offer he will not reject, in exchange for the information I want about Professor Hunt. Of course, if *you* obtain that information, I will not have to spend any more time with Davis. Or money. . . . Tell me how you met Davis's son?"

"He spends some time here in Antigua with his parents when he is not in the U.S. studying at his university. I met him in Guatemala City last month at the U.S. embassy party honoring Guatemalan students who have been admitted to universities in the U.S. I have received a Fulbright scholarship for my study at Florida."

"Did you spend much time with Thomas Davis?"

"No, I didn't know who he was until later at the party and I was in a small group talking generally about Guatemala and the U.S. Thomas was in that group and mentioned his father once worked for the U.S. government.

"One of my Guatemalan friends whispered to me, 'His father worked with the CIA. My dad was in Guatemalan intelligence work and knew him then.' Our conversation with Thomas about his dad didn't go any further. But I did make an effort to talk to Thomas. He is studying at Vanderbilt, and he said his school will play football at Florida this fall. He plans to come and see the game. He invited me to go with him, and, in turn, I invited him to a party after the game. I will have a report for you after that meeting."

"You have done well, Luisa. I am encouraged that we will find out what we want to know about Hunt while you are in Gainesville."

"I knew you would be pleased that I have started a relationship with the son of a CIA agent who has the information you need."

"I am *very* pleased. . . . Now let me show you how to use the Glock pistol I'm giving you. You cannot carry it on the plane to the U.S.; it will be taken in a diplomatic pouch to Washington and then delivered to you in Gainesville."

32

LIVINGSTON, MONTANA

KEN RANGLEY IS THE CHIEF DETECTIVE OF the Park County Sheriff's office in Livingston, Montana. Thirty miles north of our Mill Creek cabin, the city of Livingston hosts some 7,000 residents. Livingston arguably might better be called a town. The word "city" sounds too urban. Livingston does not have the characteristics of urban life—gridlock, tall buildings, Starbucks, a few trees that survive despite great odds, and a frenetic pace induced by unneeded prescription drugs.

Livingston has a sister city in Naganohra, Japan, which most Livingstonians have never heard of and cannot spell or pronounce. Nor does one find many Japanese walking the streets of Livingston; they're far more likely to be at Disneyland.

Anyone disappointed with Livingston need only travel an hour west on Interstate 90 across the Bozeman Pass to reach Bozeman, which deserves to be called a city. It is overrun with a rapidly increasing population of about 37,000, plus something like 15,000 Montana State University students. That means some 15,000 Ford 150s, or equivalent, on the streets from August to May.

Livingston remains to some degree what it started out as in 1882, a railroad town created by the Northern Pacific Company. Passenger service ended, but the town is on an important east-west freight line.

One of the most attractive features of Livingston is the Yellowstone River which, after a long flow north from Yellowstone Park, turns sharply east in Livingston and heads nearly 400 miles to be absorbed by the Missouri River just beyond the border in North Dakota. The Yellowstone River portion from the park to the town is one of the country's pristine fishing waters. The part east of the town is OK, but becomes increasingly warm until the trout disappear.

Lucinda and I live about two miles east of the Yellowstone River on Mill Creek Road. We can tow our drift boat, *Osprey*, and be on the river in thirty minutes at the Emigrant launching ramp.

Emigrant clearly isn't a city and doesn't have enough population to be a town or perhaps even a hamlet, although "hamlet" is not a word used often in Montana. Emigrant is best known for its single blinking traffic light that marks both the entry and exit to the town. It's the only light between Livingston and Gardiner at the entrance to the park, a distance of about fifty-four miles. That's 0.185 lights per mile, if a blinking light even counts.

Bozeman's main street, on the other hand, has something like a dozen lights in about two miles. None are blinking lights. That number of lights per mile is closer to New York City's number than to Livingston's.

I settled on Mill Creek a dozen years ago, having landed at Bozeman and decided it was too big. When I reached Livingston and turned south on route 89, I was approaching Emigrant when I was stopped by Rangley. He has a daughter, Liz, who was the age my expected daughter would have been but for the accident that took the life of my pregnant wife, El.

Ken and I talk a couple of times a year, and he now knows the story of Elsbeth. Liz is at Montana State University in the same year as Elsbeth at UF.

He and I also discovered at that first meeting that we each preferred being on a drift boat than in a car, and the ticket he might have written for driving dangerously *slowly* on local speedway 89 was quickly forgotten. We since have spent many days, but not enough, fishing together on the Yellowstone.

Eight years ago Ken was promoted to Chief Detective. That was after his boss, Park County Chief Detective James W. Shaw the Fourth, aka Jimbo, was discovered to have murdered one of the Shuttle Gals, the five women who moved drift boat vehicles and trailers from launching sites to the takeouts. Shaw was convicted and executed.

It was time I called Ken; we hadn't talked since Lucinda and I arrived in Montana in late April. As with Grace Justice, not keeping in contact with Ken and his assistant Erin Giffin was another inexcusable and embarrassing absence of good manners.

Lucinda was off to have lunch with Elsbeth, her friend Sue, and Ken Rangley's daughter, Liz, at the Chico Hot Springs resort where they all were working for the summer. I took the time to call Ken.

"You must want something, Macduff. I thought you would have called by now."

"Sorry, Ken. I'm a pro at putting off some items I should have at the top of my list. Like calling both you and Erin."

"I'll forgive you if you tell me when we can drift Mallard's Rest to Carter Bridge on the Yellowstone."

"Three days. I had a cancellation."

"OK. Booked! You're forgiven. How are Lucinda and Elsbeth?"

"Elsbeth's working the main desk at Chico Hot Springs. Lucinda's having lunch with her as we speak. Your daughter Liz is with them. And Elsbeth's friend and roommate Sue. Say hello to Elsbeth when crime brings you to this part of Paradise Valley or you're visiting Liz."

"Any recent deaths on your boats, here or in Florida?"

"Not even one. But. . . ."

"But what?"

"Do you know anything about airboats?"

"Not around here. Did you bring one to Montana?"

"No. Apparently you haven't heard about the two airboat murders in Florida. Actually, one was before we came out last year. But I wasn't involved and never mentioned it to you."

"Now you're mentioning it."

"Yes. I think there are some things you ought to know."

"Tell me."

It took me an hour to tell Ken about each of the two murders and answer some of his questions.

"So now you've told me all. What are you worried about?"

"Withholding evidence."

"You haven't withheld anything. You reported on Channel 16 the airboat and body in Pine Island Sound. Plus, a boat arrived with two FWC officers. You answered what little they asked. They didn't ask you to stay. I can't see any reason for worrying. The murder near your cottage is more troubling, especially with the sheriff you mentioned, Turk Jensen. Listen to Grace Justice. And if you need to, call that Muirhead lawyer."

"What are you going to say if you get a call from the Ft. Myers or St. Augustine authorities?" I asked him.

"Why would they do that?" Ken asked. "I'd tell them I knew nothing about either case and that, unless there's a link to us here in Montana, there's no reason I should know anything."

"They may want you to send us back to Florida. Presumably so they can get enough information interrogating us to press charges."

"That's ridiculous! Call your lawyer friend. See what he says."

"I will. Thanks. By the way, how is Erin?"

Erin Giffin is Ken's best assistant and is certain someday to be his successor. A few years ago Erin helped me through some bad days when Lucinda was in a coma and then had amnesia. She's become very close to Lucinda.

"She's fine. She's not in. Give her a call and say hello sometime."

"Say hello for me."

"No. *You* do that! You're terrible about keeping in contact with friends."

33

THREE DAYS LATER

FOR A DAY AFTER TALKING TO KEN, I MOPED about. I should have been as thrilled with the conversation as was Lucinda when she arrived home from lunch with Elsbeth.

The dilemma with the airboat murders caused frustration on the part of the Florida authorities. They wanted to solve the horrible murders, and while currently no light was at the end of the tunnel for them, before they set either case aside as a cold file, they would want to talk to Lucinda and me.

I decided I had to talk to Grace Justice and tell her about my conversation with Ken. After putting together some notes so I wouldn't forget Ken's views, I called Grace one afternoon. She answered on the first ring.

"Wish you'd come out and stay with us," I said. "We'll take you drifting on the Yellowstone."

"Someday I will. After I finish the local airboat case."

"Tell me about that, but first let me tell you about my conversation with Ken Rangley at the sheriff's office in Montana. He felt strongly that Lucinda and I have nothing to worry about," I told her. "I also expressed my concern that Ft. Myers or St. John's County might try to get me back to Florida for questioning and wherever that might lead."

"Your friend Ken's right," said Grace. "Both Florida jurisdictions are frustrated. I am, too, but more because of having to deal with Turk Jensen. If anyone contacts you, tell them you'll be back in early December and will talk to them. And consider retaining an attorney for any conversation with the authorities about anything. Please don't tell my co-workers or Jensen or any state attorney people in Ft. Myers I said that."

"Remember the gill net case?" I reminded her. "I used Bill Muirhead from St. Augustine. He was great. I think his tattoos and pony tail make others think he's a soft touch."

"Since you used him a couple of years ago, he hasn't lost a major case," she said. "When we have a moment sometime, I'll tell you about his last triumph over Turk Jensen."

"There is one final thing, Macduff, about the airboat murder here. Want to hear the latest? I won't keep you if you're headed off to the Gallatin or Madison to fish."

"I'm fishing with Lucinda on the Gallatin late today. Caddis hatch, I hope. . . . I have time. Tell me about the case."

"You know the boat owner, Franz Gerber. I told him I wanted to arrange a time to inspect his dock where he kept the airboat in a sling, next to two PWCs. He turned me down, said to stay off his property unless I had a warrant. I got one, and I'm going to inspect the pier and dock soon."

"What do you expect to find?"

"Don't know. Anything related to the murder. . . . Gerber has threatened to file a civil suit against our office for what he alleges is harassment. We have his boat and need to keep it a week or two longer—as evidence. We've talked to him several times, but he never is cooperative and always cuts short our questions. His attorney, Wolf Solis, an old friend of his who has recently been re-admitted to the bar after a suspension for improper conduct before a half-dozen judges in this area, is more of a problem than his client. Solis is living on the edge of another suspension, this time more likely to mean disbarment."

"Is Solis telling Jensen to get his act together?"

"Nope. They're fishing buddies. Enough said."

"What about Gerber? Is he mad because he can't use his airboat?"

"He claims he needs it for business. But two weeks ago he bought another new airboat. A neighbor told us he won't accept the old one being returned. He wants the county to pay for the replacement."

"Gerber sounds challenging. Keeps you out of trouble."

"He's trouble! Why did you help him install the propeller?"

"He asked for help. Until he gave me reason not to help, I was willing. Now I have reason. I'll stay away from him."

"And your fingerprints must be all over the boat. Jensen's coming over to look at the boat tomorrow."

"He won't find prints. The prop was wiped down."

"Damn, Macduff! We don't have the funds for lengthy, drawn out law suits. Gerber will use every device he can to run up our legal costs."

"Won't the judges control him?"

"They don't like his lawyer, Solis, but they're afraid of him. He pushes them, and in my view the judges give him too much leeway. . . . Macduff, enough of Gerber and Solis and Jensen."

"Grace, be careful. Gerber has two guard dogs that run free on his property, including access to the pier and the dock."

"Thanks for the warning. We'll take care of the dogs. Best to Lucinda. Go fish!"

34

MOVING EAST AND THE FALL TERM AT UF

THANKSGIVING DAY WAS A REMINISCENCE FOR Lucinda and me of our first meeting at her Mill Creek ranch exactly eleven years ago. The date is more fixed in my memory bank than even our wedding date of. . . . Oh! I know the month was March, and I *think* the day was the twelfth, but I'm not sure.

When Lucinda reminds me what day it was, she also adds the exact hour and minute we exchanged rings. My left hand's fourth finger jogs my memory about the rings part of the ceremony, but she claims some vows were also exchanged. She makes them up as she goes along. I do remember that the ceremony was held at a church that sits with conquering majesty on top of an old Indian mound in Oyster Bay, Florida.

That evening we sat on our cabin porch and inhaled the last pageant of fall along Mill Creek, but when eight inches of snow fell on Black Friday, the day after Thanksgiving, while others were shopping, we were following snowplows east and turning south as often as possible. We lost the snow long after we lost the spectacle of white burnished mountains. White flakes followed us south into Texas, where ultimately we had to turn east again or find ourselves in Mexico.

After a two-hour doze at a rest stop outside Dallas, we decided to push on without a lodging stop until we reached Florida. It was a wise decision because another snow storm was determined to overtake us. We managed to stay barely ahead of its eastern edge—frequently looking at the storm through our rear view and side mirrors that warned us in stenciled print along the bottom that "Things in this mirror are closer than they appear." The darkness on the rear horizon kept pace with us all the way across the country.

Finally, we escaped the storms by turning south in Jacksonville. An hour later, at two in the morning, we were sitting on our cottage porch sipping Gentleman Jack and Montana Roughstock Whiskey, still dressed in mountain attire.

Our housekeeper, Jen Jennings, had cleaned the cottage so thoroughly it looked ready for the annual St. John's County spring open house tour. Within a week we made it so "lived in" that any scheduled house tour would have to be canceled. The cottage wouldn't look "Jennings clean" again until we arrived from Montana the following year.

When the sun rose the next morning, we took our French vanilla roast coffee to the porch and realized we had walked in on a fall spectacle of trees tinted with colors we rarely expected to see in Florida, variations of orange, purple, and yellow, mixed among gradations of reds—scarlet, maroon, and mauve—on the foliage of our maples, oaks, and sweetgums, their leaves hanging on to their final days. It's a welcome surprise each fall for us and for our visitors from the North who believed Southern state tree colors went directly from green to dead each fall.

Lucinda called Gainesville as soon as we thought it would not wake Elsbeth. She and Sue were luxuriating in their Golf

View rental, the very same house El and I owned for the decade prior to her death and where I remained for another decade of melancholic grief over my loss. During that latter decade I never knew Elsbeth survived and was being raised in Greenville, Maine, by a loving family named Carson. How could I have imagined that during her years at UF Elsbeth would take El's place in our former house?

Elsbeth increasingly has been drawn to the legal profession because of my commitment to the rule of law and twenty years teaching at Florida's pre-eminent law college. I never tried to "recruit" her to this study, but she knew my feelings about her choosing to apply to UF for an additional three years. For the last year I'd had little time to talk to her about her future; she was enthralled with being at the London School of Economics for the academic year, as was her roommate and closest friend Sue about her year at LSE's sister school, King's College, almost in sight of LSE near the Aldwych on the Strand in London.

Soon after the beginning of the fall term at UF, where Elsbeth and Sue returned as juniors, conditioned on the transfer of credits from London, they visited us at the cottage for a weekend. Sue wanted additional beach time, and Elsbeth undoubtedly wanted additional money. Elsbeth explained to Sue how easily funds can be shifted from my account to Elsbeth's. She never asks for enough money for more than a month because she likes to badger me every four weeks and see how easy a touch I am over the course of a term.

After my wallet had become thinner and her purse fatter, she told Lucinda and me about a reception planned at UF's law college for early in the fall term. She was looking forward to attending.

"Dad, the college's International Law Society invited both law students and interested undergraduates at UF to a reception at a private home. The law students were invited to bring friends, and especially parents who, after all, would have to fund three more years of university. Would you two come with Sue and me?"

Elsbeth's invitation surprised Lucinda and me. She knew our concern about going to Gainesville for any purpose.

"Dad, you both *have* to come. I need your advice and so does Sue. Her parents live in Wyoming and aren't lawyers. She respects your opinions for law questions. After all, you *have* encouraged her to think about law school."

"Tell us about the reception. You know the trouble Lucinda and I have about being in Gainesville and especially anywhere near the law school."

"But you both go to Gainesville for UF soccer games. The stadium is a five-minute walk, at most, from the law buildings. And we're going to a house that's nowhere near the law college buildings."

"I don't know. What do you think?" I asked, turning to Lucinda, who was enjoying, as she often said, "hearing Elsbeth twist her dad around her little finger."

"Macduff, you haven't taught at UF for over a decade. The law college has changed," Lucinda reminded me.

"It has," Elsbeth responded. "I checked. Obviously *none* of the students who were there when you were, Dad, are still there. They're all off in scattered places practicing. Or likely retired and long dead."

"Oh, stop that! I'm not that old. My former students are still alive, at least most of them. . . . I'm more concerned with the faculty. There might be some I knew who will attend the reception."

"When you left UF, five faculty, including you, Dad, were teaching international law subjects. The oldest, Axel Smith, died two years ago and has been replaced by a woman from Oregon's law school. Not one of the other three is still on the faculty. One took a position in D.C. as counsel at the Organization of American States, one was given a chair in international law to teach at Vanderbilt, and the third is now in Brussels as a lawyer with NATO."

"How do you know all this?" I asked her.

"Don't ask. I have my sources. I've been at UF long enough and dated a couple of guys studying law."

"Lucinda, help me."

"I think you're missing something," said Lucinda. "Dean Hobart Perry must still be dean. He knows about your dad once being law Professor Maxwell Hunt."

"He's not here," Elsbeth interrupted. "According to the law college website, Perry stepped down and two weeks ago began teaching for a year in Nebraska or one of those states we try to rush through on the way between Montana and Florida. You won't run into him at the reception. . . . Dad. Lucinda. I'd love to have you both go to the reception with us. Sue and I'll protect you!"

"*That* worries me," I moaned.

Lucinda nodded and rolled her eyes when I added, "OK, we'll go."

That evening, after Elsbeth and Sue headed back to Gainesville, Lucinda put down her book and looked at me as though I had done something I'll regret.

"Macduff, I was amazed at your agreeing to go to Gainesville. When we've gone to soccer games, you dressed so you wouldn't be recognized—sunglasses and a floppy, wide-brim

Gator hat. You looked around all during the game. I had to keep telling you to sit still and watch the field like other spectators. . . . Remember what happened with Herzog's nephew a decade ago?"

"We were never compromised. It was the two of us who identified Martín Paz and foolishly followed him toward the law school."

"He died next to the law school, shot by someone who saved us by killing Paz. Do you want to go through that again?"

"No," I said in a near whisper, and after a long pause, added, "This is different. It's ten years later; Herzog is now President of Guatemala and doesn't have time to chase us. Besides, now that we're married, I know you'll protect me."

"Don't be so sure of that! There are times I wish Martín or that mental case Park Salisbury who tried to shoot you while you were floating the Snake River in Wyoming was a better marksman."

"You'd miss me, and you know it! Your life would be dull. Shouldn't we all go to the reception?" I asked.

"I guess . . . we can't live a life of hiding. . . . Macduff, have you ever thought of beating Herzog to the punch?"

"Every day. But killing the president of a country? . . . Just as *he* has to wait until his presidency is over to come after me, I think *we* have to do the same."

A week later we were in our SUV headed for Gainesville. Lucinda looked stunning, wearing a simple black knee-length dress with the bottom dozen inches punctuated with pleats. The sleeves went down just below her elbows. The neck was high but scooped, setting off a necklace of black and dark red beads. She would be a distraction to anyone looking toward me. If they did look at me, they would see a middle-aged man of inconsequential character wearing clean pressed baggy clothing—Lucinda had scared twenty pounds off me.

My darkish tan pleated trousers were a size too large that made me look lost inside them. My French blue button-down shirt was far too big at the waist, and I hid folds in the shirt beneath the jacket, a Harris Tweed herringbone with leather elbow patches. The jacket draped more than enhanced my now fit frame. My tie, the first worn in months, was the one I reached for in a dark closet at home on a tie rack covered with Lucinda's scarves. The tie was dark blue with red figures of soldiers called ragamuffins or rags by the club it represented, where I always stayed when in London a decade and more ago.

Wearing sunglasses I started our drive, but Lucinda reached over and removed them.

"I thought sunglasses would surely prevent anyone from recognizing me," I stated.

"You're not teaching at UCLA and trying to look like a star. Who wears sunglasses after dark at a reception in Gainesville?"

Gone were the sunglasses.

For the first half-hour, Elsbeth, Sue, Lucinda, and I stayed more or less together talking to law faculty or students, all persons new to the college since I left.

I was concerned when a thirtyish woman joined us and introduced herself as Rebecca Nadal, the new interim dean.

"Are you two ladies interested in law school?" she asked, looking at Sue and Elsbeth.

"We've just come back from a year studying in London at LSE and King's," explained Sue.

"What did you study?" Nadal asked.

"I'm Sue, and I studied philosophy."

"I studied international law. My name is Elsbeth."

"Elsbeth!" exclaimed Dean Nadal. "Do you know the name Professor Maxwell Hunt?" she asked.

I grabbed and squeezed Lucinda's hand, an impulsive reaction expressing my concern for trouble.

"I don't," answered Elsbeth, as though the question were merely social talk. "This is my first time in the law buildings. I was raised in Maine, started my university training at the University of Maine, and transferred here with my friend, Sue, at the beginning of our second year. We were both tired of frigid winters."

"It's just a coincidence," Dean Nadal said. "A Maxwell Hunt, whom I didn't know, was a prominent professor here and was married to a Norwegian whose name was Elsbeth. It's most unusual."

"More common than you think," Elsbeth stuttered. "Immigrants once Americanized their names; Elsbeth or Elspeth became Elizabeth. That's not true today."

"I didn't mean to pry, Miss?"

"*Carson,* Elsbeth Carson."

Dean Nadal left to meet other students. I turned to Elsbeth and asked, "Why did you use Carson? You're registered as Brooks."

"The dean's meeting so many people she'll never know. I'm registered at the university, not the law school. I didn't want to add 'Brooks' to the mix when she mentioned Professor Hunt."

I squeezed her hand and nodded at her, proud of her determination to protect me.

Lucinda and I moved on to talk to other groups and let Elsbeth and Sue talk alone with other students. We drifted to the food table where Lucinda nudged her elbow against my side, and said, "She's a special young lady."

"You're much the reason for that. She never knew her mother, who was the most important part of my life for more than a decade. I've told Elsbeth everything I could remember about El. She cherishes her image of El, but she considers *you* to be the person she wants to have as a mom now."

"Who would you like to have me for?" she asked, turning to me with concern in both her voice and expression.

"The person I will spend the rest of my days with," I whispered in her ear.

"Maxwell!" The single word came in a shrill, female voice as Lucinda and I were filling dinner plates at the buffet table.

I began to turn away from Lucinda, her face contorted with anguish from hearing that single name called out. She grabbed my arm and whispered, "Ignore her; don't look up. Don't respond."

I couldn't ignore the voice because I didn't want her to call out again.

"I'm sorry, but my name is . . . ." I caught myself about to say Macduff. . . . "My name is not Maxwell."

"Of course it's Maxwell," she said too loudly and attracting looks from other guests. "Don't you recognize me? Brenda Stafford. I'm Jim's widow."

Jim Stafford and I joined the law faculty the same year. He taught property law. He was a fine teacher but a disappointing scholar. Once he earned tenure, he never wrote another word for publication. Jim died in a car accident a month before I was reported as dead from a stroke in D.C., after my rescue in Guatemala from the hands of Juan Pablo Herzog. El and I never saw much of Brenda and Jim during the decade El was alive. When she died, I rejected all social invitations and never saw Brenda again.

"Mrs. Stafford, I think you believe I'm someone else."

"You're Maxwell Hunt. You taught here for twenty years. A month after my Jim died, you were reported as having suffered a stroke in D.C. It was unusual because no body was brought back here for burial. And the day after you allegedly died, there were two strange men in your office and house; you must remember that we lived next door to you in Golf View.

"They wouldn't talk to me—they said they were representatives of Hunt's estate. They wore dark charcoal suits, white shirts, and each had some combination of red, white, and blue for a tie. They looked rumpled. I didn't like them."

Then she leaned close to me and whispered, "Just between the two of us, I never believed you died, but I respect your wanting privacy for some reason or other. I'm happy for you."

"I'm Lucy, Mrs. Stafford," Lucinda interrupted. "Ronnie here and I have been married for thirty years next month. We have a nephew here at the university who lost his parents two years ago. We've tried to fill in for them. This is our first time in Gainesville. We live in Minneapolis."

"You two can play any games you want, but you *are* Maxwell Hunt," Brenda again asserted, looking at me.

Lucinda was pulling on my jacket cuff.

"Ronnie, we have to find our nephew," she said. "We promised him dinner, and our reservation was for twenty minutes ago." Looking at Brenda, she added, "Sorry we caused you to think we're the Hunts."

Elsbeth and Sue saw us head for the door and met us in the foyer, out of sight of Brenda Stafford.

"You two look like you've seen a ghost! Are you OK?"

"Keep walking ahead of us and ignore us. We'll tell you in the parking lot."

We hurried to our car, Elsbeth and Sue behind at a distance. They had parked next to us and without saying a word got into Sue's car and drove off. We waited a few minutes and followed, Lucinda on her cell phone, calling Elsbeth.

"What are you two up to?" inquired Elsbeth. "I have the speaker on my phone on," she added to let us know Sue would hear what we said. I didn't want to bring Sue into this although she knew much about my background.

"We're fine," I said. "I had a dizzy spell. Not a problem, but I wanted to leave before I fell. You two go back if you wish. I'll call tomorrow from the cottage. Sorry to upset you and have to leave early."

Lucinda and I had agreed with Elsbeth a couple of years ago that if anything dangerous to me arose, I would feign a dizzy spell. Elsbeth knew she would find out more as soon as we could tell her.

"Dad, we were through anyway and going to suggest we all leave for dinner. We can do that another time. I'll call you tomorrow. But before I let you go, I want to tell you about someone I met at the reception. Her name is Luisa. She's a graduate law student from Guatemala. She really was nice, and Sue and I talked with her about UF. She hasn't been here long, but she seemed to know more than we did."

"Elsbeth, you know that for us the mere mention of Guatemala sets off alarms. Should we worry about what you talked about?"

"No. I told her my name was Carson. I use Carson whenever I don't need to give someone my real name."

"Did you tell her you're first name?"

"Yes, and she said it must be a way of saying Elizabeth she'd never heard before."

"Did she give you her last name?"

"Yes. Solares."

"Anything else you think I ought to know?"

"No. She was so nice. Obviously from a well-educated and prominent family. I assumed that when she said her uncle was the President of Guatemala, against his suggestion that she not disclose their relationship."

"Do you know the name of Guatemala's president?" I gasped.

"No. I don't know much about the country except for what you told me about how beautiful it was when you were there as a visiting professor years ago."

"Elsbeth, the president's name is Juan Pablo Herzog. Luisa Solares has to be his niece."

35

THE NEXT MORNING AT THE COTTAGE

GRACE JUSTICE CALLED THE COTTAGE WHILE I carried the last dishes from the washer and set them on the shelves. Doing the dishes and emptying the dishwasher were what I accepted as my responsibilities when Lucinda offered to be the family nutritionist. I didn't realize that meant *she* would choose our food, which eliminated most of what I like—burgers, bacon, burgers, fries, burgers, hot dogs, and burgers. Plus thick, creamy milkshakes.

Lucinda had left for an eye exam in St. Augustine. I was soon to head for the one place in the county where I could buy gas that didn't contain the dreaded ethanol that contaminates fuel and shortens the life of outboard engines. I welcomed the chance to talk to Grace, but not until Lucinda returned from her appointment.

"Macduff, you two OK? I wanted to run something by you about the first airboat murder in Pine Island Sound," said Grace. "And then talk about the case here and Turk Jensen."

"We're both fine," I said.

Lucinda had returned and sat down, a little wobbly from drops in her eyes. And she'd been driving! "What's new about the Pine Island Sound murder?" she asked.

"I don't think there's a link between the two murders, Grace said. "But maybe that's because I can't find very much evidence about either case to think otherwise."

"What did you want to ask us?" Lucinda queried.

"I have some thoughts about Cassell and Cartwright as the killers of Prescott," Grace replied. "And it brings into the discussion the fact that there were two Prescotts, which the Ft. Myers authorities seem yet to acknowl. . . . "

I interrupted. "I don't know any more than Martin R. Prescott, Swenson's partner, seemingly fled the area, believing *he* was supposed to be the victim murdered on the airboat. Swenson may not know he fled, believing that the Prescott who many liked *was* his partner."

"The Ft. Myers state attorney's assistants either don't know or don't believe there was a second Prescott," commented Grace. "Maybe they're satisfied with having the file sit on the cold case shelf. It may be a matter of allocating funds, lacking what's needed to pursue the Pine Island Sound Prescott killing without some new information."

"It may not be lack of funds for investigating, Grace. Cassell and Cartwight are the only suspects they have, except maybe Swenson. Cartwright has friends, mainly because of his politically powerful father."

"What do *you* think about Cartwright?" Grace asked.

"I think he's missing some marbles. I don't think Cassell was comfortable working with Cartwright. We've learned Cassell was so ecstatic about becoming an FWC officer that he agreed to partner with Cartwright. No one else would. . . . Grace, do you think he's a murderer?"

"No. He's not that brutal or clever. But even if he's not a murderer, he may be dealing in drugs."

"What about Cassell?"

"Short fuse, but viewed by his superiors as having gone straight. Fair job evaluations as an FWC officer. No sensible reason to suspect him. He likes his job and wants to keep it."

"And Swenson?"

"I don't trust Swenson. I'm not sure why, but I don't like him," she said.

"Any specifics?" I asked.

"Hard to pin down. Swenson believed he had reason to do something bad to his partner Prescott. Did Swenson try to murder his partner but killed the wrong Prescott? That seems like fantasy. He knew what his own partner looked like."

"But Swenson might have hired someone to do the killing and *he*—the *murderer*—killed the wrong Prescott," I suggested.

"Grace, another thought: I remember reading online about some of the characters in Gibsonton. They don't have much side-show work anymore. One, called Monkey Face, may still be in Gibton doing mostly odd jobs for different people. That could include working for Swenson, and the odd job could include murder. Can you use your contacts and look for a former carny in Gibsonton named Monkey Face?"

"Your mind's in the world of genre detective fiction, Macduff. But I'll run a check for info on anyone named Monkey Face."

"What's up with the second airboat murder? It *is* in your jurisdiction. Have you identified the body? Any suspects? Why hasn't Turk Jensen contacted me?"

"One at a time, Mac."

"Except for Jensen, the quick answer to your other questions is we haven't identified the body, but we may be close. No suspects yet. None are likely until we identify the body. Dealing with Jensen's a different matter. He called and asked for my view on investigating *you.* He wants an arrest warrant solely because of the body found on your burned flats boat a couple of years ago with the gill net murders."

"I *was* near the scene, Grace, but not the day of the murder. I'd talk to Jensen at his office if he'd call and ask. Bill Muirhead will go with me."

"Muirhead's part of the problem. Jensen's experience dealing with him is dismal. I think Jensen knows you're not involved in the second murder. He sees going after you as payback for being embarrassed when you tangled with him—and you won—when your boat burned. It's nothing more than harassment. The trouble is that, when you put someone in office like Jensen, he's going to abuse his power."

"Should I call him and tell him Muirhead and I will meet with him anytime?"

"He wants to show up at your cottage with lights flashing, put you in cuffs, rip your place apart purportedly to conduct a lawful search, and drag you away. I wouldn't put it past him to shove you down your cottage stairs and claim you fell. But he won't when Muirhead is around. Calling Jensen might be a good idea, but get Muirhead's advice."

"What do you think he intends to charge me with? Murder? Of who? How can someone be charged with murder when you can't identify the body?"

"But there *is* a body, or at least parts, even though we can't identify who it was. The old law of 'no body, no murder' has changed. Where there's no body but there was an alleged killing, it's possible the would-be victim might show up alive. But in our case we have enough parts of a body to conclude that there was a body and whoever the person might have been, he was murdered."

"But, speaking hypothetically," I postured, "if John Smith is believed to have murdered someone who's missing—or mostly missing as in our case—and there are parts enough to make a reasonable inference that they came from that person, there should be no problem with going forth. But if Smith denies any participation, without some link between Smith and a body that can't be identified, I doubt that there would be an indictment. That may not be justice. . . . What if Smith *admitted* to a murder, and there's no body to support his claim?"

"That's different," Grace said. "*If* we have enough body parts to conclude that *some* human being was murdered, and Smith admitted to being the killer, Smith gets tried and likely convicted. . . . That's not the case here; *no one's* come forth and admitted to a killing."

"Do you have *any* suspects, Grace?" I asked.

"As I said, it's hard to answer that until we know *who* was murdered. The neighbors of the airboat owner—Franz Gerber—routinely complained to the police about the noise Gerber made at night running the airboat, often well past midnight. He was not liked. But *he* wasn't killed.

"The killing may be unrelated to the problems people have with airboats. It could have been a killing of someone for any motive one person has to kill another. The airboat was a sensational way to carry out the act. Something that would make the public horrified."

"Were Muirhead and I to meet with Jensen and he tried again to get an arrest warrant after we talked, is *any* local judge going to grant the arrest warrant request?"

"Only one. Judge Ripley Bones. He and Jensen hunt together."

"Won't he dismiss himself because of their friendship?"

"Not a chance. Bones is what we see too much of in judges. Not the most successful local attorneys run for office and give up a lucrative practice. It's the ones who can't get a practice established, aren't making enough money, and see a judgeship as a way to earn a modest amount and pay the bills. Sometimes they do a good job. Bones is not one of those. His first priority is paying back favors. Then currying friendships. A distant third is something that escapes him—assuring a fair trial."

"Your advice?"

"Call Muirhead."

"As soon as we finish talking."

Finished discussing murders and monkeys, we talked for a few minutes about our mutual passion for fly fishing. Grace is as serious when fishing on the flats as she is when tracking down a suspect. I'd like to fish with her again. She often asks me to take her.

Lucinda is certain to insist on coming along.

36

THE SAME TIME—LUISA REPORTS TO HERZOG

LUISA SOLARES WAS SETTLED IN GAINESVILLE and enjoying law classes. One of twelve students in an LL.M. program limited to foreign law graduates, she quickly developed friendships with a fellow LL.M. student from Costa Rica and another from Spain, attracted to one another by their common language and cultures.

In her first month at UF, Luisa had talked on the phone only once to Tío Juan in Guatemala. She had nothing to report other than working hard on her studies, learning how the law college functioned, and meeting many LL.M. and JD students.

But as the weeks passed, by mid-September Luisa thought she could benefit from Tío Juan's advice and hopefully praise. Finished with preparation for her next classes, she dialed his private number.

"Luisa, I was expecting you'd call and let me know if you have any news about Professor Hunt."

"I have several things to tell you, Tío Juan. First, as you suggested, I went to the places where María-Martina and Martín were killed. The door to the roof of the law building was kept locked, but I checked it every day and last Thursday found it open. I went to the edge of the roof where I could see down into the courtyard where both the law dean and the University president sat during the dedication of the new building. If María had not been shot, she easily would have killed at least the law dean.

"I found something that upset me. There was a three-foot high concrete wall at the edge of the roof. I estimated where María must have been hiding and preparing to shoot the two men. Kneeling against the wall as I thought María would have, I noticed several chips in the concrete that must have been from pistol shots fired by whoever killed María. There were faded, darkish red traces on the concrete that I think were blood. Several bullets must have passed through María, and she fell against the wall, bleeding."

"I'm sorry you were distressed; it was exactly where María was murdered," Herzog said with an edge to his voice. "It was Professor Hunt who shot and killed her. The newspapers never mentioned a name, but it had to be Hunt. Who else would have been on the roof searching for María?"

Luisa thought there were several possibilities about who shot María, not the least of whom was a member of the campus police. But she had learned never to challenge her uncle. It would not bring María or Martín back.

"Another time I went to a UF soccer game, so I could gain a sense about where Martín discovered Professor Hunt in the stadium seats and followed him away from the soccer field and past the tennis courts near the law buildings."

Luisa was unaware that Lucinda and I had discovered Martín sitting at a soccer game and constantly searching the crowd for me. Frustrated, he left. We followed him, and at the tennis courts he confronted us with a gun, but was himself shot and killed by an unknown party. I have always believed it was a CIA agent Dan Wilson sent to watch us, but he insists no such agent was so assigned or involved. Lucinda believes it was Juan Santander from Jackson Hole.

Santander was a former Navy Seal who was severely wounded and disabled in combat in Iraq. I met him when I was helping combat-wounded, disabled vets in Wyoming as part of Project Healing Waters. We became friends and have often fished together. Lucinda says he feels he is my protector and in Gainesville he shot Martín to save our lives.

A few years later Santander may have been the one who killed Whitman in D.C. And a couple of years after that, it may have been Santander who saved Lucinda and me from two crazed Druid-worshiping zealots who had kidnapped us, tied us in wicker baskets emblazoned with mistletoe, rigged them with explosives taped across the front of the wicker, and set us drifting down the Yellowstone River on the summer solstice.

We were rescued by a figure that jumped into our boat from the low Mill Creek bridge and pulled us away from the explosives. Lucinda insists it was Santander; though at first doubtful, I'm increasingly inclined to believe her.

"Tío Juan," Luisa continued, "one thing happened that may be useful for you to know," Luisa continued. "I went to a reception for law and undergraduate students. It was at the home of a young, new law professor who is advisor to the law college's international law society. One conversation I had included two juniors who are interested in law school after another two years. One was named Sue, the other *Elsbeth*. Does that mean anything to you?"

"I'm not sure, but I don't believe so," Herzog responded. "When Professor Hunt allegedly died, it was ten years after his wife's death. She died in a boating accident in Wyoming. She was expecting. Her body was never found and the soon to be born child obviously perished. I think Hunt's wife's name was Elizabeth. But, let me think about this. I might want you to meet this Elsbeth and Sue again, perhaps to ask them to come to the law school and sit in on a class you're taking. Then you could take them to lunch. Let me think of what you might ask them. . . . Anything else to tell me?"

"Yes. You may not have heard that last spring Dean Hobart Perry stepped down as dean. He is not at the law school this year but is expected to return next fall. Rebecca Nadal, a respected member of the law faculty and Perry's associate dean, will serve as interim until a new appointment is made, someone who will assume office next summer. Do you have any idea how I might approach Dean Nadal to find out about the report done years ago when you offered to fund a chair in honor of Professor Hunt and insisted on seeing a thorough report about his purported death?"

"Luisa, I tried to steal that report after Martín was killed. I was never given a copy. I hired someone who entered the dean's office one night and broke into his locked filing cabinet. In it was a section marked 'Deceased Professor Hunt Report for Donor J.P. Herzog.' But the file was missing. Perry may have had it at home. Our break-in caused enough damage to warn the dean what we were looking for. He must have hid or destroyed the file. But it was a public record that he should have felt obligated to retain.

"What you must do is talk to Dean Nadal. I realize now that it will be necessary for you to tell her you're my niece and how you've heard from me about how sorry I have always been that the funding I offered was disapproved. She may deny any knowledge about it or admit that a report was completed but can't be disclosed. It could even have been transferred to the UF president's office for safe-keeping. Tactfully asking about it may help us.

"Don't push the issue. We have other ways of learning who Professor Hunt is, such as retired agent Thomas Davis in Antigua who was part of the CIA staff that helped Hunt enter some kind of protection program.

"Another thought is you might find an employee who was in charge of maintenance of the law buildings when Hunt allegedly died and who might accept a generous bribe for information. I am prepared to pay that person enough to comfortably retire. But only if the report is produced.

"I look forward to your coming home for the Christmas holiday. Call me when you arrive, and we will meet during your vacation. I am pleased with what you have done so far, Luisa.

"As the Americans say," he added, "'keep your eyes and ears open.'"

37

AT THE UF LAW COLLEGE

ELSBETH RECEIVED AN EMAIL FROM INTERIM Dean Nadal a few days after the law reception, asking her to make an appointment to talk at the dean's office. Elsbeth had never been in the law school buildings, and she was nervous both about talking to the dean and running the risk of meeting Luisa Solares.

After making the appointment she called us and said she would be meeting Dean Nadal the following day and wanted any advice we might give her.

"What do you suppose her interest is?" Elsbeth asked. "She's too busy to interview every potential student, and I have another couple of years before I'm ready for law school. She didn't ask Sue to join me. I don't know why."

"We left Dean Nadal at the reception with doubt in her mind about your relationship to me when I was Professor Hunt. She may have something in mind, or perhaps it's only curiosity about a former law professor."

"But I told her I was Elsbeth Carson, not Brooks. Or Hunt."

"How did she address the email?"

"She used my email address at the law school, which is ebrooks@law.ufl.edu. That means she learned or guessed that Elsbeth Carson is Elsbeth Brooks."

"Can you tell if she was guessing and sent it to other addressees?"

"I can't tell; the email came only to me as far as I know. I suspect she will ask me about using the Carson name."

"It wasn't hard for her to discover that there was no Elsbeth *Carson* registered at UF, but there was an Elsbeth *Brooks*. Did you have to include a photo when you applied a few years ago?"

"No, because of something related to admissions based on race, which a photo may disclose. I can't think of anywhere she could find a photo of me."

"Tell her you're in the process of being adopted by a distant aunt and uncle named Brooks who raised you since your mother and father—the Carsons—died several years ago. You've changed your name recently because you've been with the Brooks for three years and love them. You thought this would be a nice way of thanking and honoring them."

"But that's an admission I'm a Brooks."

"You've effectively admitted that already. You're registered at UF as Brooks. To deny that would be an admission you filed a fraudulent application. You might be suspended or even dismissed."

"Then how should I approach our conversation?"

"Don't offer any information she won't find in the university records. Convince the dean you don't know as much about the Brooks as you would were they your parents since birth. If she raises any question about Lucinda's and my lives before you joined us three years ago—which is true—tell her you simply haven't been made privy to that information and cannot provide her an answer."

"Dad, isn't she more interested in my first name than whether I'm a Carson or a Brooks?"

"Yes, but our concern is that if she thinks you're related to Professor Hunt, she would have to track that through the Carsons' family tree and would come to a dead end when she learned they were deceased. You had no siblings; the Carsons couldn't have a child. But the dean might be able to learn that they were in Jackson Hole when El died."

"Dad, is there anything you'd like to tell me that she would know about because she's the dean with access to all the law school records?"

"Yes, I'll tell you briefly."

I told Elsbeth details about the report Herzog demanded five years ago and that I was fairly certain that Dean Perry had shredded the original and all copies.

I could have told her more, but I didn't want to cause her any more stress than necessary. I don't believe she knows anything about the deaths of a niece and a nephew of Herzog—first María-Martina's death on the law school roof and the later killing of Martín near the tennis courts.

"When we're together next time, Dad, you have to tell me everything you can remember about you and Herzog that you've omitted. Promise?"

"Promise," I answered softly, but sincerely.

"Elsbeth, I know you're a mature young woman, but Herzog is beyond anything you should have to deal with. Keep that Carson name alive; you may want it back."

"Just try to make me. I'm a *Brooks!*"

The next two days passed with lightning speed, and Elsbeth soon found herself sitting in the Dean's suite with concern that she might give away something that would hurt her dad. And maybe Lucinda.

Dean Nadal opened her office door, walked up to Elsbeth smiling, shook her hand warmly, and, gently touching her arm, took her into the dean's private office. They both sat away from the dean's desk, in comfortable chairs circling an oval coffee table with a spectacular ceramic pot in the center. The pot had subtle images of a gator wrapped around from bottom to top. Two large oriental rugs divided the office between the sitting area and the dean's desk. Florida art covered the walls. Last week in Elsbeth's art history class, the focus was on Florida art, and now she felt as though she was in a museum.

"From my classes," Elsbeth said, "I know about Herman Herzog's and Martin Johnson Heade's work in Florida, but this is the first time I've seen Audubon's bird with the St. Augustine fort in the background."

"These are on loan from the art museum here on campus," said the dean. "I admire them every day. . . . Let's talk about Professor Maxwell Hunt and your father, Macduff Brooks. Do I have your attention?"

"More than that. I don't know what to expect," Elsbeth said, visibly trembling at hearing the name "Brooks."

"Before we talk about specifics, Elsbeth, let me tell you a few things I know about Professor Hunt. He was a fine professor here for twenty years, although he became quite reclusive after his wife died. Her name was Elsbeth, the same as yours, but she was called El. I came here to teach a few years after he left, which has been eleven years. When Dean Perry retired and I was appointed interim dean, he told me a few things about

Professor Hunt he thought might arise during my time in the dean's office. He was very guarded; I sensed he was telling me only part of what he knew, possibly to protect someone.

"Dean Perry asked me to his home and gave me a file which he asked me to read while I was there and return to him. It was clear he did not want it copied. I read the file, which he apparently kept at his home. It did not cover anything about Professor Hunt or the law college. It was solely about a Guatemalan man named Juan Pablo Herzog who offered a donation to this law college. You know who I'm speaking of?"

"*Who* is Mr. Herzog?" Elsbeth asked, not wanting to lie by telling her she had never heard of Herzog, but to learn how much Nadal knew. She was prepared to lie if it protected her dad and Lucinda.

"I think you may know about Mr. Herzog. What I will tell you involves Juan Pablo Herzog and a niece and a nephew of his who were shot near here on campus. We have a graduate law student here this year from Guatemala. Her name is Luisa Solares. She is also a niece of Herzog. Between the two of us, I am watching her because I do not know if her interest being here extends beyond her law studies.

"Luisa Solares's uncle was furious when we turned down his generous proposed gift of $4 million. To this day he may believe we have information that would help him locate Professor Hunt. I'm not going to play games with you, Elsbeth. I have learned enough about Professor Hunt to believe he survived the beating he received from Herzog and did not die as the result of an alleged stroke, as the State Department and this college reported.

"I believe Professor Hunt is in some kind of protection program. When Hunt was here, he traveled occasionally for the state department to foreign lands. It was travel as part of what our government called AmPart, where prominent people from the U.S. in many disciplines were sent abroad to lecture. Professor Hunt's travel suggests that he went for reasons additional to giving lectures to law faculties, businesses, and government groups. Our deans never knew that his travel was for more than lecturing. None of his colleagues here knew, as far as I am aware. I suspect his wife El did not know, but he did most of his travel for the government after she died."

"Have you talked to anyone in the State Department about Hunt's alleged work with them?" Elsbeth asked.

"No. Dean Perry must have had contact with someone at the CIA, but he destroyed all records here that named names. Except one. I found one email Perry must have overlooked. It was correspondence with a man named Dan Wilson."

Elsbeth gasped. Dan Wilson had helped her make contact with her dad at a time Macduff didn't know she had survived.

"How did this Mr. Wilson fit into the picture?" Elsbeth inquired.

"I don't know. I have tried to talk to him, but when I did finally reach him, he suggested I had confused him with some other Dan Wilson. I know enough about the CIA to understand that further pursuit with him would be useless."

"Dean Nadal, you've told me about Herzog, his attempted gift, his anger, and the deaths of his niece and nephew. I assume that's all part of the law college's records, especially related to the law college's fund raising. Do those records refer to Professor Hunt?"

"Not a word. He is only referred to in the general faculty files, such as the composition of committees and office assignments. Even the proposed gift makes no mention of Professor Hunt, although Herzog wanted the endowed chair to be in the name of Hunt. The only record Dean Perry saved referred to a donation without reservation. But I now know there were two reservations insisted on by Herzog, from the records Dean Perry was willing to share. First, the chair was to be named for Hunt, and second, we were to undertake a thorough investigation regarding Hunt's alleged death of a stroke in D.C."

"What is your belief of any connection between Professor Hunt and my father?"

"If I had to guess, I'd venture that your father is Professor Hunt and that you are his daughter."

For a moment Elsbeth was unable to speak. . . . "What evidence of that do you have?"

"Circumstantial. I checked your age and date of birth. You allegedly were born in Greenville, Maine, the same day as the accident on the Snake River in Wyoming when your real mother was lost. I think *you* survived."

"But my birth is recorded in the Greenville, Maine, hospital records."

"Where Mrs. Carson—your adoptive mother—worked. I suspect she had your birth added to the files or did it herself."

"Why are you now interested in Professor Hunt?"

"I'm interested in one thing. I do not want Juan Pablo Herzog to succeed in finding out that Professor Hunt is Brooks. Or that you are his birth daughter. Also, there is his current wife to consider. I believe you are fond of her."

"Yes. Very much. I have talked in the past few days with your former dean, Hobart Perry, who was wonderful to me in finding Dad," Elsbeth said. "I called him at the law school where he's visiting this year and asked him one question: How much could we trust *you*? He told me he holds you in the highest regard, that you would never disclose what he told you, even though he had not mentioned the name Brooks. When did you link Hunt with Brooks?"

"At the reception where I met you," Dean Nadal replied. As soon as you said your name was Elsbeth. But at first I only thought that it was a pretty name. When I associated Elsbeth with Professor Hunt and you so emphatically said you were 'Elsbeth *Carson,*' my intuition said something was not correct, and it was probably Carson."

"But I *am* a Carson. At least I was for eighteen years. Now I have three mothers," Elsbeth said, her voice cracking. "I was born in Wyoming on the banks of the Snake River. I *was* the daughter of Elsbeth Hunt. But until three years ago I had no thought that I was anything other than a Carson. Then Dan Wilson contacted me, and I learned that I was Professor Hunt's daughter. . . . More recently, my widowed father's second wife, Lucinda, entered my life, and in time I realized I wanted to be a part of the Brooks family."

"At the reception you told me you're a Carson. Why?"

"Yes, I was scared to mention the name Brooks."

"But you are registered here as Brooks."

"True. There are nearly 50,000 students at UF. I assumed I would become lost among them. There are seven Brooks at UF."

"But you came to the law school reception. Wasn't that risky?"

"Yes, but it was not my meeting you that proved troublesome, but my meeting someone else."

"Who was that?"

"Luisa Solares, niece of President Juan Pablo Herzog of Guatemala."

38

A FEW DAYS LATER

ELSBETH'S MEETING LUISA SOLARES AND HER conversation with Dean Nadal were sufficient to prevent me from sleeping, but there was a further matter that added to my anguish.

Lucinda and Grace had been inseparable for the last month. I didn't know what they did or said or were planning when they were together, which was at least weekly. They weren't fly fishing. Maybe they talked about me. It was likely their conversations were nothing more than the rebuilding of a friendship between two women. Becoming good friends like Elsbeth and Sue. I'll pass it off as girl stuff. Girl stuff I don't understand.

I spent time alone on my flats boat. When she was at the cottage, Lucinda seemed disinterested in or distracted from asking about what I caught and what flies and what weight and sinking rate lines I was using. My fly tying table was busier than at any other time since my initial move to Montana.

She hadn't come home one evening early enough to share time on the porch or dock as the sun faded. At dusk I had poured a Gentleman Jack and took it down to the dock, stepped aboard our flats boat, *Sandpiper*, and envisioned adding some kind of forward casting platform.

The apogee of my self-pity crumbled incrementally with successive sips of the Gentleman Jack. I heard two cars drive in, but I didn't make the effort to turn around and look. I could hear laughter and identified the two as Lucinda and Grace.

I listened to them climb the stairs and five minutes later come back down talking, then silent as they walked the two dozen yards to the dock. Reading a long downloaded email about fishing in Cuba, I still didn't move.

"Are we invited to join you? You seem preoccupied with something," Lucinda said.

"Nothing much," I answered, not raising or turning my head.

"Could we attract your attention with some information about the airboat murder near here?" Grace responded.

"If you've solved it, you don't need me. If you haven't, you have nothing new to tell me," I responded, cryptically, immediately regretting my attitude.

"If I told you Grace and I know who was killed on the airboat near here *and* who did it *and* why, would you at least turn your head and acknowledge we're here?" said Lucinda, rolling her eyes in exasperation. "And stop worrying about Turk Jensen?"

"Muirhead returned my call today—a strange, brief message," I said. "Jensen had assured Muirhead there would be no arrest. And no search warrant was sought. Muirhead said Grace and he had talked to Jensen and told him in no uncertain words that, if Jensen pursued you, they would see him challenged and likely dismissed. Isn't that true, Grace?"

"It is. And, Macduff, you also owe a debt to Lucinda. She said you were depressed about Turk Jensen's causing trouble again and where publicity might lead. Lucinda pushed me. We confronted Jensen at a good time, pressing on his weaknesses. Don't worry about him for the moment. But I'm making no promises for the future. He'll be after you sometime."

I looked at Lucinda and then Grace. And Lucinda again. I felt a relief I hadn't realized I needed.

"Thank you, Grace. Now entice me with some information, such as who the body parts belonged to."

"Grant Borders."

"Who was?"

"Owner of a sixty-foot-long sport fishing boat registered in the Bahamas with the home port in Nassau. It was frequently docked at Camachee Cove—in sight of Grace's condo. Borders owned houses in Key West and Grand Bahama."

"No one reported Borders missing," I asked.

"No one was interested."

"Wife?"

"Included."

"She didn't report him missing?"

"No," Grace said. "His *boat* was reported missing in the Gulf Stream between Grand Bahama and Palm Beach. Other boaters saw it burning and sinking. Off the record—he was missing but not missed. At least not by his wife, Jane, who two days before had agreed to a divorce and a settlement of about $3 million. Nothing was signed. Now she stands to receive closer to $30 million."

"She didn't report him missing?"

"Correct. She considered the report of the boat sinking to include an obvious loss of its skipper—her husband."

"The captain went down with his ship?" I surmised. "But not with his money."

"If you wish to call it that," Grace said, grinning at my phrasing.

"What does this have to do with the airboat murder?" I asked.

"Borders *wasn't* on his boat when it sunk. He was abducted at Grand Bahama *before* he made the crossing. The boat was set for an auto-pilot course to Palm Beach and loaded with explosives, to go off when it was in the Gulf Stream, half-way to Florida."

"*Who* stopped Borders in the Bahamas and *how* did he end up tied to the airboat propeller near here?"

"The *who* brought the *him* to Florida, presumably on a *different* powerboat," Grace replied, exasperated. "We think they brought him into the St. Augustine Inlet at night, ignored customs, shifted him to a small flats boat, sped down the Intercoastal, and, a mile after the Matanzas Inlet, turned west and headed through the marshes to where the airboat was hanging in a sling on Gerber's dock."

"This is pure fantasy. . . . Go on," I said, now fully attentive, but still edgy.

"Remember that most of this is unproven. Grant Borders was subjected to what you won't enjoy hearing. First they cut off his fingers," Grace continued. "Then they removed his teeth. He wasn't responding and was almost certainly dead. But his captors continued as planned. No dental work or fingerprints were left for identification. His body was tied and placed in the propeller cage of the airboat. Both boats started back to the Waterway, but the tide was going out, and they went aground. We think they planned to leave the airboat drifting on the ICW and return north on the flats boat. But they panicked and ran the airboat aground near or on the owner's—Gerber's—property. Gerber was away on business.

"Why did they go to the trouble of using an airboat to dispose of Borders?" I asked. "There were easier ways."

"Someone desperately wanted Borders to suffer and die," said Lucinda. "The airboat was a statement. No simple poisoning or self-defense shooting."

"You're implying it was his wife who planned his death?"

"She had an obvious motive, protecting the inheritance she would receive only if the settlement wasn't finalized. And one more reason, she had a lover named Julio Jones," added Grace.

"She could have had Jones hire some thugs to do the dirty work," said Lucinda. "Jones apparently didn't want to be there when Borders was abducted. If the police question him, he has an alibi. He wasn't near the Bahamas or Palm Beach. He was in Atlanta with, if you can believe it, *another* married woman."

"Pretty dumb if Jones's Atlanta girlfriend wasn't wealthy. But maybe he thought Jane Borders was going to dump him," I observed.

"From what we learned, Julio Jones had more testosterone than intelligence," Lucinda added.

"That is an interesting story, Grace," I conceded, "but how did you conclude that the dead person was Grant Borders. The body had no teeth or fingers?"

"Killers often forget to cover all their tracks. In this case it didn't help us identify the *killer*, but it did the unidentified *victim*. We got a warrant and finally searched Gerber's pier and dock. Ironically, Turk Jensen helped us convince Judge Bones to issue the search warrant. Jensen was confused and overwhelmed about the whole matter.

"Yesterday, we searched Gerber's pier and dock. We didn't find anything on the airboat or dock until we climbed down on the dock framing. Then we saw something small lodged in a cross beam under the boathouse and removed it. It was the tip of a finger! It was only one part of one finger. But it might lead to a finger print. That or a DNA match is essential to identifying the body. Both would be better."

"That leaves missing from your story the 'who.' Who was behind Grant Borders' killing?" I asked.

"We have some ideas about that," Lucinda attested.

"But before we talk about that," I suggested, "what you've told me so far seems to verify that the two airboat murders were not connected."

"You're right to a point. But Borders' killer almost certainly got his idea from the Prescott murder. Borders' death was little more than a copycat murder."

"Lucinda and I shouldn't have to worry anymore about being drawn into Borders' death. Or should we?"

"You're free of any link between the two murders," assured Grace.

"Link? You know we had *nothing* to do with *Prescott's* death."

"An argument can be made you didn't report what you saw."

"We saw a body and reported it to the FWC."

"Two FWC officers responded. They'll say you were not cooperative."

"We'll respond that they were not professional. But, Grace, you're more likely than we are to learn about anything newly discovered about Prescott. Do you have anything?"

"I've talked off and on to the state attorney in Ft. Myers, hoping to get something useful in addressing the murder here. But now that the Borders case is close to being solved, I doubt I'll have reason to talk to people in Ft. Myers anymore."

"Borders' case is solved? Maybe half-solved at best. You still haven't shared with me *who* killed Borders?"

"Hired killers from the Bahamas. Hired by the most obvious suspects—Jane Borders and her lover Julio Jones," she offered.

"*Obvious* doesn't mean *actual.* Is there a better suspect?" I replied.

"Borders owed money to some bad people. I don't know how much. Or who he owed. They may be out of the country. To tell the truth, Mac, I'm so busy that I'm not going to worry about solving Borders' murder. It took place in federal or international waters, whatever that part of the Gulf Stream is considered. *It didn't happen on my turf.* As far as my office is concerned, Borders was already dead and dismembered when his body was placed on the airboat in *this* county."

"So much for the way the wheels of justice turn," said Lucinda quietly. "And you two are lawyers!"

"Wasn't justice served?" I asked. "Borders made no contributions to society. He's dead, and he won't be missed, especially by his wife, Jane."

"But his killers are *alive,*" Lucinda declared. "And so are Jane Borders and the two further along the chain of adultery—Julio Jones and his other mistress."

"We'd like to know who the hired killers are," agreed Grace. "But as far as we're concerned, Jane and Julio and whoever they're playing around with can continue to play with each other."

"Jane will soon be able to *afford* to play a lot more," I said with a shrug.

"One final matter," Grace added. "You two don't know about this, Lucinda. The state attorney in Ft. Myers has asked me to convince you two to drive down and talk to him about the Prescott murder."

"What do you suggest?" I asked.

"Go! Get things cleared up."

39

MEETING WITH THE FT. MYERS STATE ATTORNEY

THE NEXT MORNING STARTED WITH TWO CUPS of coffee, nurtured in shade on the slopes of the irrepressible volcano Agua in Guatemala. Finished, I called Sam Jester, Chief Assistant State Attorney in the Ft. Myers, Lee County, 20th Judicial Circuit offices. He was in.

"Sam, this is Macduff Brooks in St. Augustine. We haven't met. You know Grace Justice. She's a good fri. . . ."

"When can you be here?" he interrupted loudly. As I would soon learn, his voice contrasted with his diminutive appearance. Two cushions on his chair raised him a few important inches. Yet he looked like a third grader at his teacher's desk. What he had been denied in stature he made up with unseemly developed vocal cords.

"Thursday, two days from now?" I suggested.

"Be here at nine," he ordered firmly, and hung up.

I was thinking more like meeting in early afternoon. Five hours of mostly interstate panic, dodging eighteen-wheelers, meant leaving the cottage Wednesday and staying over.

"Lucinda!" I called out toward the bathroom. The door opened and steam poured out, followed by a towel-wrapped head.

"You always pick a good time to ask me something," the head said, muffled by the towel.

"I'm on the phone—at least I was—to the state attorney's office in Ft. Myers. I told him I can be there at nine Thursday morning. He didn't say anything about expecting you to be with me. Do you want to go?"

"Not especially. I'm innocent. You were skippering our flats boat when we saw the airboat. Not me. Anyway, I'd want an attorney with me. Wouldn't you?"

"Remember that *I'm* an attorney. At least I was in an earlier life. I even remember a little lawyer-speak," I added.

"Maybe if we went in together, we might catch him off guard. We have my irresistible charm plus your experience in understanding the trickery of practicing law. But don't admit to Jester you're a lawyer. He'd ask about your legal background."

"You're very smart, even with nothing on except a towel wrapped around your head."

"I could go the way I am!"

"I'll go alone. By the way, I'll be staying at Tarpon Lodge."

"Tarpon Lodge!" she exclaimed. "Why not in Ft. Myers?"

"Since I have to stay over Wednesday night, I thought I might deviate a few miles and stay on Pine Island. I can drive to Ft. Myers in about an hour Thursday morning."

"And you're also having dinner at Tarpon Lodge?"

"Of course. I have to eat. You often remind me about that as my nutritionist. I remember what I had the last time; I'll have it again. Blue crab and roasted corn chowder, Pine Island clams, and shrimp pasta. And I hope they have flan for dessert."

"That is unfair!"

"Then come with me."

"You betcha! You've bribed me once again."

We survived the drive to Pine Island the following day and checked in at Tarpon Lodge. I had my chowder and clams and shrimp pasta. Lucinda had crab cake sliders and crabmeat tortellini. We were doing our best to support the local shellfish industry.

The next morning we arrived at Jester's office at 9:10.

"Your appointment was at nine," said his secretary, setting down her purse and turning on her coffee maker.

"You got here with us," I reminded her. "If we'd been on time, the office door would have been locked. You unlocked it!"

"You should be punctual. Your appointment was at nine."

"Please tell Mr. Jester we're here."

"State attorney Jester just called. He's at Starbucks. He'll be here in thirty minutes."

Jester arrived forty-five minutes later, carrying a Starbucks cup and a bag with a croissant. He was wearing a green plaid suit, a blue shirt with white cuffs and collar, and a lavender and pink stripped tie. He was not color conscious; maybe he was color blind. What impressed us most were his elevator shoes, which raised him an impressive three inches. He never looked at us or said a word as he walked past his secretary's desk and into his office.

"Our appointment was at nine," I reminded his secretary. "It's exactly 9:56 now. Call Jester and tell him we are here and are prepared to see him now. And, that at 10:00 promptly, four minutes from now, we will leave. And we will not be back."

Jester opened his door at 9:59. A croissant crumb was wedged in his moustache.

"I'm Sam Jester, Chief Assistant State Attorney for the 20th Judicial Circuit. Come into my office. . . . Gertrude," he said, turning toward his secretary, "get me a coffee."

We entered quietly without saying a word. He walked around his large desk, sat down on the cushions, leaned back, and said, "This meeting is for one male named Macduff Brooks. Period. What are you doing here, lady?" he asked, turning toward Lucinda.

"I'm Lucinda Brooks."

"I don't much care," he said. "Why are you here?"

"I thought I might have something worthwhile to contribute as you question Mr. Brooks. Especially since *you've* been so unsuccessful in investigating the airboat murder of Mr. Prescott."

"That's totally incorrect,' he stammered. "We know who did it. Mr. Brooks was ordered here simply to substantiate some of our findings."

"And what findings are those," I interjected, before Lucinda caused Jester to have a stroke.

"Prescott was murdered by a couple who had a Hell's Bay flats boat and were photographed at the scene."

"You've mentioned two things," I stated. "First, who the alleged killers of Prescott were—an unidentified couple on a flats boat. A man and woman? Two men? Two women? Second, you make reference to a photograph."

"Photographed *by* whom and *of* whom?" Lucinda asked before Jester could respond to Macduff.

"Taken by a Florida Wildlife Commission officer who fortunately happened upon the scene of the murder."

"He would be Tommy Lee Cartwright?" I offered.

"How do you know that? We have released no information that identifies Cartwright."

"Undoubtedly because Cartwright's daddy could easily have you sent back to being a public defender if you did release it," Lucinda said, continuing her testy comments.

"Be careful, lady. That daddy is my uncle. Tommy Lee is my cousin."

"You may not have released Cartwright's name," Lucinda interjected. "But the newspapers have identified him, along with a younger FWC officer named Cassell. . . . May we see the photograph?"

"No, that will be used at trial."

"The newspapers have printed a photograph. I assume we're talking about the same photo."

"Maybe."

"We're getting nowhere. You said you have questions."

"Have you visited a man named Rod Swenson?" Jester asked. "He lives in Gibsonton."

"I have met him," I responded.

"Why?"

"I heard he sells airboats. I wanted to ask him about purchasing a used boat."

"Have you ever owned an airboat?"

"No."

"Ever been on one?"

"No."

"I don't believe you were there to buy an airboat. Did you talk to Swenson about Prescott's murder?"

"Briefly, Prescott's name came up because it's been the talk of the airboat community."

"Who did Swenson say did the killing?" he asked.

"He didn't. Unlike you, he didn't presume to know," Lucinda added.

"Do you know that Swenson arranged for Prescott's murder?" asked Jester.

"Have you arrested him?"

"Not yet. He worked with two others."

"Do you know who they are?"

"Of course. The couple on the boat."

"Do you have the names of the two?"

"No. That's why you're here."

"And what do you want from us?"

"Admission that you were the two on the flats boat and an admission you were part of a plot to kill Prescott."

"You're kidding! Are you playing games, Jester?"

"You're a murderer, Brooks," he said, losing his temper and standing. I *know* you did it. You might as well admit it."

"Did Swenson give you our names?" I asked.

"No. He won't talk."

"So where you are today is that you *think* Swenson arranged the killing, but you have no proof. You *think* a couple carried out the killing, but you have no proof, and you *think* Lucinda and I were the couple on the boat, but you have no proof. Am I right?"

"I *know* you two were the two on the boat. Do you deny it?"

"We *were* on a flats boat that day."

"Where?"

"Pine Island Sound."

Lucinda was staring at me in disbelief.

"Near Black Key?"

"Yes."

"Did you see an airboat?"

"Yes, two."

"Did one have a body in the propeller cage?"

"Body parts."

"So you're guilty!"

"Of being in the vicinity after the fact, yes. We also called Channel 16 and reported what we were looking at. Cassell and Cartwright showed up shortly after our call—wearing FWC hats on an airboat with FWC markings."

"So you admit to *being* at the scene of a crime?"

"I admit only what I have just stated. Observing a mutilated body on an airboat, one would assume a crime had been committed. Meaning, yes, we were at the scene of a crime, *after* it was committed."

"You didn't report this to the police?"

"The FWC has police powers so, yes, we reported it to the police. Cartwright had taken charge, and he had backup. He told us to leave. We did as he ordered."

"Do you expect me to believe this?" he said, turning to Lucinda.

"We don't much care," she responded, worrying me that she might hit him. "Your belief and what happened are poles apart. You have turned this into your own fantasy," she added. "Don't you have better things to do? Like giving out parking tickets."

I had rarely seen Lucinda so offended by another's speculations. She is more effective than having Swenson's pit bull.

"Mr. Jester," I stated, "we've answered your questions. If you have further interest in us, we will be accompanied by Attorney Ted Thomas from here in Ft. Myers. I understand you know him."

"I have no comment. . . . You're free to go," he mumbled.

"May I make a suggestion about the case?"

"I doubt you have anything to add, but go ahead," he said.

"Swenson owned an airboat company. Correct?"

"Yes, but he had a partner."

"Did they get along?"

"I wouldn't know."

"They did not," I offered. "Do you know the name of his partner?"

"It was *Prescott*."

"Was?"

"He was killed on the airboat."

"Do you know Prescott's full name?"

"What are you trying to do?" Jester asked.

"Swenson's partner's full name was Martin R. Prescott," I explained.

"I think that may be right," he conceded, not knowing what that meant.

"And you believe that Swenson killed or ordered the killing of Prescott?"

"I've already told you that."

"What would you say if I told you Martin R. Prescott is alive."

"That's outrageous! And it's ridiculous. His mutilated body was found on the airboat."

"I agree that the dead body of Prescott was found on the airboat."

"Then why are you so confused," he asked.

"Do you have the medical examiner's report?"

"Of course."

"Who does it say was killed?"

Jester pulled out the report and looked at the first page.

"This is the report for Prescott," he said.

"What is Prescott's full name?"

"*M. Raymond Prescott.* It says so right here. So, you're wrong."

"But you agreed that Swenson's partner's name was Martin R. Prescott?"

"What's the difference? M. Raymond Prescott or Martin R. Prescott?"

"The difference is that the former was a CPA working here in Ft. Myers. If you don't agree, check."

"So what?"

"The latter, Martin R. Prescott, was Swenson's much hated partner. He was not educated and certainly not a CPA."

"Are you saying there were two different Prescotts?"

"Voila! You finally understand," Lucinda exclaimed. "We're making some way."

Jester scowled at her. "I know Swenson wanted his partner named Prescott dead. So who wanted the CPA named Prescott dead?" he asked.

"I have a theory," I said.

"Which is?"

"Swenson hired a man in Gibsonton to kill his partner, Martin R. Prescott. But the hired person mistakenly killed a *different* Prescott," I contended, watching Jester's contorted expression.

"But Swenson would learn as soon as he next saw his partner, who he thought was dead, that he hadn't been killed on the airboat." he said, sitting back smugly.

"I agree. But if Prescott learned that a man with his name was killed on an airboat, don't you think that Prescott might flee?"

"Where is he?" Jester asked.

"I don't know. I'm not a detective. That's your job. You can initiate a search for him. I think you will discover by talking to Swenson that he is yet unaware that his hired killer murdered the wrong Prescott."

"Swenson will flee."

"Not if you get to him first. You now have reason to hold him."

"I can't *prove* Swenson killed the CPA," Jester conceded. "I was hoping our conversation would help."

"Who would be the best person to pin the blame on Swenson?"

"The hired killer."

"Of course. Do you wish our thoughts about him?"

"I do."

"Lucinda," I nodded to her, "can do better than I can about this."

Jester turned toward Lucinda.

"When Macduff and I were in Gibsonton," she began, "while he talked to Swenson, I went into a local bar that was apparently the watering hole for former carnies. I met one, a fifty-something white male who had grown his facial hair and shaped it to look like an ape's face and added some clever makeup. Everyone called him Monkey Face. I talked with him briefly, and one thing he said has come back to me repeatedly, but at the time I thought it not relevant. We were talking about the airboat murder.

"Monkey Face said he had seen Swenson's partner Prescott in a bar in Ruskin, south of Gibsonton, the day *after* the murder. Monkey Face also said, 'I was drinking and using crack a lot at that time. I'm off it all, as of today. I didn't believe what I was seeing. I figure it was the drink and drugs. I was scared and left and came back here.'"

"That isn't enough to convict him," Jester said.

"That's your job, if you ever find him," I advised.

"At least we know where Swenson is," said Jester.

"He won't talk. He has an alibi. Maybe Monkey Face will rat on him."

"But we have *you* two."

"So you do," I said. "Do you really believe we were involved in the murder?"

"Depends on how you mean 'involved.'"

"Were we in any way *aware* of the incidents that led to Prescott's death?"

"Not to my knowledge. But you still may have been involved."

"If you came across a mutilated body on a public tennis court you were going to play on," I surmised, "called 911, and reported what you had just seen and where it was, waited until the police arrived, and, after telling them what you saw, they said you were not needed anymore, and you left, were you *involved*?"

"Yes."

"Had you committed a crime?"

"Not necessarily."

"What would it require for the police to believe you had committed a crime?"

"Motive."

"Motive to kill the person you found on the tennis court?"

"Yes."

"What motive do you believe *we* had to kill Prescott."

"You were curious. You didn't go home and forget it. You visited Swenson. Your lady looked around Gibsonton. . . . Did you ever go back to Pine Island Sound?"

"Yes, to fish at Cabbage Key. You're not talking about motives, but occurrences *after* the murder."

"Did you ask anyone at Cabbage Key about the murder?"

"An employee at Cabbage Key."

"Who?"

"Ted, the manager. I didn't get his last name."

"What did he tell you?"

"Absolutely nothing to add to what you know."

Jester was quivering, visually breaking down. After he regained some composure, he said, "I have an idea. Want to hear it?"

"Sure."

"I'll find you free of any suspicion. You'll no longer even be persons of interest."

"Sounds good."

"But . . . "

"But what?"

"You've given me some ideas. Things I would, of course, have thought of in time. I want to check out Monkey Face and find out more about Swenson. If I call you, you agree to talk to me?"

"About?"

"My thoughts on where we are in the investigation. Anything about the case."

"What about Cassell and your cousin Cartwright? Are you going to pursue them?"

"No. They didn't do it. Cartwright is working for the FWC only because of his father's influence."

"Cassell?"

"Needs a different partner. Good kid. Has a future with the FWC."

"What if I told you I think Cartwright was 'involved'?" I asked.

"How?"

"In a different manner."

"What do you mean?"

"Drugs."

"Drugs? How?"

"Do you know his background with drugs?"

"Yes, but that's in the past."

"Did you find traces of cocaine on the airboat?"

"Yes."

"Where?"

"All the lockers."

"Did you think it was connected with the murder of Prescott?"

"Yes, but we found nothing more to link the two."

"Could Cartwright and Swenson have been collaborating on dealing in drugs separate from the murder?"

"Possible."

"Are you reluctant to go forward because of Cartwright's father?"

"Possible."

"All I'm suggesting is something's still missing, and it relates to drugs."

"I'll look into it."

"You do that. Lucinda and I are through. No more talking about the murder with Swenson. Or with Ted at Cabbage Key. Or with anyone. Good luck with the case."

"One last thing. Thank Grace Justice when you see her. You owe her big time," he concluded.

"For?"

"Talking to me about you two. She likes you both. She used some strong words to convince me to back off."

"What had you planned?" I asked.

"I have warrants for your arrest—both of you."

"Charges?" Lucinda asked.

"Obstructing justice."

"The warrants?" I inquired.

"Tossed out after I talked to Grace."

"You might change your mind." Lucinda observed.

"*Not* possible."

"Why not?" she asked

"I guess I need to be on good terms with you in the event you hear anything or have something to suggest. But even more, I want to stay on good terms with Grace. Someday she's going to be *the* State Attorney for Florida. That means she'll be my boss."

As we left Jester's office, Lucinda looked at me and said, "He knew we weren't involved. I don't believe he had arrest warrants. He wanted our agreement to be on his side if he has questions. We were called here for one reason: to do his job for him."

"You were tough on him."

"I can be that way. On you, too, if needed."

"Ouch! Do you believe what he said about Grace?"

"Yes."

"Did we waste our time coming," I asked.

"Not one bit. We're out of it. We zip our lips about the Prescott murder and unzip them only if Jester asks us for help. We can discuss it ourselves, but there are better things to talk about, such as tomorrow. And the day after tomorrow. And the day after that."

We felt relieved but exhausted leaving the building and getting into our SUV for the tedious drive home on the bill-board boulevard, more commonly known as I-75.

"I have an idea," suggested Lucinda as we drove out of the parking garage. "You know it's my birthday tomorrow."

"Oh! Let's stop at a drugstore and I'll buy you a gift."

"A gift? How sweet."

"I was thinking of a card. If they're on sale." I knew a blow was coming.

"Could we stop and have lunch in Gibsonton? And, with zipped lips, try to overhear any talk about where Monkey Face might have gone?" I suggested.

"Bad idea. Jester might be there this afternoon," she said. "We don't want to run into him anywhere near Swenson or Monkey Face. One more mention of any of those names and you owe me."

"You're right; it's a bad idea. It's because you're getting wiser. That comes with each new birthday. We'll see the difference tomorrow."

"I'll ignore that. But I've always been wiser."

"A Ph.D. trumps a JD?"

"In our case, of course. Do you have any better ideas?"

"Always. Right now we drive to Captiva for lunch at Doc Ford's Rum Bar & Grill."

"Who's Doc Ford?" she asked.

"A fictional character thought up by a former guide turned writer. Name's Randy Wayne Wright. Doc Ford gets into more trouble than we do."

"Is Wright good looking?" she wondered, grinning.

"Compared to who—Monkey Face?"

"We agreed not to talk about him," she concluded. "You owe me. I think I'd like to meet Wright."

The traffic to Sanibel from the mainland was unusually light. Crossing the bridge Lucinda turned toward me, placed her hand on my arm, and commented, "We're going to have a late start for home. Do you mind the night driving? You said you have cataracts you've done nothing about."

"I won't have to drive at night if we stay over," I responded.

"Are you asking me to sleep over with you?"

"You bet!"

"But I didn't bring my toothbrush or pajamas," she smirked.

"I'll stake you to a new toothbrush. I won't do the same about the pajamas."

"What'll I wear?"

"It's your birthday. Wear your birthday suit."

By the time we reached Doc Ford's at the entrance to South Seas Plantation on Captiva, I had called the plantation and reserved a room.

The luncheon crowd at Doc Ford's was clearing out and we chose a table in a quiet corner. Our waiter was mid-forties, clean shaven, large ears, and full lips. He appeared shy when he asked for our choice.

"A bowl of your clam chowder," ordered Lucinda.

"That will be fine for me as well," I added.

"Are you OK?" I asked when the waiter left. "You look as though you've seen a ghost."

"I need to make a phone call. Right now."

"Whatever for?"

"You'll hear."

She dialed and listened.

"This is State Attorney Jester."

I grimaced, dropped my napkin, and drew a finger across my throat, whispering, "Why are you calling him?"

She held up her hand with the palm facing me, then covered her cell phone, and quietly said to me, "Please! Listen."

"Jester, this is Lucinda Brooks. Macduff and I are sitting at a table at Doc Ford's in Captiva. Our waiter is Monkey Face. We just ordered and should keep him busy for an hour."

"We'll be there in forty minutes."

They arrived in thirty-five. To the astonishment of the diners, Jester arrested a shocked and resisting Monkey Face, put him in handcuffs, and led him away. Within five minutes the diners had returned to their meals. Some, including us, had a new waiter.

40

MID-OCTOBER GAINESVILLE FOOTBALL FROLICS

VANDERBILT'S FOOTBALL TEAM CAME TO Gainesville in mid-October for their annual afternoon of embarrassment. If scorekeepers factored in football players' GPAs, Vandy would be perennial SEC champions. The NCAA would not appreciate that idea. Only when money speaks does the association listen. Would Harvard abandon the Ivy League and join the SEC if the college could share in the SEC's revenue?

Luisa Solares had invited Thomas Davis, Jr., to both the game and a post-game party at a friend's fraternity. He arrived late Friday night and slept on the floor of a high school classmate's condo. A pre-game party around the pool kept him awake until 2:00 a.m. At 9:00 a.m. his friend shook him and handed him a bran muffin and a plastic cup of Bud Lite.

Because he was to sit in the UF students section, he left his Vandy labeled shirt in his bag, wearing instead a black knit shirt and golden-hued khaki pants that closely resembled the Vandy colors. He would *not* give up his ragged hat emblazoned with a "V."

Luisa, Thomas, his friend, and his friend's date planned to meet at the Swamp restaurant before heading to the Swamp playing field. UF fans took their gators and swamps seriously.

The four arrived for lunch at about the same time and were lucky to find an empty table. Thomas's friend Mitch was top-to-toe in orange and blue, wearing a blue baseball cap with an orange "F," an orange tank-top with blue "Gators" on the front, alligator embellished orange and blue shorts, and blue flip-flops. His deeply sun-bronzed date, Tessa, had an orange visor with a blue "F," a scooped blue sleeveless blouse that showed off the top half of her breasts, orange short-shorts that showed off the bottom half of her butt, and blue sandals with little gators on the strap. Luisa, absent of any tan, wore a silk dress that showed nothing—a habit bred among the wealthy in Guatemala that would permit no deviations.

The four made it easy for the frenzied waitress by all ordering the Hawaiian pork quesadillas, which surprised Luisa because she didn't know quesadillas had made the leap from Mexico to Hawaii.

All four also chose the same drink—Swamp Juice, a mix of coconut, pineapple and lemon juice, banana liqueur, and raspberry rum. Luisa had never tasted a drink so exotic. She sipped hers slowly and didn't join the others for a second round. But when Thomas was nearly through with his second, she said, "Thomas, if you'll order another, I'll share it with you." She poured half into his glass and took an occasional sip from her half, but poured most into a plant behind her chair. Thomas quickly finished his.

U.S. football was incomprehensible to Luisa. As best as Thomas was able, considering the alcohol he consumed during the game by mixing rum—snuck into the stadium in two zip-lock bags—with purchased cokes, he explained to Luisa what was happening on the field. Luisa stood on the seat along with all the students, occasionally glanced at Thomas, and hoped he would loosen his tongue that evening and talk about his father.

The game ended after three-and-a-half hours. Thomas said it was a long game because of all the passing, which Luisa didn't understand. She knew the game itself lasted only sixty minutes. But much of the time the clock was running and the players stood around in a circle talking. Even when they lined up facing one another, they didn't move much before the ball was lifted from the field. No wonder so many players were obese, she thought. If they ran a little more, they might be in better shape. Strangely, the game ended with all the players standing around while the last half-minute or more clicked away until the clock reached zero.

The best part for Luisa was the half-time show. If she went to another game, she would try to arrive shortly before the half and leave the stadium as the band left the field. One thing she quickly understood about U.S. football came from watching the form of "football" played in Guatemala, called *futbol,* where a player would lay on the ground writhing in pain faking an injury, only to hop up after a few minutes and continue playing as though nothing had happened. The Gators had perfected faking injuries as efficiently as executing their plays.

After the game Thomas suggested they go back to the Swamp restaurant for a few drinks, but Luisa successfully pleaded to let her buy some food at Publix and have a picnic by Lake Alice on the edge of the campus. They agreed and were the only people picnicking. Thomas told Luisa most of the other fans were still in the parking lots or bars drinking. She knew she had to keep Thomas from sobering up; the picnic supplies she bought included more than enough beer to achieve her goal.

When the four arrived at the fraternity at 7:00 p.m., Luisa wondered how so many people already showing the effects of alcohol had room for another drop. But there was much more than drops flowing freely at the fraternity. Mitch and Tessa disappeared soon after they arrived, making it a good time for Luisa to talk to Thomas.

"Thomas, you haven't told me much about you, other than you live in my country, Guatemala. Is one of your parents Guatemalan?"

"No. My father worked for the U.S. government and sherved a few years in Guatemala," Davis said, speaking deliberately but slurring some words from the effects of the alcohol. "It ish not unusual for people who work at a federal agency and are shigned abroad to like a country and deshide to retire there. Thash what he did; only he chose Antigua over Guatemala City."

"Antigua is beautiful. . . . Do your parents worry about the violence in my country?"

"Yesh, but they lived in other places more dangerous. . . . Luisha, my mother ish invalided. She had a dishabling stroke soon after they moved to Antigua. Now she ish confined to her bed and hash round-the-clock care."

"It must be hard on your father?"

"Yesh. And he also ish not in good health," he answered and added nothing more.

"My uncle," said Luisa, "President Juan Pablo Herzog, told me about his love for America. Did you know he went to graduate school here?"

"I di … didn't," Davis replied truthfully.

"And he became very good friends with a professor named Hunt at the law school. Hunt had lost his wife in an accident and was very lonely."

"Thash a shame," muttered Davis, swallowing a half cup of daiquiri. Luisa didn't think he would last long and she needed to be more aggressive with her questions.

"They were such good friends that my uncle decided to donate money for a chair in Professor Hunt's name. All he asked for in return was *assurance* that Hunt had died as reported. He didn't want to establish a chair to honor a deceased professor and then learn that he actually had survived."

"Thash a good idea," Thomas said after taking another sip.

"Hunt had been visiting in Guatemala and was beaten by thugs and flown back to Washington. It was reported that he died of a stroke in D.C., but my uncle had heard that wasn't true, and before he gave the money—which was several million dollars—he wanted a thorough investigation and written report about the alleged death."

"Thash OK. Thash fair," Thomas muttered, spilling his drink on Luisa's dress.

"Has your dad ever talked about meeting a Professor Hunt?"

"Yesh. Dad wash with the CIA. Your uncle knows that. Dad sometimes shat in on a meeting when a CIA person got hisself compromised, and the CIA people talked about giving the pershon a new name and making him live shomewhere else."

"Was there such a meeting about Professor Hunt?" Luisa asked excitedly.

"I sink sho," he muttered, looking as though he was about to pass out.

"It must be exciting to help someone in such a case. Where did Professor Hunt decide to live, and what was his new name?" Luisa asked, realizing she was being overly direct.

"I guess sho," he said, not sure of what she had asked.

"I wonder why a law professor would choose to do all that—have a new name and move—in such a case. What would you do?"

"D… D… Dunno," he stuttered.

"What would your dad. . . . Thomas, are you OK?"

"I doan feel so good."

"I'll find a couch you can lie down on."

The fraternity was crowded with members and their guests, but they found a place for Thomas to stretch out.

"Thomas," Luisa said, shaking him, "we were talking about your dad and Professor Hunt. Are you awake?"

"Yesh."

"What did Hunt decided to do for work?"

"Fish, I tink. Fish," Thomas said, and passed out.

"Holy Mary, Mother of God," whispered Luisa. "So close! *So* close! But I *know* what Hunt does. Something about fishing."

Luisa called Thomas' friend who, with the help of some fraternity brothers, carried him off to bed. Luisa went home.

Thomas woke the next morning with a horrendous headache. He remembered talking to Luisa and that she was interested in something about a professor. He didn't recall what he had said. From conversations with his father, he knew he occasionally worked with the CIA's protection program. One time his father had mentioned a person being placed in the program who was a prominent law professor from somewhere in the South. When asked what he wanted to do with a new identity, the professor simply had said, "I'll fish." Thomas didn't know any more, but he liked Luisa and would help her if she asked.

That noon, an hour before he flew back to Nashville, he called Luisa and apologized for his behavior.

"That's all right, Thomas. I had a good time. If you get here again—call me." She disliked his drinking and hoped she would not have to date him again.

"I'd like that," Thomas responded. "What were we talking about when I crashed?"

"I asked about a Professor Hunt from here a dozen years ago. He nearly died in Guatemala from a beating. He was rushed back to the U.S. The CIA decided his life was still in danger and placed him in a protection program. Do you remember?"

"Yea, but I was a little dizzy."

"You passed out just as you were mentioning that Hunt decided to become involved in fishing, and you mentioned the place and his new name," she lied, "but you were mumbling and I didn't hear. What were you trying to tell me?"

"I wish I could help Luisa, but I really don't know his name or where he decided to live. My father only told me that the man would fish. He didn't explain that."

"It's *so* interesting. When you talk to your dad next, would you ask him?"

"If it would help, of course. But it won't help."

"Why?"

"Dad has Alzheimer's. He can't do anything to help my invalid mother. They have in-home care, and he spends his days painting watercolor scenes of Agua, our nearest volcano. His memory mostly is gone. I saw them three weeks ago, and for the first time Dad didn't recognize me. I doubt that either he or my mother will survive long."

"Dios lo maldriga!" she exclaimed and quickly realized it was not an appropriate remark for a lady to make. "I hope you have some time left with them. I wish I could help, Thomas. Goodby."

She hung up and even though it was only mid-day poured a large glass of *Ron Zacapa Centenario Gran Reserva* from a bottle Tío Juan had given her when she left Guatemala. She would call him and relate her good news.

But not before she finished more of the rum, which she hoped would soon mean she didn't care about anything.

41

A WEEK LATER BACK AT THE COTTAGE

AFTER WE RETURNED FROM FT. MYERS, NOT A word was spoken between us about the two airboat murders. We assumed that our roles were over and that we had left the stage.

The two cases had few comparisons, except for the use of airboats to murder and dismember someone. State Attorney Jester in Ft. Myers was inept and devious. Lucinda and I were pleased to be through with him. He achieved little on his own and was always suspicious of us. The truth is we helped him solve the murder, but by nothing more than pointing out the obvious.

On the other hand, State Attorney Grace Justice was effective and transparent. We did nothing to help but listen to her. Our connection to the murder was no more than being neighbors with Gerber.

Lucinda and I were thankful for Grace's keeping the matter as far out of the hands of County Sheriff Turk Jensen as she could. She achieved a great deal, and I didn't need attorney Muirhead to help. Yet!

Another week passed, and we decided one day to have dinner sitting on the porch at Aunt Kate's on the Intracoastal Waterway north of St. Augustine, but only after feeding Wuff promptly at 5:00 p.m..

After Menorcan clam chowder, we started on grilled mahi-mahi, often the fisherman's catch special of the day, meaning whichever fish was most available. Sometime in the future, mahi-mahi will go the way of such once popular menu items as snook and pompano, now eaten at home only when caught non-commercially. Commercial fishermen are self-destructing. Without restrictions they are destined for oblivion, like chimney sweepers.

The Mahi-Mahi was followed by Key Lime pie, consumed slowly while we gazed across the waterway and counted small, private aircraft, no more than silhouettes beside the setting sun, practice taking off and landing at the airport on the far shore.

On the drive from the cottage, Lucinda had run into Publix to pick up a few groceries and the local St. Augustine *Chronicle*. We found all the "few groceries" that consumed six large bags, but no *Chronicle* and settled for *U.S.A. Today*. At our table, anticipating the chowder, I had pulled the paper out from under Lucinda's bag and after desert while waiting for the check opened to state news.

"Lucinda!" I exclaimed, loud enough to turn heads. "There's a piece about the Prescott murder in Pine Island Sound. Should I break silence and read it to you?"

"Only if *we're* mentioned. What's the headline?"

"It says: 'Year Old Ft. Myers Airboat Murder Solved.'"

"Oh, go ahead and read it," she conceded.

"We may not like what we read," I replied before addressing the article:

State Attorney Sam Jester of Ft. Myers announced at a quickly called press conference yesterday that he had solved the long festering investigation of the grisly airboat murder of a CPA named Raymond Prescott that occurred a year ago near Black Key in Pine Island Sound, a popular fishing and boating location.

Jester outlined in detail the arrest and confession of a former carnival employee who lived in Gibsonton, Florida, ten miles south of Tampa. Jester stated he had been looking for the carny, colorfully known as Monkey Face, for months, but was unable to locate him. 'I correctly had concluded that he killed Prescott and believed he had remained in the area after the murder. That also proved correct; he was working as a waiter at a restaurant on Captiva. I took two men with me, and I personally arrested Monkey Face—his proper name is Rutherford Hastings—while he was working serving lunch. I, of course, owe a great deal to my staff members who supported me as I unraveled this terrible murder.'

Hastings' arrest quickly was followed by the arrest of Rod Swenson, the owner of an airboat business. Swenson allegedly hired Hastings to kill Prescott, who was his partner in the business. The two partners had become antagonistic towards each other.

Jester said he came to the conclusion that there had to be two persons named Prescott and that Hastings, under the influence of drugs and drink, misidentified the two Prescotts and murdered the wrong one. The intended Prescott victim fled and has not been found. Jester also told how he had first thought it might have been two fishermen found at the scene who were the perpetrators, but upon further investigation he dismissed that idea. The two have not been named.

The Chief State Attorney in Tallahassee praised Jester and said he would submit a request that Jester receive the highest honor—the Sherlock Holmes Award— given to State Attorney offices' personnel.

"Don't like it!" Lucinda exclaimed when I finished reading. "The article's *perfect.*"

"Do you agree with what Jester said?" I asked.

"With not one word!" she shot back, "except that we're innocent. Does it mean what I think it means?"

"It's over," I said. "Isn't it good to have such erudite state attorney officials? Jester certainly can solve murders. He had thought of everything and was correct every time."

"Shall we celebrate?" she asked.

"Of course! I'll pay for half of our dinner."

"You're too kind, Macduff."

"Always a gentleman," I agreed.

"I really don't want ever again to talk about these two murders," she added, "but I'm still curious about one thing."

"Which is?" I asked.

"Why the FWC hired Cartwright?"

"Influence," I said.

"Meaning a politician daddy?"

"Meaning a politician daddy with money."

"Sooner or later Cartwright will be caught. . . . doing something illegal," she commented. "But not because of anything you and I do," she added.

"You're right, as usual."

We were tired and ready for bed as we reached our gate. But the gate was broken open, the lock had been cut and chain tossed aside. I sped the two hundred yards to the house to confront whoever might have broken in, if they were still there. Lucinda took her Glock from her purse. I tried to think where I had left mine.

A county sheriff's car was in the driveway, lights flashing. A spotlight was directed onto our cottage porch and bathed the front door in blinding light. Crouched behind the car, looking over the hood and up toward the door, gun in hand, was Turk Jensen. He was shouting through a megaphone in the direction of the cottage, demanding we come out with our hands where he could see them. The commotion he made kept him from hearing us arrive.

I got out of our SUV, walked up behind him and grabbed his gun, emptying the cartridges and handing it back to him. He stammered, abnormally speechless. Until he recognized me.

"Dammit! Who the hell do you sink you ar. . . . Brooks? Why you not in your house? You are under arrested, you murderer. I'm puttin' cuffs on you," he said, pulling them from his belt and dropping them onto the rain-soaked mud covering the ground.

"Are you crazy, Jensen? Pulling a *gun* on us? . . . You've been drinking. On duty! And pointing a gun?"

"I shed you under arrest for murderin' Fran Gerder," he said, words slurred and eyes red.

"Franz Gerber? He's alive, Jensen. At least he was early this afternoon when I saw him at a grocery store. He looked fine; he wasn't bloody and lying in a pile of corn flakes. And maybe you mean *Grant Borders. He* was killed on Gerber's airboat weeks ago."

"So I got 'em meshed up."

He pointed the gun at me again, forgetting I had removed the cartridges.

"Why are you pointing that gun?"

"I shed I'm arrestin' you."

"Where's the arrest warrant?"

"Don't need a damned warrant. Judge Bones ish my buddy. He gonna give me one later."

"Lucinda?" I turned around. She was pointing her cell phone at Jensen.

"I've got it all on my cell phone, Macduff. It should make the best of U-Tube for this week. Jensen's not very photogenic."

"Gimme that phone," he demanded stepping toward Lucinda and falling, covering the front of his uniform with mud.

"Get up, you disgrace," I demanded. He did so, slowly.

"I want that phone," he said, again raising his gun.

"You can have the phone. I've sent my video to Grace Justice," Lucinda said. "You want to call her and explain all this?"

"Jensen," I said, "I suspect this is your last day in office." I grabbed his handcuffs from the ground and cuffed him to the door handle of his police vehicle. Then called Grace.

"Macduff! Am I seeing what I think I'm seeing?" she said.

"You are."

"I'll come and get him and take it from there," Grace said. "Jensen's through when this hits the media."

"It's in your hands as far as we're concerned," I said, turning to Lucinda who was nodding. "We're tired and going to bed."

"When he sobers up, he'll be one angry man," Grace warned. He'll head straight to his supporters, try to get this video suppressed, and deny what happened."

"Can he do that?" Lucinda asked.

"He could before just a minute ago when I forwarded the video to the *Chronicle* and to my boss," Grace answered. "The state will step in and take over, probably have an interim sheriff appointed. It may be quieted down in exchange for his resignation from the force. The county sheriff's office will be all the better. For the most part it's a good group of officers who I suspect will applaud Jensen's departure."

I reached inside Jensen's vehicle and turned off the flashing lights and spot light, then followed Lucinda up the stairs to the cottage. We went inside and turned off the outside lights, leaving Jensen slumped by the side of his car, sitting on the ground in the dark.

He was in no condition to drive, but he was gone when we looked the next morning.

42

THE NEXT WEEK - THE BAHAMAS

"DO YOU THINK WE OUGHT TO CALL GRACE and see if she's read the Ft. Myers article about how Jester single-handedly solved the Prescott case?" I turned my head and asked Lucinda as we were heading to the St. Augustine Jeep dealer. I had misplaced one of the two ignition keys, and Lucinda was sure I'd do the same with the remaining one. I also needed a new lock for the gate.

"Yes, we should call her," Lucinda replied, setting down her water bottle and dialing.

"State attorney's office," a voice said.

"Grace Justice, please."

"She's on her way back today from the Bahamas. Leave your number, and I'll have her call."

Five hours later Grace called. I answered and flipped on the speaker phone.

"Don't ask me about Jensen. The video you forwarded to me has gone viral on U-Tube. Jensen's finished. On to better things. Are you two still married?" she asked.

"Are we?" I asked, turning to Lucinda.

"Some of us have to suffer, Grace. While you bask in the Bahama sun, I have to put up with Macduff."

"I wasn't basking in the sun. I was investigating. Grant Borders was killed either in the Bahamas or in international waters, while making the Gulf Stream crossing to Florida from Grand Bahama. Maybe he took his last breath after he reached Florida, but he almost certainly was not killed in the United States. . . . If someone is shot at the airport in Mexico City and makes it to Tampa where he dies, where was he killed?"

"Did you find out *who* killed Borders?" I asked, ignoring her theoretical questions.

"When I went three days ago, I didn't know where he was killed, who did it, who ordered it, or much of anything else. Much of the trip was a waste of time, except I did learn about who runs Abaco, and I want to go back and fish."

"Who runs Abaco and why does it matter?"

"From what I learned reading some reports we have in the office, including the CIA Country Report on the Bahamas, Abaco is in the pockets of a Reginald Covington the third. Don't forget to add the III after his name, or he won't listen or talk to you. His grandfather was Reginald and his father Reginald *Junior*. The grandfather was the most prominent black in the Governor General's rule. When the Bahamas became independent in 1973, the grandfather was part of the new country's government under his friend Lynden O. Pindling.

"The Bahamas developed rapidly due to tourism and foreign investment. Apparently, Reginald Covington was an honest man and neither corrupt nor involved with the drug trade.

"But within a decade after Pindling and Covington left office, the country began to become involved heavily with the drug trade flowing through the Caribbean on the way to U.S. consumers. Drugs invariably mean *corruption*. Covington Junior was a developer who profited enormously from the tourist expansion. But, allegedly he became involved selling drugs. The current Covington either isn't involved in the drug trade or he has hidden it cleverly. He doesn't need the money—he inherited the huge fortune his grandfather and father accumulated."

"Grace," I interrupted, "it sounds interesting but not unusual in developing countries. Did you gain your impressions from actually meeting with him?"

"Don't be so impatient. I met him. It was not pleasant."

"Was he abusive?"

"To the contrary. He was the consummate gentleman. At least until he suggested I stay over with him on his yacht. I learned later that he's been married four times and is currently on the prowl between number four and whoever will become number five."

"Did he see you filling that role?"

"*Macduff!* I met him *once* and turned down his invitation."

"So you came away with nothing, not even a marriage proposal?"

"No proposal, and maybe nothing specific about Grant Borders. But I learned we might as well drop the matter. I don't have the inclination, funds, or experience in international issues to get us involved."

"Tell us what happened."

"I had heard that before Borders went to Grand Bahama Island, where he most likely was abducted, that he had been fishing out of Hope Town on Elbow Key at Abaco."

"Was Covington a friend or business partner of Borders?"

"I'll get to that."

"Why don't you start with your meeting with Covington? What did you two talk about?"

"Patience!" Grace said. "I'll try to reconstruct every minute of the time—maybe all of one hour—I was with him."

"I flew to Nassau," she began. "Several Bahamian government officials refused to talk to me about the Borders case. They said it was pending, and they had nothing to report. . . . I didn't believe them.

"That evening, I was sitting in the British Colonial Hilton lounge overlooking the placid blue-green water when a secretary from one of the government offices I had visited that afternoon sat down next to me and said she might be able to help. She wouldn't give me her name and was clearly nervous, looking around the lobby every minute. I suggested we go to a more private spot, and we took a taxi to a small bar she recommended on the outskirts of Nassau and started drinking Goombay Smashes. By the time she was sipping her third, I knew she would tell me what she wanted to but couldn't get started.

"What she wanted to tell me was that there were rumors on the island that the disappearance and probable murder of Borders may have started in Hope Town."

"Anything more than rumors?" I asked Grace.

"Some. After talking to her, I knew I had to go to Hope Town and poke around. She gave me the name of a friend—the wife of a high ranking official in Nassau. The friend had a house in Hope Town. It sounded large, but not as large as the house next door, which she said belonged to Reginald Covington III. She didn't tell me anything specific, but she said her friend was scared of Covington, who had tried to hit on her several times, including all during the year-and-a-half duration of his fourth marriage.

"The friend warned me that Covington was outwardly charming but privately vicious and described how she once watched him out her second-floor bedroom window. Coming out of his house angry because his dog was barking, he took a piece of anchor-chain and beat the dog to death. Then he stuffed the remains in a black plastic garbage bag and set it out with the trash. She's avoided any contact with him since.

"When we were finished—I promised not to mention our conversation—I went to my room, packed a few things, and took the first morning plane to Marsh Harbour on Abaco and then boarded the ferry to Hope Town where I was greeted by a sign: 'Hopetown is a very small island that does not have a town drunk so we all just have to take turns.' I could taste the Goombay Smashes. . . . I wanted to talk to Covington and wasted no time going to his house. It was enormous. Not surprisingly, there was a gate and two guards. One burley guard told me to leave. No guns or clubs; burley was enough."

"What did the guard say?" I asked.

"If I recall correctly," Grace began, continuing her narrative, "the guard smiled and said, 'Mr. Covington the third does not see anyone without an appointment.' I smiled back. He smiled again and went on, 'However important your concern is, I can't disregard his orders regarding his privacy.'

"'I understand,'" I told him, and turned away, took one step with my head dropped in contemplative failure, and ran into a large, elegant man. He was a good six-and-a-half-feet tall.

"'May I help you?' he asked, taking my arm to keep me from falling. He was black. But perhaps not. His skin had a dark golden hue common to the tropics. He spoke with the baritone of Pavarotti and the felicity of an Oxford don.

"'I'm very sorry, but I had hoped to see Mr. Covington,' I told him.

"'Mr. Covington *the third*, madam,' he said firmly.

"'OK. The third,' I responded, a bit loudly.

"'I'm Reginald Covington the. . . . '

"'The *third,*' I interrupted, turning and taking a step toward the street.

"'Oh! Come in. I can't disappoint a pretty lady,' he said and added, 'What did you say your name was?'

"'I didn't. . . . I'm Grace. Grace Justice . . . *the first.*'

"He laughed and said, 'Come with me to the house, Grace Justice the first.'

"'Am I safe?' I asked.

"'We'll find out,' he responded. . . . Even his walk was spellbinding, like a sergeant major in the British army. . . . We entered through the front door, walked past walls lined with impressive art from floor to ceiling—like the *Doria Pamphilj* in Rome—and walked out onto a terrace that looked west beyond Anna's Cay to the emerald Sea of Abaco. As soon as we sat down, a waiter came and asked what I would like.

"'Will drinking a pina colada affect my safety?' I asked Covington.

"'It depends on the size,' he said, and, turning to the waiter, added, 'A small pina colada for the lady. There,' he added, looking back at me, 'you're safe. . . . Now, what do you do that brings you to my house?' he asked.

"'I'm an assistant state attorney in Florida, based in St. Augustine,' I told him.

"'That would be where Mr. Grant Borders used to live,' he volunteered. 'You're here because of his recent death?'

"'Yes. Did you know Borders?'

"'I've done business with him. He owned a house here and often kept his boat in our harbor,' he answered calmly.

"'Do you have any idea who might have killed him?' I inquired.

"'Why would you want to know?' he responded, grinning.

"'My job is to deal with murders,' I told him.

"'But he was not murdered in the United States,' he said. 'It appears to have occurred either in the Bahamas or in international waters. Florida would seem to lack jurisdiction.'

"'There could be charges,' I suggested. 'Such as *conspiracy* to commit murder, which occurred in the U.S.'

"'That would mean anyone from any nation could undertake an investigation anywhere else based on your conspiracy theory. . . . Have you talked to our Ministry of Justice about obtaining permission to undertake an investigation here?' he inquired, smiling.

"'I'm actually here for a few days' vacation,' I told him, returning his grin. 'Once here, my curiosity was aroused. It *was* a grisly murder and since the body, or a few of the body parts, were found in St. Augustine and I was the state attorney assigned to the matter, I thought I would ask whomever I met what they knew or who might know more.'

"'And I was one who was purported to have an interest?' he asked.

"'Yes.'

"'By whose reference?' he inquired.

"'I can't say,' I answered. 'Mostly because I don't know. I was at my hotel in Nassau, which had a large message board in the lobby welcoming a number of mentioned guests and a note about their professions. I was so listed. . . . I was having a drink when a person came to my table and said they had some comments on Borders.'

"'Was this someone male or female?' he asked.

"'If I answer, will you next ask more, perhaps about the person's characteristics?'

"'I might, but only for the same reason you mentioned you have made some inquiries—curiosity. What is it that you Americans say? Curiosity killed the cat?' He smiled again.

"'I'm not a cat,' I said.

His mood abruptly changed. Covington turned to his servant and said, 'Ms. Justice has to leave. Please escort her to the gate. And if she has no transportation, have her driven to town to her lodging.'

"'That won't be necessary. I'll walk,' I said, and left."

"That's my story!" Grace said to us. "What do you think?"

"Did you catch any bonefish?" I asked.

"Macduff!" said Lucinda sharply.

"Actually, I hoped you'd ask," said Grace. "I had one day bone fishing out of Hope Town with a guide named Bonefish Dundee. He was superb. I landed a dozen plus before my arm gave in. Throwing bonefish flies and stripping them in were exhausting. But great fun! I'll never forget it. Maybe we could all go there? . . . Think about it. Hey! I've got to go. If you have anything to add, call me. Our office has stopped further investigation about the murder unless something comes up unexpectedly. You two were never involved anyway. Get on with your lives. Let me deal with Turk Jensen."

"I won't ever forget the image of Prescott's body in Pine Island Sound," Lucinda exclaimed. "Whenever I'm with Macduff in our flats boat and pass Gerber's land where they found Borders' body parts, I know the horror will come back."

"And I won't ever forget Turk Jensen slumped against his car, sobbing," I added.

"I'll deal with Jensen," Grace again assured me.

43

A FEW DAYS LATER IN ANTIGUA

AFTER RECEIVING THE CALL FROM LUISA IN Gainesville, Juan Pablo Herzog focused his attention on Thomas Davis Senior. Thomas Junior had been too drunk at the party to tell Luisa much, but he did say—when asked about Professor Hunt's future—that his father had said Hunt intended to fish.

That could have meant he was retiring and would spend his days fishing much like others would play golf. Or it might have meant he would in some way be involved in business that involved fishing, such as working for a fishing equipment company, like Simms or Orvis. Another view might be that he would work in some public service role, such as a fish and game warden.

What was disappointing to Luisa was that Thomas had told her nothing about Professor Hunt's new name or residence and that her Tío Juan wouldn't learn that information from Thomas's father who had Alzheimer's and was under round-the-clock personal care. If that proved true, Herzog would have to consider another way to learn about Professor Hunt's name and whereabouts.

First, Herzog needed to make a personal visit to Thomas Davis's Antigua house to learn for himself how disabled the senior Davis had become.

Herzog called his private secretary, Carlota Boschmann, and instructed her to set up a meeting with the senior Davis. He was willing to go to Davis's Antigua home.

An hour later Boschmann returned his call and said she had called the Davis home and talked to a person named Rosa Morales who said she was a full-time nurse at the home. Señora Morales was willing to meet with President Herzog and suggested the following day at 9:30 a.m.

At 9:27 the next morning, a polished black Hummer pulled up to the front entrance of a two-hundred-year-old house hidden behind large entry doors and surrounded by a high, centuries-old stone wall, the top of which was covered with glass bottle fragments to deter thieves trying to climb over the wall and break into the house.

A man dressed in black and wearing wrap-around sunglasses slid down from the Hummer's high front passenger seat and, after looking around carefully, walked the few steps to the immense, old, grandly carved wooden front doors, and rang a bell that quickly brought a servant who opened the small barred window in the door and inquired whether President Herzog was in the car.

Herzog lowered his rear window a few inches and, overhearing the servant, quickly got out of the car, hustled the few steps, and entered the opening door.

"Please come with me," said the servant, who introduced herself as the housekeeper, Señora Anna Toledo. She led President Herzog into the vaulted ceiling living room. Sitting in a chair by a window that looked out on gardens and a bubbling fountain capped by a carved stone pineapple was a man Herzog knew from Guatemala's foreign residents' records to be sixty-seven, but who was thin and gaunt and appeared to be in his late seventies.

Herzog pulled a desk chair around in front of the man to face him no more than four feet away.

"Mr. Davis, I am President Herzog. I have something to discuss with you that is a matter of national security," Herzog lied.

The man showed a broad smile and with misty eyes stared intensely at Herzog, but said nothing.

"A decade ago you worked on a case that involved a man named Professor Maxwell Hunt. He was being placed in a protection program because your agency thought he was in some danger. That proved not to be the case. I would like you. . . . "

"Presidente," interrupted Señora Toledo quietly, wringing her hands and nervous because she knew the terrible temper that would be unleashed at the slightest provocation, "Señor Davis has not been well, but I believe he understands you. I do hope you will speak slowly and clearly so he does understand."

"As I was beginning to say, Mr. Davis," said Herzog, ignoring Toledo, "I want you to tell me about Professor Hunt."

"Ye, Ye, Yes," Davis replied, slouching in his chair but never abandoning his smile."

"Can you tell me what name you gave Professor Hunt and where he intended to live?" asked Herzog, wanting to quickly get the answers he needed and return to Guatemala City.

"Max . . . Max . . . Maxwell!" Davis replied with visible emotional satisfaction and turned his head away and again stared out the window.

"*No!* I know Hunt's name was Maxwell. Tell me his *new* name," said Herzog, raising his voice, drawing a grimace from Señora Toledo, and attracting to the room a person who stood in the doorway and glared at Herzog.

"Please, keep your voice down. Señora Davis is dozing in the next room," demanded the woman. . . . "I am Rosa Morales, the Davis's nurse."

"And *I* am the President of Guatemala," said Herzog, staring angrily at Morales. "Señor Davis was about to tell me something I *must* know about. Do *not* interrupt!"

At that Davis rose from his chair and excitedly waived his arms at Herzog.

"Go, Go, Go!" Davis blurted, water from the glass he was trying to drink dribbling down his front.

"What is wrong with this man?" Herzog shouted at Morales. "Is he playing games with me?"

"He's not well, Presidente Herzog," said Señora Toledo.

"He doesn't appear to have fully lost his memory," said Herzog.

"You apparently don't know that Señor Davis has advanced Alzheimer's," said Morales, without the slightest hint of fright by Herzog's conduct. "You must leave. You have excited him. He understands a few words but is unable to respond with more than a stutter."

"When will he be able to tell me what I must know?" Herzog demanded.

"I don't believe he ever will be able to tell you anything; he is under significant medication."

"What if you stopped his medication?"

"Without the medication he would suffer and die. You will have to learn what you wish to know from some other source."

"Does he have lucid periods when he could tell me what I want to know?"

"No." she said, lying because she did not like the president's arrogance. "*Please* leave."

Herzog rarely accepted any challenge to his intentions and needs. But this time he was so frustrated and set back by Morales's defense of Davis that he rose, quickly walked to the door, and returned to his vehicle where his secretary, Carlota Boschmann, was waiting. He vented his exasperation on her, but finally quieted, looked at her, and gave her instructions.

"Boschmann, first thing tomorrow morning start investigating who other than Davis and a second person named Alan Whitman were at the meeting of the CIA in D.C. those years ago when Professor Hunt was having his name, profession, and location all changed. We know he chose a new profession, something to do with fish or fishing.

"Alan Whitman, a CIA agent, was at that meeting and, a few years later, after being forced out of the CIA, was about to tell me that information when he was killed by the CIA.

"There had to be more than two agents at the meeting. Remember the name *Dan Wilson;* my contacts tell me he was there and in charge of placing Hunt in the protection program."

"Where is this Wilson person?" Boschmann asked.

"He's still with the CIA. He travels frequently. Some of that travel may be to visit whoever Hunt has become. Put someone in Washington to tail him. I want to know everywhere he goes."

"Anything else, Señor Presidente?"

"I want to talk to Coronel Carlos Alarcon, the head of our police archives, the Archivo Histórico de la Policía Nacional. You may have heard about Alarcon; he graduated with distinction from our military academy and was sent to the U.S. Army School of the Americas at Fort Benning, Georgia.

"Alarcon also is currently the senior official of an intelligence gathering unit—the Kaibiles—which is part of my General Staff. He has worked with the U.S. CIA and presumably has American friends in D.C. The CIA helped us build our new military intelligence school in Guatemala City, next to the La Aurora Air Base. There is a plaque inside the school thanking the CIA for its help."

"I will call Coronel Alarcon as soon as we return to Guatemala City," Boschmann said, "and will instruct him to report to your office at 9:00 a.m. tomorrow."

"How could I get along without you, Carlota?"

Boschmann smiled and nodded, thinking that within a month's time she would flee Guatemala and begin living hidden in a small hilltop town in Southern Spain where she would forget Herzog. She knew that would take a long time.

Maybe never.

44

THE FOLLOWING DAY IN GUATEMALA CITY

THERE WAS NO QUESTION where Coronel Carlos Alarcon was the following morning at 9:00 a.m. With his hat tucked under his left arm, wearing his dress uniform bedecked with ribbons from illusionary campaigns, he stood rigidly in front of President Herzog.

"Coronel, you look splendid. Place your hat on the side table and come and sit at my dining table. I have ordered us breakfast."

Alarcon was nervous as he obeyed Herzog, never having seen him so cordial in dealing with a subordinate. He set his hat on the table as instructed and sat down carefully at the dining table just as a servant wheeled in a meal fit for a king, which made Alarcon grin: Everyone in the military knew Herzog thought of himself as a king.

Both began their breakfast without conversation. Alarcon watched Herzog carefully and thought that the president seemed disturbed by something.

"You lead the Kaibiles, Coronel Alarcon," noted Herzog, setting his empty coffee cup on the table, leaning back in his chair, and looking as though he were talking to the person who would finally provide the information Herzog sought, at whatever cost in lives—American or Guatemalan—that price might be.

"You did a remarkably efficient job when you headed our counter-insurgency unit and quieted the indigenous Indio terrorists in the highlands. Regrettably, it created tens of thousands of widows and 150,000 orphans."

"A time of loyal service to my nation, Señor Presidente. And besides, there are thousands more in the mountains when we need them for labor."

"Coronel, do you have good connections with the U.S. CIA mission here in Guatemala?" Herzog asked.

"Very good, Excellency, and also with many at the Agency headquarters in Langley."

"I have only one request: Bring me the name and location of a man who spied for the CIA against our country some dozen years ago."

"I don't understand," Alarcon said. "A name should be easy to obtain."

"You are right, but it has proven not to be so easy. I have been trying to find that information for over a decade. It is the most painful failure of my life."

Over the next hour Herzog laid out his history as a student, friend, and later adversary of Professor Hunt. As the minutes passed, increasingly Herzog perspired, even though he turned the air conditioner down twice. First a touch of moisture had appeared on his forehead, and soon his sharply starched and pressed shirt showed sweat stains until they embarrassed him.

"Any questions, Coronel?"

"Yes. You have tried to get information from two CIA agents who were at the meeting where Hunt was present and his future was discussed—that information is what name he would take, where he would live, and what he would do.

"The first person at that meeting you learned about was Alan Whitman, who was shot and killed by a sniper before he said anything other than confirming that Hunt had survived the beating you gave him. The other person is Davis, who you have told me is likely to be of little use because of his Alzheimer's.

"How many others were at that meeting?" Alarcon asked.

"I have no idea, but that is important. I'm certain that a man named Dan Wilson was present. He is a CIA agent and apparently the man responsible for Hunt's protection. . . . We should further assume that there were others at the meeting."

"Why not go after Wilson?" Alarcon asked, "Abduct him and bring him here. My men know how to make him talk."

"We may do that. I would prefer to find someone from that meeting who doesn't have to be tortured. Someone I can pay generously. With government funds, of course."

"Use the aid money the U.S. government sends us," Alarcon suggested, laughing guardedly. "There is no effective accountability for how we spend that. . . . Do you have *any* knowledge about other agents present at that meeting?"

"None. Apparently it is one procedure that is closely protected."

"I will find out the names, Presidente."

"How?"

"It's better we do not talk about that. But I will do it. Do you wish all the names?"

"Of course. But we can proceed with any one."

Alarcon was making notes and smiling. He had not had an assignment as encouraging as this for several years. He could put himself in line for the presidency when Herzog finished his term. Of course, he didn't know that Herzog intended to be president-for-life.

"I apologize, Coronel, for my emotions. It is like this whenever I talk or think about Hunt. . . . No greater service can you provide me than by bringing me the *new* name of Professor Hunt. And where he lives. And what he does. Then I will settle with him—finally."

"I will start today, Excellency. I have no reason to doubt that I will find what you wish."

"Do not fail me, Coronel. Your career is at stake," Herzog declared.

Herzog thought a more accurate way to state that would have been "Your life is at stake."

45

THE SAME DAY IN ANTIGUA AT THE DAVIS HOME

SOON AFTER HERZOG HAD LEFT DAVIS'S HOUSE the prior day, his secretary, Carlota Boschmann, had decided she must do something to help Señor Davis avoid another unhealthy meeting with the President. She had learned much about President Herzog in the short time she had been his private secretary, and there wasn't anything she liked.

During a night unable to sleep, she rose from her bed, walked onto her terrace, and looked out at the country she loved, the volcanoes outlined dramatically by a full moon, then returned to her bed for another hour of struggling with sleep. She decided that in the morning she would call the CIA offices in Langley and try to find someone who might help her, hopefully the man Herzog had mentioned—Dan Wilson.

At 4:00 a.m. Boschmann gave up trying to sleep, rose, showered, dressed, and went to the kitchen. After trying to eat, she waited until it was 9:00 a.m. in Washington. With some effort she called D.C. She was transferred from one office to another a half-dozen times before she was connected with Wilson.

She told him who she was and that she was at the Davis's house the previous day. She expressed her decision that she couldn't remain Herzog's private secretary because of the way Herzog tried to obtain information from the senior Davis. Also, she mentioned the earlier comment by Thomas Davis Junior to Luisa, made in Gainesville, that Hunt was now involved with *fish*. She thought that Herzog was closing in on Hunt, and before she fled her country for Spain, she wanted to do whatever she could to deny him success.

"What more did the senior Davis tell Herzog?" Dan Wilson asked Boschmann, delighted she had unexpectedly called.

"He began by stuttering Hunt's first name: Maxwell."

At least he didn't stutter "Macduff," Wilson thought.

"Did Herzog say what he wanted Davis to tell him?"

"Yes, what Hunt was now called, where he lived, and what he did."

"And you're certain Davis said nothing?"

"Yes. It was his son who had told Luisa that Hunt was now doing something with fish."

"Damn," exclaimed Wilson. "What were the son's exact words? That's important."

"What I recall is only that when asked what he would do he said 'fish.'"

"How is the senior Davis today? Might he be able to talk?"

"I assume he's about the same. But he has lucid moments."

"Would he be able to respond to Herzog's questions another time?"

"Marginally possible, but only if Señor Davis was having an unusual moment of comprehension and memory. Your question is best answered by Señora Rosa Morales, Davis's nurse."

"But you believe it could happen?"

"Yes, it could. Davis might be able to speak very rationally, but for a very brief time."

"Keep Davis away from Herzog, Ms. Boschmann. Can you do that?"

"Not for long, Mr. Wilson. I'm terrified of Herzog and what he would do to me if he discovered where my loyalties lie."

"I'll have an agent in Davis's house within twenty-four hours. Then you're free to leave as you planned. And thank you for calling me, Ms. Boschmann. I may call you so we can talk again."

"I admire Señor Davis and his wife," she said, her voice breaking. "I don't want them harmed."

"Anything else to tell me, Ms. Boschmann?"

"Yes, Herzog has asked me to arrange for you to be followed in D.C. and wherever else you go. . . . One other matter. Herzog's niece, Luisa, is ruthless. She has been trained for years by Herzog to do his bidding. Today that means finding out about Professor Hunt. After that, who knows what? Beware of her, Mr. Wilson."

She hung up, went to her bedroom, and began to pack for Spain.

46

THE FOLLOWING AFTERNOON

DAN WILSON CALLED ME AND SOUNDED LIKE he had a cold or laryngitis or age had taken over his voice box. But it wasn't any of that; it was dealing with Juan Pablo Herzog.

"I was with my boss, Mac. He doesn't know the details of Professor Hunt's changes—need to know and all that. He knew something was bothering me, but Macduff Brooks doesn't exist to his knowledge."

"What if you're gone? Do I not exist anymore?"

"Only until Herzog finds you! You know I destroyed all records of your meeting with the protection people. So beyond me you don't exist. But, and there's always a 'but' in this organization, I have authority over appointing someone as a local contact whenever we have a person in the protection program. You remember Paula Pajioli?"

"She was the first person killed in the wicker man and mistletoe murders," I said.

"She was replaced by Jack Ivonsky. We haven't needed his help."

"I met him once, a couple of years ago. Nice to know he's still around."

"He obviously knows you're in a protection program. But he doesn't know who you *were,* meaning he doesn't know you were once Maxwell Hunt. I assume you've never told him."

"That's right," I said. "What if something happens to you? Other than Ivonsky, no one at Langley knows about me."

"That's true. But there's one thing I've not told you about. If anything were to happen to me, my personal lawyer has an "open in the event of my death" envelope. Inside is a complete description of your conversion, but *not* your former name, Maxwell Hunt. He would know you only as Macduff Brooks. The lawyer would get in touch with you and you'd decide whether to let the Agency know about your history with us. I can assure you that the Agency will appoint someone to take over for me. That person would only know about people in the protection program if they contacted us or if we maintained files on them that named names. If you decided to go it alone and you told Ivonsky, that would end the relationship."

"In my case I'd want to keep some contact with your office," I said, not sure what that contact might be.

"Maybe not. What if Herzog died? You wouldn't need us."

"True."

"But we might need you. Remember Isfahani? We might want you to do something similar."

"Be a hired assassin? I don't think so."

"You might not like the alternatives," he said with an edge to his voice.

"We've had two narrow escapes, Mac," said Dan. "First, Alan Whitman in D.C. four years ago when he was about to tell Herzog about you, but was shot and killed, and now this incident at Davis's home two days ago. . . . I'm worried. Before I called you, I called one of our agents in Guatemala City and instructed him to stop whatever he was doing, go to Antigua, and dressed as a doctor pretend to monitor Davis's health. But mainly he will watch for any further attempts Herzog might make to get Davis to talk.

"I've talked to Herzog's private secretary," Dan commented. "Her name is Boschmann. She's terrified of Herzog, enough so that she's planning on leaving soon for an undisclosed retirement abroad. She said she will lie about Davis's health if Herzog inquires before she leaves, telling him Davis took a turn for the worse after Herzog left Davis's house, blaming it on Herzog's presence and aggressive questions. Davis is actually stable. Our agent has moved into the Davis home."

"It all sounds like Agatha Christie's *Ten Little Indians and Then There Were None,*" I murmured. "Whitman's gone. Davis is not far behind. And then there were eight!"

"You're wrong, Mac. Now there are *seven* other agents I have to evaluate; they're all the remaining ones who were present when you were placed in the protection program. . . . The only one who concerns me immediately is Herman Miller, the agent who retired to live in Florida. He's in Key West and spends much of his time deep-sea fishing around the lower keys."

"Why are you worried about Miller?" I asked.

"Some months ago I told you about him. He was a problem when he was working for us and was forced to retire. That or be fired. Something similar to Whitman earlier. He's unhappy, but he needs his pension. If Herzog gave him more than his pension, he might talk about you. We don't believe Herzog would be so generous. He wasn't willing to give Whitman what he demanded. But now he has access to national funds."

"Dan, how would Herzog know the name of Herman Miller? He learned about Alan Whitman because Whitman sought him out. And he learned about Thomas Davis from Alan Whitman.

"We were monitoring Whitman before he was shot," said Dan. "As far as we know, Whitman told Herzog about no other agent who was present at the protection program meeting."

"What do you recommend?" I asked.

"Let me think about that. I want to deal with Davis first. I have a couple of ideas I want to explore. I'll get back to you in a few days."

Wilson immediately gathered his closest staff members, agents he believed were unquestionably loyal. But years ago he had incorrectly believed in the loyalty of the members he appointed when he formed the committee to determine Hunt's future. It proved untrue with respect to Alan Whitman.

More recently Thomas Davis talked too much to his son. He told Luisa what his father had said about a protection program and a professor getting a new name, occupation, and location. Davis Junior didn't seem to know about the name or location, only that the former professor planned to deal in some way with fish. Davis Senior didn't say any more; he didn't know what he was doing at the meeting with Herzog in Antigua two days ago.

Wilson turned his attention to what Miller might do if Herzog approached him.

He shuddered at the thought.

47

A CALL FROM ELSBETH A FEW DAYS LATER

AFTER DAN CALLED, I GAVE MUCH THOUGHT to how good life would be without Herzog. He's part of a large family. I suspect none share, or even know about, his paranoia about killing me, but if any of his relatives thought I killed their Juan Pablo or María-Martina or Martín, I would have new adversaries. Luisa Solares might be one.

Assuming any threat to me from Guatemala ended, presumably I would be set free by the CIA. But not fully. The friendship I've built over the years with Dan Wilson wouldn't end, but I would be free to resume my life as Maxwell Hunt. Would I choose that route? Not a chance! I like what I've created, especially the family Lucinda and Elsbeth and I have become. Lucinda and I look forward to seeing Elsbeth through college and maybe marriage and starting her own family.

I also value my life. How many are fortunate to spend summers in Paradise Valley, Montana, and winters in St. Augustine, Florida? The only downside is the twice a year drudgery of four to five days driving across the country. I like guiding, especially my work for Project Healing Waters. But the years take a toll on the body of a fly fishing guide.

When I was in the classroom daily, I taught scores of soon-to-be lawyers now in their seventies and eighties who continue to be fully active. I don't know of more than a handful of fly fishing guides the same age who can go eight or nine miles in a drift boat six to seven days a week throughout the frantic, short summer season and in all kinds of weather, including being caught on a river half-way between the launch and takeout sites in late afternoon lightning-illuminated thunderstorms.

You don't row ashore, seek shelter under trees, and wait out a storm. You remain cowering in your seat, your fishing rod ready to attract more lightning strikes than trout. A decade ago I could face all that, but now I have accepted fewer floats and average three a week.

Wondering how Lucinda would feel about dealing with these choices, when she got back from some shopping, I made her a glass of iced tea, took her by the hand to a chair on our porch, sat her down, and asked her. The uncertainty of moist eyes affirmed she had given the choices some consideration, but not enough to discuss them with me.

"Oh, Macduff! My God! I've never given Herzog's death and our freedom any serious thought," she exclaimed. "I've assumed that he would go on forever. . . . But his death is a wonderful thing to contemplate! . . . Would I be Lucinda Brooks or Lucinda Hunt?"

"Or Lucinda Lang," I added.

"What does *that* mean? Do you plan to kill Herzog and then declare our marriage a fraud? Or to use *your* language: *ipso facto, ab initio,* whatever? I have a little of my own language: *till death us do part!*"

"If death us 'do part,' you could choose whether to be Mrs. Brooks or Mrs. Hunt. Maybe Ms. Lang. Or, if Elsbeth left and moved back to Maine and took you with her, you could become Lucinda Carson. And, of course, you could become Mrs. Elsworth-Kent again. Robert, your former husband, is in prison or looking for you. Or he's dead."

"Don't remind me of him. I am indelibly Lucinda *Brooks*. It's taken time, but it's comfortable. Like an old shoe."

"I think I've said enough. . . . Mrs. Lucinda Brooks. . . . But maybe. . . . "

The phone graciously intervened. It was Elsbeth.

"Do you *have* to keep checking on us?" I asked teasingly.

"I wondered if Herzog got to you, Dad," Elsbeth responded. "Then Lucinda and I could split your assets. . . . And I *am* going to check on you every day of your life. I need to be sure you're not abusing Lucinda. Or Wuff. . . . But that's not why I called. I had an enlightening talk with UF's interim dean, Rebecca Nadal. She called me."

"Was the discussion about Luisa Solares?"

"Mostly about Sue and me going to the UF law school. But we did get to Luisa, and Dean Nadal apologized to me for having to live in the same town with Herzog's niece. She emphasized that Luisa is here for only one year and will return to Guatemala in the spring."

"Did the dean say why she wants the two of you to apply to the law school?"

"She suggested law as a good career for women. But more provocative was her insistence that I'm now a Brooks and that I was one time about to be the daughter of Professor Hunt. She added that whatever he had done with his life, he once was honored here as a law professor."

"It's clear she knows who you are," I said, worried about what that meant.

48

AT THE CASTILLO IN ST. AUGUSTINE

ENGLISH ELIZABETHAN PRIVATEER FRANCIS Drake sacked St. Augustine twice in the 16th century. While I repaired some cottage porch railings, Lucinda and a friend went to St. Augustine for a ceremony about Drake's actions and the determination of the Spanish settlers to resist Drake and see their settlement rebuilt. The ceremony was at the Plaza de Armas inside the fort, or more properly the Castillo de San Marcos. Later prominent for housing Geronimo and his Chiricahua Apaches, the Castillo is now a National Monument.

When Lucinda returned to the cottage in mid-afternoon, she acted distant and confused. I was sitting on the porch and got up to greet her, but without looking at me she brushed by into the cottage and went directly into our bedroom where she closed the door. Fifteen minutes later, I went to the door, knocked, and called out, "Lucinda? You OK?"

Not a word came in reply. I put my ear to the door. She was crying. I opened the door a bit and saw her sitting in a chair beside our bed, staring out a window toward the marshes. She didn't turn her head or say anything, hiding her sobbing. I didn't want to disturb her, but if asked was ready to offer help.

I softly stepped over behind the chair and placed a hand on her shoulder. Her body was trembling. What troubled her may have been something she preferred to keep private. If so it was the first breakdown in our communication with each other since we married. I sat on the edge of the bed, touched her shoulder again, kissed the back of her neck, and walked quietly back to the living room, closing the door behind me. She would let me know when she was ready to talk.

Fully an hour passed before she came out, her face reddened and her eyes moist. Not a trace showed of her trademark Cheshire cat grin. She moved a small rocking chair over next to my chair, sat, and leaned on my shoulder.

The first words had to be hers.

It was another thirty minutes before she whispered, "I saw him!"

"Tell me about it."

"At the fort. I *saw* him. He was standing in the crowd a dozen people in front of me. I grabbed my friend's arm and said, 'We have to leave. *Please.*'"

"Who was it?"

"It was *him!*"

"Has someone been stalking you?"

"It's him," she said, convulsing into tears again.

"I can't help you unless you tell me who."

"Robert!"

"Ellsworth-Kent?"

"Yes," she said, burying her head against my neck.

"Are you sure?"

"Yes. I was married to him. I'd recognize him anywhere."

"We thought he'd fled the country after the wicker man and mistletoe murders out West," I said quietly.

"If he did, he's back," she sputtered, barely more than a whisper.

Years before we met, Lucinda worked in the investment business in London. She was swept off her feet by a dashing British army hero, a graduate of Sandhurst—England's version of our West Point. During the Falkland's conflict with Argentina, he was wounded and awarded the Distinguished Service Order for bravery.

He and Lucinda married two months after they met, but she quickly learned he had violent nightmares about the war and began to abuse her. They parted after two months, and she quickly received a divorce. He was soon in serious trouble and sent to prison on the Isle of Wight off the Southern coast of England.

Several years ago out of the blue, she received a letter from Ellsworth-Kent saying he was coming to America to find her and take her home to England to live with him. He disavowed the legitimacy of the divorce, learned Lucinda and I were living together, and made it clear she was going to return with him.

With a woman Ellsworth-Kent met in New Orleans, they began what became known as the "wicker man and mistletoe" murders. On different Western rivers on successive solstices and equinoxes, they kidnapped five different people I knew, placed them in a drift boat, and covered them with a wicker basket and mistletoe, an old method of sacrifice used by primitive peoples in the Orkney Islands off the northern coast of Scotland. On each basket explosives were tied, set off with a timer as the drift boat floated down one of the different rivers.

Five people I knew lost their lives, first on a summer solstice on Montana's Madison River, three months later on the autumnal equinox on Wyoming's North Platt River, another three months on the winter solstice on Clark's Fork in Montana, then next on the spring equinox near Henry's Fork in Idaho, and lastly on the summer solstice on the Yellowstone

River near our Montana cabin exactly a year after the first death. Lucinda and I finally deciphered the identities and plans of the culprits and narrowly escaped similar deaths. Ellsworth-Kent and the woman disappeared and to our knowledge have not been heard from since. They were never apprehended. Now it appears Ellsworth-Kent is back.

When Lucinda calmed and was able to speak, she looked at me through weary eyes that had seen horror.

"Did he see you?" I asked.

"I don't think so. We entered the fort late and never worked our way forward to where Robert was standing. He turned sideways, but didn't look back toward us."

"Would he have any reason to be in St. Augustine?"

"Hopefully no more than as a tourist. Many British come to St. Augustine on holiday tours."

"Does he know we live here part of the year?" I asked.

"I hope not, but he must. He learned about me and you when he tried to take me back. . . . This is not like our problem with Juan Pablo Herzog, who wants us but doesn't know who we are or where we live. Robert knows both. . . . What do we do, Mac?"

"If it were Robert you saw, why hasn't he gone directly after you rather than seeing the sights of our town?"

"I don't know. But it *was* him."

"We can contact Grace and tell her about him. He has to be on some wanted list. He did kill five people in the West."

"I hate to bring Grace into this. All five of the wicker man murders were on Western rivers, meaning there's no reason to bring them up with Grace."

"But it's serious. Robert is a dangerous *fugitive*. . . . How about calling Dan Wilson?"

"Yes, he knows all about the murders by Robert. Dan was in your hospital room in Bozeman when I first received the letter from Robert that said he was coming for me."

I called Dan immediately and apologized for doing so late on a Saturday—he was called in by his wife from their yard where he was beginning spring garden planting. After hearing Lucinda, he agreed to assign an agent to St. Augustine to work with local authorities and renew the search for Ellsworth-Kent. He would claim a CIA interest in the matter because it was an international issue involving an American and a foreigner. If Grace were brought into it by the CIA, Dan promised it would be without naming Lucinda or me.

Dan must be sick of us. In the past few weeks he's had to send one agent to Guatemala to protect me and now one here to protect Lucinda. I wonder what he's thinking about us.

It was a good time for some Montana Roughstock Whiskey and Gentleman Jack. But too exhausted to even open the bottles and pour, we crawled into bed at nine.

At 2:00 a.m. Lucinda turned to me and whispered, "I can't sleep. Sorry if I woke you."

"You didn't. I've watched the clock on the bedside table as it turned 10:00 p.m., 11:00 p.m., midnight, 1 a.m., and now 2:00.

"What are you thinking?" she asked.

"I've got to find and kill Ellsworth-Kent."

49

A FEW DAYS LATER

LUCINDA REMAINED UNSETTLED FROM HER sighting of Robert Ellsworth-Kent, her former husband of two months. We had contacted Dan Wilson later the day she saw Ellsworth-Kent, after she had regained some composure, and Dan immediately sent an agent, Meredith Jones, to St. Augustine.

Jones was not told about my background or Lucinda's disagreeable history with Ellsworth-Kent, but only that a British citizen wanted for multiple murders had been sighted at the Castillo San Marcos by someone who both could identify him and was a survivor of his one unsuccessful murder attempts five years ago. Agent Jones brought photos of Ellsworth-Kent and at various St. Augustine locations began asking if he looked familiar.

Lucinda thought she would share her frustration with Grace and called her, turning on the speaker.

"Before you tell me why you called and I forget to mention it, there's news from Ft. Myers. Have you heard it?"

"Well, Jester hasn't spoken publically, and I haven't read anything about it," I answered. I don't read the Ft. Myers papers.

"I can't wait. What's the news?" interjected Lucinda.

"Monkey Face escaped."

"How? And what about Swenson?"

"He's still in custody awaiting trial. He denies any participation. Says it was a personal feud only between Monkey Face and Prescott. Swenson's been acting strange. He may have suffered a minor stroke in jail. He's to be examined more thoroughly in the next few days."

"But Monkey Face did kill the wrong Prescott!"

"That's still murder. The Prescott he intended to kill—Swenson's partner—hasn't been seen since."

"How did Monkey Face escape?"

"He was in jail in Ft. Myers. Supposedly in maximum security. You know, when he was arrested at your lunch table at Captiva, he had hidden all his facial characteristics and removed any make-up that enhanced his appearance as an ape when he was in the circus sideshows."

"He was clever," I added, listening in. "When he waited on Lucinda and me in Captiva, he was borderline handsome, at least clean shaven and hair trimmed."

"That cleverness helped him create a new disguise."

"As a what?"

"The fat lady!"

"You're kidding."

"I'm not. You know he was a pretty trim fellow. . . . He somehow got a woman's outfit for a *very* large lady. Where he got it isn't clear. Anyway, he hid it where he was working in the jail laundry.

"Monday's the big laundry day. Near the end of his work shift, which was a few minutes before the evening meal, he climbed into a hamper that had the fat lady garb in the bottom. Changing clothes, he left his jail outfit in the hamper and put on his fat lady's disguise. No one looking in the laundry hamper would be surprised to see his jail outfit. He added padding to look fat, plus a wig he either made or had someone bring him on a visitor's day. Some eyelashes, rouge, and bright red lipstick finished his new identity."

"So he's in the bottom of the hamper," I assumed, "covered with dirty laundry, but now looking like the circus fat lady. He still had to get out of the jail complex."

"He had help. The jail had a show after the dinner, like Johnny Cash used to do in prisons. This show was presented by carny folk from Gibsonton all bedecked in their old carnival side-show outfits. One was even dressed as Monkey Face! They also had the usual sideshow couple: he seven feet tall, wearing clothes too small that made him look even taller; she a midget, wearing clothes too big. Seven carnies started the show, but eight left the jail after it was over. The eighth was our Monkey Face. Nobody counted them going out.

"One jailer remembered that one of the female carnies had to go to the bathroom during the show. Our guy was hidden in the bathroom and followed the gal on her way back to the entertainment. Word has it that Monkey Face joined in the show and acted out his fat lady role for a half-hour before all the carnies left, including Monkey Face. Obviously, he was missing at bed check."

"I suspect Jester was not pleased that the full story was sure to get out."

"He wasn't, and that's why he called me and asked me to tell you Monkey Face was on the loose."

"Why would *we* want to know?"

"Jester said Monkey Face may know that you two turned him in when he was your waiter at Captiva. What do you think?"

"Monkey Face appeared to be in shock when Jester and two police arrived, surrounded our table, and arrested him. They placed him in handcuffs and escorted him off. He never yelled at us or showed any indication that he thought we were involved."

"That's a relief."

"He had no reason to recognize us. Remember, Grace, Lucinda saw him in Gibsonton, but I never saw him before he was our waiter. But I'd seen photos of him. Even if he figured out that we might have been the reason he was caught, he doesn't know who we are. I paid the bill in cash."

"I'd hoped to hear something like that," she said.

"Does this mean we're *really* through with the Prescott murder?"

"I think so. They may not catch Monkey Face. He's good at disguises and if he's smart he's nowhere near Florida. He knows the country; he traveled with the circus for a dozen years. Some of his carney buddies he once worked with on the circuit, from somewhere like South Dakota or New Hampshire, may have taken him in and are hiding him."

"What do you suggest we do? Anything?"

"Yes. I know what you should do, Macduff. "You've put Lucinda in enough danger that you ought to worry more about her murdering you than about Monkey Face. You're not through. Do something special with Lucinda. Take her to Cancun for a week."

"Cancun sounds good. I'll take her," I said, hugging a smiling Lucinda.

"Promise?" she asked, prodding me in the side. "You're in front of two witnesses."

"That's unfair. But OK. We'll go to Cancun."

50

FOUR DAYS LATER

IT WAS GOOD TO HAVE THE PRESCOTT MURDER case over for us. Not so for Jester, who vocally placed all the blame for Monkey Face's escape on the prison system.

"When do we leave for Cancun?" Lucinda asked. We were in pajamas, sitting on our sofa, she at one end facing me and I at the other facing her, our feet entangled.

"I hate to change the subject, but I think your feet smell," I said.

"Macduff! That's Wuff. She's lying at the foot of the sofa. We haven't bathed her for … I don't know how long."

"Poor dog to be blamed. But if we bathe her and the smell hasn't gone away, you owe me an apology."

"You changed the subject. You owe *me* a trip to Cancun. I want to go to the Desire Resort & Spa."

"I was thinking about the Holiday Inn."

"Not a chance. The Holiday Inn doesn't have 'Bare as You Dare' on Monday nights.

"What am I in for?"

"You'll see. Sunday nights they put on 'Erotic Circus.'"

"I don't think I'd make it past Monday night."

"You can try. I'll help you."

Before I had a chance to ask any more about the resort another phone call from Grace saved me from further embarrassment.

"One more murder case is over," she said.

"Grant Borders?"

"Were there any others? Of course it's Borders."

"Prescott was killed by Monkey Face. Did another carny kill Borders?"

"Not unless you consider Reginald Covington III a carney, which he would take issue with."

"How do you know it was Covington? Has he been arrested? By Bahamian or U.S. authorities? Where is he n. . . ."

"Mac, Mac, settle down," she interrupted. "One question at a time. . . . I talked to Covington yesterday."

"Were you back in Hope Town in the Bahamas?"

"No. He was three feet in front of me. Right here!"

"In St. Augustine?"

"Yes, at my Camachee Cove condo. I opened the door after breakfast to take the trash out, and there he was. Elegant. Pressed pleated white trousers, a beautiful pink French-cuffed shirt with an English spread collar, and a regimental striped tie."

"A little overdressed?"

"Dressed like that is *never* overdressed!"

"How did he get to your place?"

"Not hard to find my address. I *am* a public employee. He flew from Abaco in his jet—under the radar—directly to Hastings."

"Hastings! That's cabbage country a dozen miles west of St. Augustine. Why would he fly there?"

"No customs to bother with. He has an interest in some Hastings farm land. He bragged he often left his plane in a Hastings hanger built for crop dusters."

"Why did he come?"

"To tell me *he* killed Borders."

"I don't believe you. Why would he do that?"

"Well, there was another reason. He wanted me to fly back with him and live at his Hope Town house."

"He wants to marry you?"

"He didn't suggest marriage."

"What did you tell him?"

"That I appreciated the offer. No one before ever had flown illegally into the U.S. to make me such an offer. I think he remembered my mentioning that Hope Town was one of my most favorite places on earth."

"And that you would shack up with him in order to live in Hope Town?"

"He didn't use that language, but yes."

"Did he walk away after you turned him down?"

"No. I invited him in for coffee."

"I'll bet he loved your erotic Indian miniature paintings."

"They were the first thing he noticed. He looked at each carefully."

"Weren't you worried being in your condo alone with him?"

"Not at all. He was a gentleman."

"Who had committed murder."

"Yes. But I can live with calling it 'justifiable homicide.'"

"That's incredulous, Grace. You're a state attorney. . . . He wanted you to trade living the life of luxury with him for who knows how long, for his admission of guilt?"

"Something like that."

"Tell me about Borders' death."

"Borders and Covington had some business interests in Abaco. Orange groves that produced delicious fruit and were safe from freezes. Plus cheap labor. It was going well until Borders talked Covington into selling their company to another orange grower."

"And?"

"After the sale went through, Covington learned that the undisclosed owner of the purchased business was Borders, who fraudulently had convinced Covington to sell out for a very low price. Four months later Borders sold his larger company for a huge profit. Covington lost a chance to gain several million dollars. He was not pleased."

"And he killed Borders."

"Yes," she said.

"Why using an airboat?"

"He wanted to do something gruesome. He had read about the Pine Island Sound airboat death and thought a copycat killing would link the two murders and cause confusion about who did it."

"I know Borders was kidnapped and wasn't on his boat when it exploded and sank in the Gulf Stream. Did Covington come to the U.S. to participate in Borders' death?"

"Maybe not his death, but certainly his dismemberment. He told me he wouldn't miss it. He cut off Borders' fingers."

"How did he get here?"

"He used the same airport he used to visit me!"

"And he helped strap Borders to the propeller?"

"Yes, a little looser than was Prescott, which resulted in more dismemberment to Borders."

"So Borders was killed in the U.S.?"

"No. He was dead when he was tied to the propeller. Covington botched the kidnapping in Grand Bahama. Borders died from being tied up too tightly. It broke his neck. Apparently he died on Covington's plane before they were over U.S. territory. He might have died when they were still in the Bahamas. Covington went ahead with his plan, even though it was too late to watch Borders being spun to death on the airboat propeller."

"Grace, why didn't you arrest Covington?"

"Borders died in the Bahamas or over the water out of U.S. reach. The Bahamas are calling it an accident. Any crime for prosecution in the U.S. would have been bringing a dead body—of a U.S. citizen—into the United States illegally. People frequently illegally bring things into this country from abroad, like rum or cigars from Cuba brought in by way of Nassau. Or Oriental carpets from Iran. I do homicide, Macduff. Not export or import issues."

"What about conspiracy?"

"Was there any conspiracy in the U.S.?" Grace continued. "Maybe, but we don't know and can't prove any. . . . That brings us back to Covington. . . . He surreptitiously taunted me, suggesting I arrest him. He said he would not resist. And he said I would lose my job when the Bahamian government stepped in and complained about harassing and falsely arresting one of its most prominent citizens."

"The old difference between a rock and a hard place?"

"You bet. . . . That's pretty much it, Macduff. I have the Borders file in front of me on my desk. I've just written 'closed' on the folder. Obviously, your names don't appear even once. My advice is to forget about Borders."

"We'll try to do that. Thanks, Grace."

"One more thing, Macduff. Last week I suggested you take Lucinda off on a holiday, maybe to Cancun. Do you plan to do that?"

"I've offered it to Lucinda. She is busy making plans."

"You going to Cancun?"

"We are."

"Staying at Sandals? It's for couples."

"Some other place."

"Name? Le Blanc Spa? Moon Palace? Fiesta Americana?"

"None of the above. I believe we're going to the Desire Resort."

"Take me along? I know that place. They offer big discounts to a *ménage à trois*."

"We love you, Grace, but not a chance. We'll tell you all about it," Lucinda said.

"Not quite all," she added.

51

THE NEXT MORNING

WE WERE PLEASED TO HAVE THE AIRBOAT murders off our backs. The only lingering threat was from Monkey Face, and he was more focused on eluding capture than attempting another murder. We had no reason to believe he knew about us.

"I must admit we should have offered our names to the FWC when we found the body on the airboat and called Channel 16," I said to Lucinda in our SUV, heading for breakfast in St. Augustine.

"We didn't provide our names. Maybe next time."

"You think there'll be a next time?"

"The odds favor a yes."

"Is that based on any authority?" I asked.

"I have Ph.D."

"You keep raising that."

"You bet."

"Macduff, the airboat incidents are over. But we have some remaining worries—especially Herzog!"

"Hopefully not while he's president. Guatemala needs U.S. aid. If our aid were cut off, he might be thrown out of office," I answered.

"Herzog hasn't discovered your name or where you live," she noted, "but he *has* learned you're involved with 'fish.' Is our fortress crumbling brick-by-brick?"

"The foundation's intact. I hope! We don't know what Dan may know about Herzog. He did appoint an agent to track Herzog in Guatemala and specifically at Davis's Antigua house."

"Should we call Dan? It's been two weeks since we talked to him."

"Let's," I agreed.

We caught Dan leaving his office for home on a rainy cool spring evening in D.C. He was sitting in his new Honda, trying to figure out the electronics. A voice kept giving him instructions and further confused him. He didn't know how to turn it off. He didn't want to take his hands off the wheel; as usual the traffic heading west on I-66 was gridlocked.

"There must be an accident ahead. I'm safe to talk until we move again. I'm on something called Blacktooth."

"It's Bluetooth. Remember that: Black*berry* but Blue*tooth*. What do you know about what Herzog's up to?"

"I have a daily log of his movements. He's done nothing more than go back and forth between his residence and the presidential palace."

"Thinking of a wire tap?"

"Mac, you know we wouldn't do that! I assume Herzog's people check at least weekly for bugs in his workplace and home. I get into enough trouble involving you without having it disclosed that we bugged the Guatemalan president."

"Are you saying the CIA never bugs presidents?"

"I can't talk to you about that."

"You're saying Lucinda and I don't have to be worrying. We want to leave for our week in Cancun before we head to Montana."

"I'm not saying don't worry. Herzog's been staying close to home concerned about a coup d'état if he traveled outside Guatemala. We're more concerned with the people that have been going to the palace to meet with him."

"Why?"

"They're not his advisors on historic sites or increasing coffee exports or where he's going to cut ribbons opening new buildings or ports."

"Who are these people?"

"They're from his major intelligence units. The one he's most frequently met with is a Coronel Alarcon. *Carlos Alarcon.* Remember that name? He's the head of an intelligence gathering unit that reports directly to the president. He has a long history of working with us."

"'Us' being the CIA?"

"I'm afraid so."

"Doing what?"

"Suppressing dissidents."

"Meaning killing peasants."

"If you prefer that."

"How close are Alarcon's links with your people now?"

"I don't know. Considering the way we secretly separate responsibilities here, I *can't* know."

"Have you seen Alarcon in D.C. in the past year?"

"Yes."

"When?"

"Two days ago."

"Where?"

"In our cafeteria. The same one you ate in when you were here years ago."

"How much access would he have to CIA records?"

"Of you? None because there are none here."

"Have you ever seen him talking to any of the four remaining agents who haven't retired and who worked on my case?"

"I didn't want you to ask that. The answer is yes."

"Where."

"Coming out of an office."

"Of one of the four?"

"Yes."

"One you trust."

"To be honest, after Whitman and Davis, I don't know."

52

GUATEMALA CITY – THE PRESIDENTIAL PALACE

JUAN PABLO HERZOG WAS PERPLEXED. HE WAS ecstatic about being his nation's president. Everything he dreamed of was his for the taking. He lived in a sumptuous home, the Casa Presidencial. And he worked in the regal Palacio Nacional de la Cultura, facing the Plaza Mayor in the center of Guatemala City.

Herzog's business interests, legal and illegal, had thrived, making him one of the richest men in his country, if not *the* richest. He owned a *finca* outside of Antigua where exquisite coffee was grown. Plus a penthouse on top of the tallest building in Guatemala City, although he used it little because of the residence he assumed as President. Mostly he used the penthouse for liaisons with women who didn't wish to be seen with him, such as his latest, a beautiful woman from Huehuetenango named Dolores.

Herzog recently bought a ski lodge in Aspen, Colorado, and a condo in New York to add to the properties he owns in London and Madrid. They were paid for with what he jokingly called foreign presidential aid.

What more could he want? The answer was clear: as Salome had asked for the head of John the Baptist, Herzog asked for the head of Maxwell Hunt. Salome got her wish; Herzog unsuccessfully had pursued his for a dozen years.

Juan Pablo Herzog was sitting at a grand mahogany desk in his extravagant office with the walls lined with Latin American art. He had worked hard all day, trying to find a way for Guatemala to once and for all take over Belize. If not by treaty agreement, he thought, then by force.

A decade ago the foreign ministers of Belize and Guatemala signed an agreement to allow their nations' territorial dispute to be settled by the International Court of Justice at The Hague. But planned referendums in each country, to be held within a few years after the signing, had never been held.

Guatemala was once again rattling swords over the Belize issue, as it had done for more than two centuries. There had been no recent earthquakes or hurricanes to assuage impoverished Guatemalans who dared to question why the country was not developing and why crime lords from Mexico were taking over drug trade in Guatemala, a matter of personal concern to Herzog. At least starting the war drums over the Belize dispute bought some time before some Castro-like character led peasants out of the Petén and overwhelmed the Presidential palace.

Herzog had doubts about whether the agreement to use the ICJ to settle the dispute with Belize was wise for Guatemala; several prominent international law scholars expressed a belief that the arguments presented by Belize were more consistent with international law. Herzog would not allow Guatemala to give up its claims during his presidency.

Herzog estimated but never admitted that he spent more time thinking about finding Maxwell Hunt than he did about settling the Belize dispute. In addition to the efforts of Coronel

Alarcon, he continued to expect help with the search from his niece Luisa, nearing the end of her graduate law program at the University of Florida. She was coming home from Gainesville for a long weekend, and he would see her in the morning.

Finishing breakfast the next day on a terrace that overlooked a small park filled with red blooming bougainvillea, Herzog was in good spirits. Luisa had called and said she was in her car and about to enter the private parking area of the President's elegant residence.

"My dear niece," Herzog said as a servant escorted her into his living room. "You look very well. I hope you have good news for me."

"Tío Juan, I talked to the law college dean last week and told her how disappointed you were several years ago when your generous gift was rejected. I took the liberty of suggesting to her that your offer remains outstanding."

"That's very good, Luisa. What did she say?"

"That the law school would welcome your gift."

"What about my one condition, a report on the death of Hunt? And since now we know he is alive and engaged in something to do with 'fish,' all we want to know is where he lives and his name."

"I told her very much the same, Tío Juan."

"And her answer?"

"Not encouraging. She said she would tell us as much as she knew and what the law college records disclosed. She emphasized her search was limited because of public records access laws. But she added that there were no records that covered Hunt *after* his reported death. She insisted that he died in

D.C., and the law school was informed only that he suffered a fatal stroke."

"But we know the truth is that he survived."

"She didn't agree. She said only that the State Department never announced anything further about Professor Hunt. Assuming he lived, the State Department would have that information, not the law school."

"What you have told me helps, Luisa. Our focus must be other than expecting the law school to cooperate. We must find a CIA agent who was at the meeting where Professor Hunt was given a new name and location. Alan Whitman died; Thomas Davis is close to death and cannot help us. There *must* have been others at that meeting.

"I have an excellent person on my staff who is very experienced with intelligence," he added, "and who in the past has worked with the U.S. CIA on matters of mutual interest. I believe our hope is in his hands. He has recently been in Washington at the CIA's offices.

"Go back to UF and finish the study for your degree. If I think you can help, I will contact you. Be good and be safe, my dear niece."

Luisa quickly returned to her car and left for home, wondering if she were safe from her uncle.

Colonel Alarcon was in Herzog's office within the hour.

"Coronel, I've just talked with my niece. The law college in Florida will not help. Not that they are not willing, but because any records about Professor Hunt were destroyed by the previous dean. If we don't make progress in another way, we may want to visit that Dean. His name was Hobart Perry."

"What is your 'other way,' Alarcon asked. "Am I involved?"

"You are in charge."

"How should I proceed? What is the best way to get Hunt's current name, Presidente?"

"There were about a dozen CIA agents at the meeting when Hunt had his name and location changed. Two are dead or useless. You already know a little about them.

"We learned the name of one, Alan Whitman, because he identified himself to me as someone who would sell Hunt's information. He asked too much. When we began negotiating an agreement, in an upstairs room of a tavern in Washington, he was shot and killed by someone from an adjacent building. I believe that person was Hunt, who is an excellent marksman."

"And the other? You referred to a Davis."

"Thomas Davis. We learned his name through some conversations he had with his son which he passed on to my niece Luisa. He mentioned that his father had said that Hunt had become involved with 'fish.'"

"Can't we get more from the son?"

"He apparently doesn't know any more. But we may have to rethink that."

"Do you have any names of the other CIA agents who were at that meeting?" Alarcon asked, smiling.

"That is what you will provide me, Coronel. I don't know the name of even one."

"I have begun that, Presidente. I returned only yesterday from Washington. I believe I'm close to getting a name. I do not see how finding out their names will be difficult. Once we have done so and identified who we should approach, our goal quickly will be achieved.

"I will focus immediately on getting a name. I have done a little work, mostly keeping track of Thomas Davis in Antigua and contacting Alan Whitman's family. Unfortunately he left no one closer than a few nieces and nephews. Their names are in a file in case we wish to pursue that route."

"If you succeed Coronel—you're a young man—I will support you to become president when my term is over."

Alarcon did not know that the presidency of Herzog might last until he died.

Or that Herzog had spent the previous night with his current favorite, Dolores, who happened to be Coronel Carlos Alarcon's wife.

53

TWO WEEKS LATER IN ST. AUGUSTINE

IN 1622, A SPANISH GALLEON CARRYING GOLD from Mexico to Spain, went to the bottom of the sea in a hurricane. It had been part of a twenty-eight ship fleet that carried an estimated $4,000,000 worth (in U.S. currency at the time of the sinking) of gold, silver, pearls, indigo, tobacco, and other products. The hurricane struck soon after the fleet departed Havana. The fleet was decimated and the treasure was lost, along with Spain's dominant position in the world. The hurricane approached from the west, and when it had shredded the fleet, only ten ships limped back into Havana Harbor. The others to this day rest on the bottom over a vast area.

One ship, *Nuestra Señora de la Compacíon*, did not sink off the Florida Keys but, dismasted and missing most of its crew, was carried like a ghost ship by the Gulf Stream and sank off Florida's present day St. Augustine.

Lucinda had done some photography for a wooden boat magazine about the building of a full-size replica of the *Compacíon*, to be permanently moored at the St. Augustine city marina. She and Macduff were invited to the christening ceremony.

She was likely the only person at the christening who wore part of the *Compacíon's* treasure recovered from the sunken wreck. Around her neck on a delicate silver chain hung a silver Spanish four reales coin struck from a silver bar and hammered on a coin die. The largest coins were sometimes cut in two. The real was also called a "bit," giving rise to the English slang of "two bits" for a quarter dollar.

"Do you like the silver four reales coin on my chain neckless?" Lucinda asked me. "It stands out on my black jersey."

"You can use it to buy me a cup of coffee. It's four bits, or fifty cents."

"Is that all you paid for it? A pretty cheap birthday present to give me."

"You don't want to know what it cost. A lot more than one cup of coffee."

"So the original ship used as the model for the caravel about to be christened in front of us was full of these?"

"Yes."

"Plus a lot of gold?"

"If so, the gold was never found. A gold real was worth sixteen reales of silver."

"Is my reales coin insured?"

"Yes, for more than you are."

"Macduff! That's mean."

"No. It's that you're worth so much, there's no way to set a value on you for insurance."

"Now I like it," she said, turning toward me and squeezing my elbow. . . . She began staring over my shoulder."

"Macduff, look behind you and to the left. Am I seeing who I think I am?"

"No. But he does look a little like Juan Santander. . . . He's leaving; I can't see his face."

"Whoever he is, he has a limp. Just like Juan."

"You're imagining that."

"Mac, I have to use the restroom. *Before* the christening ceremony starts. It's where that person is headed, whoever he is. . . . I'm going to follow him. I'll be right back."

She turned and quickly slipped through the crowd. I could see her, but not the person she wanted to follow. Suddenly, ten feet from the restroom building, a tall man came up behind her and grabbed her, and began to pull her away toward the parking area. He had no limp.

"Lucinda!" I cried out, turning and running through the spectators toward the restrooms. Heads turned my way as I bumped into people and left them with fading apologies. But by the time I broke through the crowd, Lucinda was gone. I circled the restrooms and headed toward the parked vehicles. Passing between two large RVs, I ran in front of an old VW van racing toward the exit. For a moment before the van knocked me aside I could see a face—the angry face of the driver. It was a face I knew too well. The face of the man who had tried to kill Lucinda and me five years ago.

The van driver was Robert Ellsworth-Kent, Lucinda's one-time British husband.

EPILOGUE

Elsbeth's Diary

At the moment Dad was hit by the vehicle near the Castillo, I was with Sue walking home from a couple of morning hours spent at the UF library. It was nearly three hours before I heard from Grace Justice in St. Augustine that Dad had been injured and taken to the St. Augustine hospital. Sue drove us the seventy miles to St. Augustine where we went directly to the hospital.

I had asked Grace where Lucinda was. Grace said she had been trying to contact Lucinda but hadn't been successful. She thought Lucinda was planning to go with Macduff to the ceremony at the Castillo, but something else must have come up. Grace's attempts to reach her by phone were unsuccessful.

Grace met us at the hospital. I wouldn't have made it through those awful times without the support and patience of Grace and Sue. Grace offered to have us stay with her at Camachee Cove so we wouldn't face the cottage with Dad overnight in the hospital for observation and Lucinda still absent. It was a kind offer, but I remained in Dad's hospital room that night.

Four days after the incident, Dad was home at the cottage. But Lucinda was not. The focus had shifted to her absence. Grace and the local police were searching for Lucinda, but it was as though Lucinda never existed. Not one bit of evidence was found near the restrooms.

The best advice I received from my dear friend and roommate, Sue, was that we both should withdraw from classes for at least the current term, to be sure Dad fully recovered and to help in the search for Lucinda.

Dad was confused and devastated over Lucinda's loss, all the more so when the letter came.

M.W. GORDON – The author of more than sixty law books that won awards and were translated into a dozen languages, he wrote one book on sovereign immunity in the U.S. and U.K. as a Scholar-in-Residence at the Bellagio Institute at Lake Como, Italy. He has also written for *Yachting Magazine* and *Yachting World* and won the Bruce Morang Award for Writing from the Friendship Sloop Society in Maine. Gordon holds a B.S. and J.D. from the University of Connecticut, an M.A. from Trinity College, a Diplôme de Droit Comparé from Strasbourg, and a Maestria en Derecho from Iberoamericana in Mexico City. He lives in St. Augustine with his author wife Buff and their sheltie Macduff.

AUTHOR'S NOTE

I enjoy hearing from readers. You may reach me at:
macbrooks.mwgordon@gmail.com
Please visit my website: www.mwgordonnovels.com
I am also on facebook at www.facebook.com

I answer email within the week received, unless I am on a book signing tour or towing *Osprey* somewhere to fish. Because of viruses, I do not download attachments received with emails. And please do not add my email address to any lists suggesting for whom I should vote, to whom I should give money, what I should buy, what I should read, or especially what I should write next about Macduff Brooks.

My website lists past and future appearances for readings, talk programs, and signings.

89967601R00190

Made in the USA
Lexington, KY
05 June 2018